Loving David

GINA HUMMER

Copyright © 2011 by Gina Hummer
All rights reserved.

ISBN: 1-4663-4330-3
ISBN-13: 978-1-4663-4330-6

A big thank you to my family for their generosity of spirit.

With love to my first friend, my best friend, my Mom.

CHAPTER 1

The late afternoon sun peeked through the majestic redwood trees just enough to make Charlotte squint her eyes and curse the fact that her sunglasses were orphaned on her kitchen counter back home. She'd been in such a hurry to make it to the grocery store for provisions before she got on the road that she'd plumb forgot the most important accessory for the drive.

Charlotte sighed and shook her head before she resumed humming to the Beatles' "Blackbird" playing on the radio of her Jeep. Balmy winds threaded their way through the open windows, tossing her tangle of long dark auburn curls into a nest around her head. She came to a stop at a light a block north of Main Street and looked around. Beautiful, sun-drenched days were a given in Southern California, but to Charlotte, there was something enchanting about springtime in Lake Arrowhead, the small mountain town ninety minutes from her home in Los Angeles.

The air was perfumed with the first blooms of daffodils and tulips that signaled the start of a new season; the azure waters of the lake were dotted with water-skiers and avid boaters who had counted the days until they could haul their boats down to the shore and launch themselves into the smooth calm of the water. Children of all ages crammed into the Sweet Shoppe for their first ice cream cones, the cool swirls of vanilla or chocolate, sometimes both, sliding down their throats, a salve for still-lingering winter blues.

Charlotte pulled onto Main Street and parked across from the Coffee Bistro, her mouth salivating for her usual skinny latte. It would be a few months before the summer tourists poked through Lake Arrowhead's veil of tranquility, so the streets remained empty except for a few locals who strolled up and down the brick sidewalks of the town's quaint shopping corridor. The air was still and serene, filled only with the sounds of chirping birds and the faint murmurings of conversation from the few scattered customers sitting at small metal tables outside Coffee Bistro. Every year, Charlotte looked forward to spending time in Lake Arrowhead and, as usual, contemplated moving to the area full-time. Maybe one day...

As Charlotte got out of the Jeep, she grabbed the two small red duffel bags from the passenger seat and flung them onto the floor behind the driver's seat. She started to cross the street, but then ran back to the Jeep and threw her old gray sweater that was sprawled across the backseat, on top of the bags. Not that anyone in Lake Arrowhead would steal anything out of a car in broad daylight, but still. Maybe she *had* been living in L.A. too long. Her suspicious nature never took a vacation.

Charlotte started again for the coffee shop when she saw Dottie Mays, owner of the Book Shelf bookstore next to the Bistro, come out pushing a cart of books out to the sidewalk in front of the shop. Charlotte waved and ran over to help Dottie.

"Charlotte! How are you?" Dottie asked as she held out her arms to Charlotte, who gave the woman a hug.

"Happy to be back! How about you? How are things?"

Dottie nodded and removed her librarian's glasses from the perch on her nose and cleaned them with the hem of her yellow peasant blouse.

"Fine, just fine. A lot of big releases are keeping people coming back every day." Dottie replaced her glasses and put her hands on her hips as she gave Charlotte the once-over. "Well, you look even more fantastic than usual," Dottie winked and ribbed Charlotte. "Must be up to something pretty good these days."

Charlotte shrugged and shook her head before she shoved her hands into the pockets of her faded blue jeans, part of her standard uniform that often included a T-shirt that she'd probably worn two days in a row. People were always telling her how good she looked and often queried her for her "beauty secrets." Charlotte did so little to maintain her looks that she was almost embarrassed to admit she washed her face only once a day—and that was in the morning. No special creams or magic potions. She kept her makeup to the bare minimum of lipstick and maybe a swipe of mascara if she was feeling inspired. Charlotte liked to think of her physique as "just right"—she wasn't reed thin, nor was she overweight. She was curvy, with a full, voluptuous chest and softly rounded hips. A few times a week she took a brisk walk around her neighborhood, mostly to keep the old ticker happy. Charlotte often kept her wild auburn curls sequestered in a ponytail, though she'd left her hair loose for the ride up to Lake Arrowhead, wanting to feel the wind whip through it. Though middle age was around the corner, Charlotte could have passed for someone at least ten years younger.

"I swear you were going to tell me you had some cute boyfriend who was keeping you young," Dottie said as she scratched her scalp through the cotton-candy tufts of her blonde hair.

Inwardly, Charlotte rolled her eyes. *Here we go again.* Charlotte was single by choice and didn't feel the need to get all dressed up to go on the prowl for a man. She had a handful of close friends, but was often happiest sitting at home alone with a good book, a glass of wine, and her phone turned off. She was more than content with her life and didn't see the need to change anything.

Instead, Charlotte smiled. "Nope, nothing different. Just enjoying life."

One of Dottie's employees came out to summon her inside. Dottie squeezed Charlotte's hand. "That's my cue. And time to let you get on with work."

Charlotte winked and hugged Dottie again. "Oh yeah. Work." Both women giggled and said their good-byes as Charlotte turned to head into the coffee shop for her caffeine fix.

The rich aroma of fresh coffee greeted Charlotte as she stepped into the Bistro. The espresso machine whirred at top speed over the faint sounds of the same oldies station Charlotte had been playing in her Jeep. There were a handful of people inside sipping coffee or surfing the Net on their laptops, courtesy of the free Wi-Fi. As she waited for the two people in front of her to place their orders, Charlotte licked her lips in anticipation of her skinny latte. She could already feel the foam sloshing across her tongue.

While Charlotte waited for her drink, she perused the display case filled with rows of the luscious golden pastries the shop was known for. She decided to put in an order for a chocolate croissant.

"Did he come in here? Did you see him?" a man yelled out. Charlotte whipped her head around at the intrusion of noise. A stocky man with khaki shorts, gym shoes, and a short-sleeve blue button-down shirt over a wifebeater had burst into the shop. Sweat poured down in rivers from atop his frizzy brown hair and down the sides of his crimson face. His eyes darted around the shop in a panic, and a massive black camera hung around his neck.

"Who are you talking about?" the coffee girl asked.

"David King!" he shouted.

"The actor David King?" the coffee girl said, surprised as she set Charlotte's drink down on the counter.

The photographer let out a snort of frustration. "Yes, David King *the actor*." His words were laced with sarcasm. The man started to search the shop, peering over the countertop and moving chairs as though David King might be hiding under one of the tables.

"A buddy of mine works at one of the inns, says he's expected. I'm waiting for him, and then I see him walking down this street, wearing a baseball cap and carrying a backpack. I ran to catch up with him and"—the photographer threw up his hands—"he disappeared." The photographer scanned the room again with no luck. "Damn it," he muttered before he ran out as fast as he'd run in.

"Who cares?" Charlotte muttered under her breath as she sipped her drink. She tried to catch the girl's attention so she could order the croissant, but it was too late. Charlotte had lost the girl to her cell phone, on which she started to text and hyperventilate about the "hot" David King being spotted in Lake Arrowhead. Without even looking at Charlotte, the girl ran into the street, hoping she'd catch a glimpse of the heartthrob.

Disgusted, Charlotte sipped her latte, but got no joy from it. She didn't get why people made such a big deal out of celebrity sightings. You'd never have a conversation with them; you'd never see them again. They would have no profound effect on your life. Charlotte sighed. Mostly she was peeved she'd missed out on her croissant.

"Probably God's way of telling me I don't need it," Charlotte mumbled to herself as she headed outside. Charlotte was stunned at the near mob scene in front of her. Gone was the peaceful street she'd been on just moments ago. About a dozen or so teenage girls, their moms, and assorted other lookie-loos had gathered in the middle of the street, their camera phones aimed in any direction, hoping to catch a glimpse of David King for all posterity.

Charlotte shook her head and steeled herself for the short jaunt to her Jeep. She clutched her drink, holding it close to her chest as she pushed her way through the crowd. Arms and elbows poked at her face as people jockeyed for position to see…anything. Charlotte nonetheless reached her car without losing a drop of the treasured latte. Muttering to herself about celebrities and chocolate croissants, Charlotte shoved her drink into the cup holder and started the car. She revved the engine, expecting the crowd to scramble out of her way. Charlotte gripped the steering wheel in an attempt to keep her cool. Upset that no one made an attempt to move, Charlotte rolled down her window and honked the horn.

"Move it!" she hollered.

The crowd thinned out a bit; one person shot her the finger. Charlotte shifted into gear, and her foot eased down on the gas pedal. The car squealed as it began to creep down the street. Charlotte prayed she wouldn't run over anyone. She uttered a few curse words to herself until she finally broke free.

"Jesus." She shook her head. "Un-*frickin*-believable."

Relieved to be clear of the insanity, Charlotte loosened her grip on the steering wheel and allowed herself to relax. She flipped on the radio and took a sip of coffee. The Stones were on, and Charlotte jacked up the volume, pounding on the steering wheel like it was a drum set. As Charlotte zoomed down the highway, she sang along to the radio as though she were strutting around stage with Mick. The song began to fade out, and Charlotte thought she heard a noise from the backseat. Charlotte frowned and turned down the radio, cocking her ear toward the back. Silence. She went to turn the volume back up and glanced in the rearview mirror. A pair of green eyes stared back at her. Charlotte screamed and jerked the steering wheel, which caused her car to veer into another lane, where she just missed swatting another car.

The blare of the car horn rattled Charlotte, who frantically turned the wheel as she tried to regain control of the Jeep, but it was too late. She ran off the road and straight into a dirt patch. Her body jerked forward as she slammed on the brakes and the car screeched to a halt. The seat belt snapped Charlotte back against the seat. Without stopping to think, Charlotte unbuckled her seat belt and yanked open the glove compartment. She grabbed a can of mace and whipped around to face the green-eyed stranger in her backseat. She stuck her hand out in front of her and aimed the mace at her would-be perpetrator. Charlotte was ready to squeeze when she stopped and noticed a familiar face smiling at her.

"Wait," she said, her arm starting to crumple a bit. "You're David King."

"Last I checked," he replied, green eyes twinkling with amusement. "Are you okay?"

Charlotte just stared at him in disbelief, saying nothing. She didn't remember leaving the doors unlocked. How had he gotten in?

"Why are you in my car?" she asked, the mace still trained in his direction.

"I'm quite sorry for doing this to you and even more sorry that I frightened you," David said, straightening up. "It's a rather funny story if you care to hear it." He stopped to look at a stunned Charlotte, who couldn't seem to make her mouth move, so he plowed on.

"I was headed up to one of the inns here when I had my driver drop me off in town and be on his way. Since it was a quiet little street, I figured I'd be able to get a cup of coffee and browse the bookstore in peace before I checked in. No such luck. Next thing I know, some sweaty man is running after me, screaming my name. And inevitably, that means screaming girls will follow. I panicked and happened to notice you'd left your car door unlocked. So I decided to hop in and hide for just a minute, but before *I* could get out, *you* got in and drove away." He hooked an arm around one of the front seats and grinned at her. "I have to say, I rather enjoyed your concert. 'Start Me Up' is one of my all-time favorite Stones tunes," he said in the charming British accent that made millions of women swoon.

Pink blazed up and over Charlotte's cheeks; she was embarrassed that he'd been treated to her shrill, off-key warbling. Charlotte had seen him in movies countless times, and now he was sitting in her car. She tried to pull herself together, worried about how ridiculous she must have looked.

He gestured toward the front seat. "May I join you? I'm afraid it's rather cramped back here."

She lowered the can of mace and nodded an okay to him, unable to do more than stare at him in wide-eyed wonder as he crawled over to the front passenger seat. He held out his hand to shake hers. "Well, thank you. And you are?"

She took his hand, surprised at its soft ruggedness. "Ch-Charlotte," she stuttered, barely able to get her name out. "Charlotte Taylor."

He grinned again and squeezed her hand. "Charlotte. What a lovely name. And lovely to meet you. And as you already know, David King."

"David King," she whispered to herself.

He leaned back against the seat, still smiling. "Most people call me David. You can do the same if you like."

Charlotte blinked and shook her head in disbelief. Was this really happening? Was David King really sitting mere inches from her, filling up her car with whatever wonderful cologne he was wearing, knees brushing up against her dashboard? And had she almost maced those beautiful green eyes? She had never considered herself starstruck. Of course, she'd never had a celebrity in her car either.

"I would ask you to drive me to the inn, but I think that plan's been ruined. That photographer and bloody who knows who else will be permanently camped out in that lobby." He reached into the pocket of his jeans. "Better call my driver, have him come back up here to fetch me."

Without waiting for her to respond, he pulled out his cell phone and started to dial. Charlotte gave him the once-over and liked what she saw:

messy coal-black hair, five o'clock shadow, and wrinkled flannel shirt... gorgeous.

"I can drive you somewhere..." she blurted out before she clamped her mouth shut. Had she really just offered to drive David King around?

David glanced over at her as he put his hand over his cell.

"I couldn't ask you to do that."

"You're not asking. I'm offering."

"Are you sure?" he asked.

She nodded, mesmerized by his British accent; she had always thought accents were sexy. She had seen David King in movies in which he spoke with an American accent; she liked his real brogue better.

"The least I could do to make up for almost macing you."

"Indeed." He grinned at her, which made her uncomfortable. Charlotte busied herself with taking a sip of her latte and buckling her seat belt, hoping he wouldn't see the effect he had on her.

"I can hardly turn down an offer like that. Except I'm not sure where to next."

"What are you doing up here, anyway?" Charlotte asked.

"At the moment I'm in between jobs...so I thought I would come up here to the inn for a little holiday. Wishful thinking."

Charlotte tucked her hair behind her ears. "Where do I take you then?"

"Maybe to the nearest town, rent a car, find a B and B or something. What do you think?" He looked right at Charlotte while she stared straight ahead.

She glanced at her watch. "The car rental place is down the hill and will probably be closed by the time we get there." Charlotte looked out the front window of the Jeep, her mind turning. It was getting too late to drive him back down the hill, and who knew if they'd encounter another mob scene. There was only one alternative. She shook her head, a warring conversation swirling around in her mind.

David noticed her moving her lips as she played out a few scenarios in her head. He laughed and poked her shoulder. A jolt of electricity coursed through her at his touch. She tried to ignore it. "Well, now you seem rather lost in thought. What are you thinking?"

Charlotte took a deep breath as she turned to face him, still not sure if she was doing the right thing. "If you just want to hide, I may to be able to help you."

"I'm listening."

Charlotte shifted in her seat. "Some girlfriends of mine are staying at a retreat up here—just a small group, very quiet, very private. I can assure you no one would know where you are or bother you while you're there." She cocked her head to the side. "It may be just the place you've been looking for."

"Done," he blurted out. "I don't care how much it is; you seem convinced I'll like it, so let's go."

She held up her hand. "You don't have to pay; it's a quiet little group of cabins. My friends go there to get away from it all. It's just a few miles up the road." She paused. "So...you're game then?" Was she really having *this* conversation with *this* person?

He gave her a light tap on her knee, and Charlotte pursed her lips to keep her composure. "Yes! Let's shove off then," he said, a broad smile stretched across his handsome face.

"Sounds like a plan," Charlotte said as she started the Jeep and got back on the road leading up to the retreat.

"So what else is on the set list?" David asked.

"What?" Charlotte asked, confused.

David rapped on the knob of the radio. "You know, for your concert?" he said, barely able to contain his laughter.

Charlotte turned red, hoping he'd forgotten about that particular incident. "That's not funny. I thought I was by myself." She gave him a sideways glance. "Like you don't sing along to the radio when you're driving."

"Well, since I don't really drive all that much, no, not really."

"What? You don't drive, or you can't?"

"I *can* drive. I just don't drive *often*," David said as he slumped a bit in his seat and drummed on the dashboard with his fingertips. "I have a driver. Traffic makes me bonkers, especially L.A. traffic. Let someone else have the hassle. New York is the best. You can just walk everywhere or hop on the Tube, or as you would call it, subway."

Charlotte pondered this for a moment and shook her head. "I love my car. And I love driving. I couldn't imagine someone driving me around all day."

"Oh, you'd be surprised at how fast you got used to it."

Charlotte chuckled. "I doubt it."

The sun had just started to make its descent into the horizon, and the warm afternoon air had cooled a bit. Just then, a cluster of cottage-style cabins came into view. There were a handful of cars parked in a variety of makeshift parking spots out front. Charlotte maneuvered her Jeep into one and turned it off.

"Well," she said as she gestured toward the cabins, "here we are."

"What is this place?" David asked as they got out of the car and he looked around. "Some sort of camp for adults?"

"No." Charlotte smiled. "Like I said, it's a retreat. Most of the ladies here may not realize who you are." She looked over at him as she reached behind her seat to get her bags. "I hope that doesn't offend you."

"*That* would be a nice change of pace." He ran over to her side. "Let me get the bags for you."

"How about you take the groceries and your backpack and"—Charlotte picked up her bags—"I'll take these."

David grinned. "Deal."

As she stood in the evening light, watching him sling his backpack over his shoulder and hoist the grocery bags, Charlotte took the opportunity to get a better view of David King. He was even more handsome in person than he was on-screen or in any of the tabloids she saw at the supermarket. He had to be at least six feet tall with broad shoulders, and even though his arms were beneath a flannel shirt, she could tell that they were muscular, the kind you could get lost in. A chunk of his dark, unruly hair kept falling into his piercing green eyes, which shone like emeralds.

Stop staring, Charlotte admonished herself as she pulled the cabin keys out of her purse. She headed toward a small cabin that was squeezed in between two much larger cabins. Charlotte shoved the key in the lock and motioned for David to come in. The scent of pine cleaner greeted them, and shadows from the fading evening sun cast themselves against the knotted wood floors. David took a look around as he sat the grocery bags and his overstuffed backpack on the small kitchen table.

"Nice place," he said. "Now what are these ladies going to think about you dropping a veritable stranger down in their midst? You're sure I'm not intruding?"

Charlotte placed her bags next to the table, deciding to sidestep the question for the time being. David started to take the groceries out of the bags and set them on the table. He inspected the bags of pretzels, cans of potato chips, and assorted boxes of pastries.

"A girl with a healthy appetite, I see."

Charlotte began to put the groceries away. "I like my sugar and my salt. Sue me."

"Should I be scared? I'm not walking into a coven of witches, am I?" he asked with a wink.

"No, no. Nothing like that."

David pulled out a chair and sat down. "So what kind of retreat is this anyway? Are you all doing yoga or something?"

"No. We're all writers. It's a writers' retreat."

He looked at her, wide-eyed. "Writers? What kind of writers? Oh dear. Don't tell me you're screenwriters," he laughed.

Charlotte felt her heart speed up; his smile took her breath away. She pulled out a bottle of Arizona Iced Tea. "Can I pour you a glass?" she asked as she pondered her answer.

"Please, thank you." David leaned forward. "What kind of writers are you all?"

Charlotte pulled two tall glasses from the cabinets and filled them with ice. "Well, we all write different things—novels, political articles, biographies." She paused. "One lady writes educational books." Distress flickered across David's handsome face. "Don't worry, David—none of us write for the tabloids or anything like that." She handed him a glass.

He exhaled. "Thank God." He held up his glass to hers. "To new friends," he said. Charlotte joined her glass with his, and they clinked. "Cheers."

Charlotte gulped her tea, not realizing how thirsty she was. David also drained his in a few quick swigs. They both plunked their empty glasses down at the same time and laughed.

"I guess we were thirsty," Charlotte said as she resumed putting away her groceries.

"Apparently." David reached for the bottle and refilled both glasses.

"Before we make our big entrance, there is something else I should probably tell you." Charlotte paused. "All of the ladies here are either divorced or widowed." She looked at him for his reaction.

"Divorced or *widowed?*" he stammered. "Would you mind explaining?"

Charlotte leaned against the counter as she twisted her fingers around her long auburn locks, trying to come up with an easy answer. "One of the ladies owns this property, and several years ago, she started bringing colleagues here for a getaway. And she soon realized all of her friends were divorced or widowed. They would spend hours discussing their struggles. She also noticed her divorced friends would end up in one part of the house talking about their problems, and her widowed friends would be in another part of the house talking with each other, and it just developed from there."

She finished putting away her groceries and joined David at the table.

"For a long time now, the group's been gathering here once a year. The widows stay together in one of the large cabins, and divorcées in the other. During the day, the two groups meet in their respective cabins to talk about their issues. We also hold book clubs, seminars—that kind of thing. But at dinnertime we all come together in the large dining cabin in the back. We all eat together and talk about our projects or play cards." Charlotte shrugged. "There really is no set plan. It's just fun."

"Fascinating." David leaned forward and looked at her. "So, why do you have your own cabin?"

Charlotte threaded her fingers together and looked down at the table. She let out a sigh. "I belong in both groups. Sort of."

David frowned. "Oh. Both?" He raised an eyebrow. "Why both?" he asked gently.

Charlotte took another sip of iced tea. "I'd been separated for about two years before my husband was killed in a car accident, so the ladies put me in the 'both' category. I'm the only one with this particular situation, so I chose to stay in the small cabin. I spend time with both groups, but my *main* job is to make all of the arrangements for us before everyone else gets here." Charlotte leaned back against her chair. "I usually come up here early and make sure the cabins are ready, clean, stocked—that kind of thing. I had to run back to L.A. for some meetings, so this is my second trip up here in as many days. I help with the travel arrangements...pick up prescriptions." She took a deep breath and released it. "I am the youngest woman here, so doing all the legwork is easier for me." Charlotte shook the ice in her glass. "I've been doing this for about three years now, and I really love it. I've learned so much from these ladies." Charlotte finished her tea. "They're like family to me."

He was silent for a moment as he drank his tea. "Which group do you talk with more?"

"Divorcées," she said matter-of-factly.

He finished his drink as though he was unsure of what to say next. "Are you sure it's okay that I stay here? This being a no-man zone and all," he said to lighten the mood.

"No," she said bluntly. "They're going to kick my ass."

David's jaw dropped a bit. "You're serious?"

Charlotte shrugged her shoulders and cocked her head to the side to indicate a beatdown was a distinct possibility.

David rubbed his hand across his chin, concern crinkling around his eyes. "Maybe I should leave; I don't want to get you in trouble with your friends."

"Oh, the ladies may bark at first, but I'll just explain to them what happened. I'm sure they'll understand," Charlotte scoffed, trying to convince them both. She glanced at the clock on the wall in the kitchen. "They should all be in the dining cabin getting ready for dinner." Charlotte stood and placed her hands on her hips. "Let's get this over with."

"Maybe you should go and talk to them first; warm them up a bit, and then introduce me." David suggested.

"I don't think so. Better to just take the bull by the horns." She held up her index finger, a thought occurring to her. "You know, I do remember two years back one of the girls brought a friend with her who was in remission from cancer." Charlotte grabbed her keys and started to walk toward the door. She was about to open it when David placed a hand on her arm and reached around to open it for her. Charlotte caught a whiff of him and closed her eyes, reveling in the woodsy scent. "Wow," she mouthed out of his eyesight. They stepped outside, and she continued her train of thought. "They were okay with that, and she wasn't a writer, *and* she had never been married." She placed her finger on the corner of her mouth. "She didn't have a penis, though," she said with a sly grin.

"Well, if they don't like me, it's bloody likely I may not have a penis as well!" he quipped.

CHAPTER 2

No one noticed when Charlotte and David opened the door to the dining cabin. Charlotte could hear bits and pieces of multiple conversations throughout the room, but no one stood up and yelled out, "Traitor!" because she'd brought a man into the mix. There were eight women in the room, ranging in age from late forties to late seventies. They all struck the delicate balance of looking both intellectual and attractive; there were a fair amount of simple black turtlenecks paired with blue jeans or slim black pants; casual French twists and short, sensible haircuts; bright red lipstick and no-nonsense black-rimmed glasses that were well suited to angular faces with brows furrowed deep in thought.

One of the women, Karen, spotted Charlotte and shot her hand up in the air to signal for her to come over. Now in her late forties, Karen had modeled when she was younger to pay for college; much like Charlotte, she had retained her current looks with scant effort. She kept her bone-straight, shiny black hair pulled back in a loose ponytail and wore a multicolored poncho over a pair of jeans, her librarian's glasses perched on the edge of her pert nose. Karen's half-moon silver pendant and amethyst crystal earrings flashed in the fading sunlight that streamed in from the room's windows. Rows of silver rings lined her fingers, filled with a variety of stones and crystals, each with a different celestial meaning. Charlotte braced herself for what she knew would be Karen's blunt reaction to David. Karen, who was never shy about sharing her opinions, stood up and smiled as Charlotte got closer. Her eyes got larger as she focused on the male intruder.

"Charlotte! What the hell?" she blurted out. The room fell silent at Karen's outburst.

All eyes turned in the direction of Karen's fury, and several of the women let out small gasps. Karen stood with her hands on her hips, irritated.

"Uh, hello—did I miss the memo where it says men are allowed to crash our tea party?" Karen said.

Charlotte started to speak. "Well, no, see—"

"I mean…come on, Charlotte; this is supposed to be *girl* time." Karen continued as though Charlotte hadn't spoken. "What are you up to?"

Charlotte tried again when Hendra, the leader of the group by virtue of the fact that she owned the cabins, stood tall and imposing, every inch of her six-foot frame filling the room. The voluminous waves of her long white hair fanned around her head like a crown. Hendra drew her slender shoulders up and stared down Charlotte and David like a disgruntled queen addressing naughty subjects.

Charlotte steeled herself as she looked from woman to woman and began to speak. "Hendra, ladies, please let me explain…This is—"

"Charlotte?" Hendra held up her hand like a cop stopping traffic. "Why in the world would you bring a man here?" she said, her tone stern. She motioned toward David. "And David King of all people? We don't want any Hollywood types here."

Charlotte gasped, surprised and amused that Hendra knew who he was. Hendra rolled her eyes at Charlotte.

"Oh, don't look at me that way. I know who he is. His poster is plastered all over my granddaughter's wall," she said, disgust punching her words. "He's some sort of teen idol person."

Horror flashed across David's face, and he cleared his throat. "Um, ma'am? I am an actor, not a teen idol," he started before Hendra cut him off with her traffic move.

"Whatever," Hendra snapped. "What are you doing here, young man?"

"Well, it's really a very funny story," Charlotte interjected. "See, I was in town, getting a skinny latte—you all know how much I love my lattes—and I came outside, and there was this mob scene of people looking for David, and I hopped in my car to come up here, and wouldn't you know, *David* had jumped in my backseat to escape, which made me run off the road, and I almost maced him, and now he needs a place to stay because everyone knows the inn he was going to be staying at, and then they'd be hounding him for pictures and autographs and the like, so I told him he could stay here and hide." Charlotte spilled the story with nary a breath and punctuated her retelling with a lot of wild gestures, hoping some dramatic flair would gain a little sympathy for David. Judging by the grins and giggles, it was working.

"He really needs to get away for a bit and just…be." Charlotte continued. "I would've asked you ladies first, but it was an emergency. Anyway, I thought he could just hide here for a while, *if* it's okay."

Charlotte smiled at the group, as did David; it was his only defense now. Hendra turned her back to David and Charlotte, her shoulders softening, and faced the group of women.

"Anyone have an issue?" she asked, her voice low.

Some of the women replied no; others shook their heads. Hendra turned to face Charlotte, her shoulders back on point.

"Where will he stay?" she asked.

Charlotte paused for a moment. "Well, my cabin has a spare room; it should be okay for him."

David nodded and took a small step forward to cash in on the positive momentum.

"Ladies, I promise I will not intrude on your time here. I will probably sleep most of the time anyway. As Charlotte said, I just need to hide for a bit. She's told me you are all people of integrity, and I can see that you are." David flashed his impish grin at the crowd. "I would really appreciate this favor."

His smooth and sexy voice, dripping in British charm to boot, draped itself over the women, lulling them into unconscious swoons; most of the women had already fallen under his spell without even knowing it.

"Wasn't he voted 'Most Sexy' a few years back?" one of the women whispered to Karen, who scoffed, still annoyed. "How old do you think he is?"

David overheard and tried not to laugh. "Yes, I was, and I'm thirty."

The whisperer, embarrassed at having been heard, turned her attention to the table in front of her.

The entire room began to fill with not-so-hushed whispers, which annoyed Hendra.

"Make him do all the dishes," Karen piped in. "At least he'll be useful." She shrugged.

Hendra gave David a curt nod. "Agreed. You will have kitchen and cleaning duties just like the rest of us; just don't get in our way. None of us will let anyone know you're here." She pivoted on her heel and headed toward the kitchen. "I'm bored with this conversation now, so let's eat."

The ladies followed suit while David and Charlotte brought up the rear.

David leaned down to Charlotte's ear. "Thank you, Charlotte," he whispered.

Charlotte smiled. "Like I said—the least I could do for almost macing you."

The dining area was a long, rectangular room with a single table that stretched from end to end. Dinner was served buffet style and usually featured a theme of some sort; tonight's was Italian. The table was brimming with heaping bowls of spaghetti and meatballs, antipasti salad laden with ruby red tomatoes, fat, juicy black olives, and thick slabs of creamy buffalo mozzarella cheese, and a basket of crusty, buttery garlic bread that snapped and melted when you bit into it. Assorted bottles of red and white wine stood guard at the end of the table, and each woman took turns filling her glass. As the women loaded their plates, they took their seats and dug in. Charlotte helped Emma with her plate and made sure she made it to her seat safely. At seventy-eight, Emma was the oldest in the group. She recently had her hip replaced and suffered daily with severe arthritis, but her pain never showed through her bubbly personality and quick wit. Charlotte then filled her own plate before she joined David, who'd already inhaled half his spaghetti.

Charlotte ribbed him. "Hungry much?" she said in a low voice.

"This is the worst food I've ever eaten. Don't tell the cook," David said as he popped a bite of bread into his mouth.

As they continued to eat, the woman directly across from David decided to break the ice.

"My name's Angela." A brunette with olive skin and a swanlike neck spoke up as she gave him a nod. "We all know just about everything about each other, but all we know about you is what we see on the covers of the rag sheets at the grocery checkout." Angela munched on an olive. "And we all know those are full of crap."

The women all laughed as Charlotte explained, "Angela's ex is managing editor for the *Tatler*."

Angela confirmed with a nod. "Yeah, and he's more full of crap than his paper." Angela pointed her fork at David. "Now, go on."

David grinned. "Well, I'm glad to hear you don't read the tabloids. As you said, they're never truthful." David took a small sip of white wine before he continued. "I was born in England; my mum was a stage director there. When I was ten, we moved to the States after my father died. Mum worked on Broadway for a while, directing and producing. I went back to London to attend the Royal Academy of Dramatic Art. Landed a few commercials, got a few telly spots, and then managed to do some ghastly teen angst films, and well..." He shrugged. "You probably know the rest."

The women continued to eat their pasta. "I think my favorite film of yours was the one you did a few years ago where you married the gal for an inheritance and you hated each other, but of course you were crazy about each other? What was it?" Angela snapped her fingers, trying to remember.

"*Love's Easy*," David and Angela both blurted out at the same time. Everyone laughed, and several murmurs of agreement went up around the table. A few women called out the names of some of David's other films and asked him for gossip about some of his costars. He obliged with a few "he wears a girdle" and "she smokes like a chimney" tales to the delight of the assembled group. Charlotte smiled to herself as she speared a chunk of mozzarella. The women had definitely warmed up to David.

David threw down his napkin and looked around the table. "Okay, ladies, that's enough about me. I want to hear about you." He pushed his plate away and folded his arms on the table. "May I ask each of you what you write and what brought you to this group?"

They all tittered and looked embarrassed.

"Oh, you don't want to hear any of that." Angela demurred. "It's not all that interesting."

"Oh, but I disagree. I have to be honest with you; I find all of this quite fascinating." He pointed at Emma, the petite woman Charlotte had assisted earlier. Her ash-blonde hair was pulled back in a simple twist, and even in her simple uniform of a man's white dress shirt tucked into slim black pants, a black cashmere sweater splayed across her shoulders, she exuded elegance and confidence. "How about you, love? What's your story?"

The woman straightened up at having been singled out by David. "I'm Emma Vaughn," she drawled in a soft Southern accent. "I was an editor for a women's magazine for about twenty years—the sixties through the eighties, the fun decades." She winked. "I'm retired now, but keep busy with speaking engagements. Hendra and I have been friends for more than twenty years, and I'm an original member of this wonderful group of ladies. I'm a widow and hate every minute of it, but my ladies here keep things interesting."

"You're from the South, then?" David asked.

Emma smiled. "Dallas, born and bred. Twenty years in New York and twenty-five in L.A. and still can't shake that Southern twang."

"Oh, honey, I'd love to have a Southern twang," a woman with a distinct Boston accent, short red hair, and milk-white skin shouted from the far end of the table as everyone laughed.

"Well, I guess it's your turn, then. And you are...?"

"Samantha Lerner, senior features writer for *What's the Score* magazine. I fall in that 'divorcée' category. I've been gracing these ladies with my presence for about two years."

"*What's the Score?* I read it religiously. Lovely to meet you."

David went around the table, querying the women about their stories. They all thrilled at being able to share a little bit of themselves with him, and plenty of whoops and hollers went around the room several times. A few were authors, some had written copy for ad agencies or magazines, and others toiled at newspapers. David seemed captivated by the women's words and asked them numerous questions, an endless well of curiosity. Even Hendra got in on the fun, her earlier animosity toward David melting away as she told tales of her days as literary editor at the *Los Angeles Times*. The hours tiptoed past the group as they plowed through several bottles of wine and even more stories. The party moved to the kitchen, where everyone took turns cleaning up.

One by one, each of the women said her good-nights. Karen stopped by to give Charlotte a quick squeeze on her shoulder and mouthed, "We'll talk later," as she gestured to David. At the end, only David, Charlotte, and Emma remained. They finished the last of the wine before Emma stood up and stretched; she looked at David.

"You wouldn't mind walking an old woman home, would you?"

David whipped his head around several times and feigned looking under the table. "I don't see any old women here."

She chuckled and shook her finger at him. "You better be careful; I could be dangerous."

David took her arm. "So could I," he said with a wink, which caused Emma to let out a full, throaty laugh. Charlotte had to suppress her own giggles.

The trio stepped outside into the icy night air. Goose bumps dotted Charlotte's bare arms, and she folded them across her chest in a feeble effort to shut out the cold. A symphony of crickets surrounded them, and the sky blinked with stars. Emma grasped David's hand as they headed toward her cabin.

"You know, you remind me of Newman," Emma said as she tipped her head back in remembrance. "First time I met him was when I interviewed him for *Butch Cassidy*." Emma let out a sigh and shook her head. "Such a charmer. Just like you."

"Well, I can think of worse people to be compared to." David smiled.

As they arrived at the widow's cabin, Emma gave David a hug and Charlotte a kiss on the cheek.

"Good night, children," she said as she gave them a wink and disappeared behind the door.

To escape the chilly air, David and Charlotte ran back to their cabin. Charlotte continued to rub her arms as she threw on her gray sweater from earlier.

"Easy to forget how cold it gets in Southern California, eh?" David asked as he buttoned up his flannel.

"No kidding," Charlotte said, her teeth chattering. She flicked on the lamp in the living room and noticed David had a huge smile on his face. "I take it you enjoyed yourself?"

David reclined against the green suede couch and chuckled. "I have to say, that was one of the most enjoyable nights I've had in quite some time." David turned to Charlotte, his face shining with wonder. "Your friends are amazing…the stories…the foul language…the wisdom." He shook his head. "I had a great time. I can see why you love this place."

Charlotte smiled as she headed to the old wooden trunk in front of the large picture window next to the door. "They're great gals," she said as she pulled out a set of sheets and a blanket. "Like I told you earlier, they're like family to me."

"Thank you for this. I can't tell you how much I appreciate it."

Charlotte nodded. "I'm glad you had a good time. Of course, after I show you where you'll be sleeping, you may be cursing me."

Charlotte waited for David to grab his backpack before she led him down a small, narrow hallway. She opened the door to a bedroom and turned the light on.

"This is your room. It's pretty small, but it'll do the job." Charlotte handed David the bedding from the trunk, which he accepted. "Sorry it's not the Waldorf."

David looked around the small bedroom, the only decor a full-sized bed and a tiny wooden nightstand with a wind-up face clock.

"After cramping around in the backseat of your car, this feels like the Waldorf." He sat the linens down on the bed. "Thanks again. For everything."

"Sure." Charlotte turned to go, but then glanced back. "Do you need some help making the bed?"

"You've done more than enough. I can manage."

Charlotte crossed back and began to unfurl the sheets. "Come on. Two sets of hands will go faster than one." David complied, and they had the bed made in a matter of seconds. Charlotte stood awkwardly in front of David, not sure what to say next.

"Good night, then." She blushed and left him alone.

"Good night," he said as Charlotte closed the door.

Charlotte went back into the front room and retrieved her bags. She could hear David moving around in his room next to hers as she rummaged around for some pajamas. She extracted an oversized flannel nightshirt and her toiletries bag. Charlotte clamped her hair back into an oversized barrette and brushed her teeth. She was about to turn out the light when she turned to stare at herself in the mirror. She ran a finger over the minute lines around her eyes and mouth, giving them a critical examination before she stepped back and looked down at her flannel shirt.

"Sexy," she muttered sarcastically before she tiptoed toward her bedroom door. She eased the door open and walked toward the kitchen. Though it had been a long day and night, Charlotte was still wound up. She didn't feel quite like going to bed just yet, so she decided to have one more little glass of wine to settle her down. She grabbed a glass out of the cabinet and went in search of the bottle of red she knew was hanging out somewhere. She opened a few doors and then spotted it on the top shelf of the pantry. She stood on her tiptoes to reach it, but the bottle was just out of her grasp.

"Damn," she whispered in frustration. She went to pull one of the kitchen chairs over when she was startled by the sound of David's voice.

"Let me," he offered. "What is it you need?"

"You like scaring me, don't you?" she teased. "The wine on the top shelf."

He grinned at her and retrieved the bottle. "Nightcap?" He winked.

"Yeah. I'm not tired enough yet. Can I get you one?"

"Sure, why not?" he replied.

She poured two glasses, and they moved to the small living room. David sat in an overstuffed black leather chair across from the couch, while Charlotte went back into the trunk for a blanket to throw over her legs.

"Still chilly, huh?" David asked as he sipped his wine.

Charlotte nodded. "I get cold really easy. There's a reason I live in California."

As Charlotte settled onto the couch and adjusted the blanket, she stole another look at David. She was still in awe over how beautiful he was. He wore a pair of gray sweatpants and a worn black T-shirt. Looking at his chiseled features in the dim light was almost too much for Charlotte. She could barely watch him without imagining what it would be like to be swept up inside those sculpted arms, bulging now against his shirt. To press up against his massive chest and to get lost in those captivating green eyes. For what seemed like the millionth time that day, Charlotte had to stop herself. *Thirty,* she kept saying over and over in her mind. She didn't remember thirty-year-old men looking like him when she was that age. She swirled her wine in her glass and then realized how quiet it was. She looked up and caught him staring at her and blushed.

"What?" she asked. "Is something hanging out of my nose?"

"Yes," he deadpanned.

Charlotte's hand flew to her nose, and David laughed. In spite of herself, she joined him.

"You're terrible," she said as she took another sip of wine.

David shrugged and smiled. "I like seeing you laugh."

Charlotte looked down, embarrassed, and then noticed him gazing at her yet again. "What?" she asked, now a touch exasperated.

He plopped his chin down into one palm. "I noticed at dinner you didn't say a whole lot about yourself."

"Oh, well, as I mentioned, I joined the group three years ago, and, well, I make a decent living writing steamy romance novels with action that I have never actually *participated* in, just heard about from these very experienced ladies—"

David cut her off. "Still vague. I want to know more about the real Charlotte. Will you tell me more?"

"What, the widow/divorcée saga?" she asked.

"If you don't mind…I'm curious," he replied.

Charlotte drained her wineglass and poured a bit more. "Well, let's see. Ben and I had been married for almost five years when I found out he was having an affair with one of his coworkers."

"Wow. How'd you find out?"

"He'd called me to say he was going to be working late at the office. He was always working late, and I felt bad, so I picked up some dinner, thought I'd surprise him and take it to him." Charlotte took a sip of wine. "He was working, all right. All over his desk."

David winced. "Ouch."

"Yeah. I had the locks changed the next morning, and he moved in with her."

"So you initiated divorce proceedings?"

"I did. But Ben just kept putting it off. Claimed he was too busy with work to concentrate on it. Even though he was living with this girl, he still seemed reluctant to move forward with the divorce. Kept saying he'd get around to it eventually."

"Maybe he was hoping you two would work things out."

"Yeah, well, that was never going to happen." Charlotte shifted her weight on the couch. "Then one day I get this call from the hospital that Ben had been in a car accident. T-boned by a semi. Died on impact."

David covered his mouth with his hands. "My God. How awful."

"Turns out, his girlfriend was in the car with him, and she was in critical condition. After I identified Ben…I don't know—I couldn't help myself. I went to see the girlfriend." Charlotte struggled to hold back tears. "She was in terrible shape—dying. Her face was unrecognizable. Neither I nor the hospital could track down this girl's family." Charlotte shook her head. "She was so alone. I stayed with her and held her hand until she died." Charlotte cleared her throat to keep from crying. "As it turned out, her parents were dead, she was an only child, and she had no other relatives—no aunts, no uncles, no cousins. So I decided to bury her and Ben next to each other."

"Wait," David interrupted. "You stayed with your husband's mistress and held her hand until she died? And then you paid for her burial, and you buried her next to your husband?" David shook his head. "That's bollocks. She broke up your marriage!"

"*They* broke up my marriage," Charlotte clarified. "He had an affair, which meant something was broken long before. I know it sounds crazy, but if you would've been in my shoes, would you have just left them there? I was still *legally* his wife—so should I have taken care of his business and left her there alone?" She held her head down and lowered her voice, surprised at the sympathy she still felt for the young woman. "She was younger than you are, and she had *no* one." She reflected for a moment. "Besides, I needed the closure." Charlotte finished the last of her wine. "And I got it."

David was silent for a moment as the gravity of Charlotte's word sank in. He set his wineglass down on the table and looked at her. "Amazing," he said.

Charlotte snorted. "Amazing…maybe. Some might say pathetic. Either way, the whole situation wasn't a high point for me. I try not to think about it too much. It's just a sad ending followed by yet another sad ending, you know?" She gave him a faint smile.

He kept those penetrating green eyes focused on her like a laser beam, never saying a word.

She began to fidget. "Why are you looking at me like that?"

"It's just…you're probably one of the strongest women I've ever met." He downed the rest of his drink and set his glass on the table.

Charlotte smiled in spite of herself, her cheeks warming at his compliments. She took a deep breath in an attempt to steady her racing heart.

"That's very flattering," she murmured. "Thank you." The moment hung in the air between them before Charlotte made a big show of stretching her legs and rearranging the frayed, itchy blanket.

"I'm tired of talking about myself," she said to raise the atmosphere. "I want you to tell me more about you. You've lived quite the life for a thirty-year-old." She leaned the side of her head against her hand. "It must be extremely exciting at times." She looked at him and waited for his smile.

She didn't get one.

"What is it?" she asked.

David leaned back against the chair and propped his feet upon the table. Charlotte couldn't help but notice he had nice feet—much better than what you usually saw strolling up and down Venice Beach on any given day.

"I feel older than thirty sometimes," he sighed. "That probably sounds silly to you, but I get tired of running around all over the planet. I long for the day that I can just put down roots and be." He stroked his chin, retreating further into thought. "I know I'm quite lucky to have the career and all the perks that come with it—especially the income. It does come with a price, as you witnessed in town. Sometimes I feel selfish for complaining; other times I want to just disappear." He sat up in his chair like a five-year-old who just spotted a bicycle under the Christmas tree, his expression animated. "Like now...I love the fact that I've *disappeared*." He snapped his fingers and popped out of his chair. He ran back in the direction of his room. "Which reminds me. I need to text William to let him know where I am. After that, I'm turning the phone off."

"Who's William?"

"My manager, who had the idea for me to come up here in the first place. When I saw that mob scene earlier, I was cursing him. Now I owe him. Be right back."

Charlotte waited in the living room while David sent his text. Charlotte could tell he was sincere just by listening to the fatigue in his voice and the excitement he expressed when talking about the experience of meeting the ladies; he really did need a break from his life.

David bounded back into the room and poured the last of the wine into their glasses.

"I'm going to take it as a good sign that William didn't text back right away; he must've made his flight." David sat down and picked up his glass. "So how long are you ladies here for?" He winked. "I guess I'm wondering how long I'll get to crash the party."

Charlotte ran her finger around the rim of her wineglass. "Well, we're here for another four weeks. And of course, you're welcome to stay as long as you like. I have a feeling you may die of boredom before that, though. I give you a week before you send up a flare to your manager to airlift you out of here." She chuckled. "Week and a half at most."

"Four weeks? That seems like a long time," David said as he stood up. "Is there another blanket in that magic trunk?"

"Yes, but let me—"

David held out his hand to halt her movement. "I've got it," he said as he walked over to pull out a fuzzy blue blanket. He settled back into the chair and draped the blanket across the lower half of his body. "Now, you were telling me why you're all up here for a month."

"Well, since the women are older and don't have husbands to rush home to, or little kids to look after, they love being here for an extended time. Gives them something to look forward to. Those who still have jobs, like Samantha, have so much vacation time that they can get away with taking a month off. Besides, when you're a writer, you can do your job anywhere."

"I have to say, I can't imagine being bored around such an outspoken group." David snuggled down into the chair a bit and looked at Charlotte. "Plus, it's nice to be around women who don't want to pull my hair or rip my clothes off."

Charlotte let out a huge laugh. "I think Emma may have wanted to rip your clothes off!"

David chuckled. "God bless Emma."

CHAPTER 3

Early morning sunlight poked through the gauzy sheers of the cabin's living room and straight onto Charlotte's face. The strong scent of coffee fluttered beneath her nostrils. She blinked her eyes several times and uncurled herself down the length of couch. She sat up, confused. Why was she on the couch? Charlotte got her answer when she saw the empty wine bottle on the coffee table.

"Oh, *man*." Charlotte rubbed her hands across her eyes, smearing the crust of sleep across her face as she did so. She yawned and stretched, her sore limbs yelping in pain.

Maybe tearing into the second bottle of wine wasn't such a good idea after all, Charlotte thought as she flopped back against the couch. She frowned when her head landed on something that definitely wasn't a couch pillow. Charlotte turned and smiled when she realized it was the rolled-up blanket that David had thrown across his legs the night before. She sat up and ran her hands across the nubby pills of the blanket, impressed by his thoughtfulness. Charlotte bit her nail and looked back in the direction of his bedroom, then crept toward the room, those glasses of wine splashing around inside her, and saw the door was open. She pushed the door back a bit and peered in. The bed was empty, though the sheets and blankets lay in a rumpled mess at its foot. She noticed David's backpack in the corner, a pair of jeans spilling from its mouth.

"Well," Charlotte mused, "he couldn't have gone far."

Charlotte stretched and yawned again before she made her way into her room to shower and dress. The steam of the shower ironed out the kinks in her muscles, and Charlotte started to hum nonchalantly while she washed her hair. After slicking back her curls into a ponytail and throwing on a pair of frayed blue jeans and formfitting red T-shirt, Charlotte bounded into the living room, ready for the day.

"David?" Charlotte called out, but was greeted with silence. She shrugged and headed to the kitchen. "Guess he's not back from his mystery mission," she muttered as she went to pull down a package of doughnuts. She smiled as she realized he'd made a pot of coffee before he'd left. For an international movie star, David King was turning out to be quite the gentleman. Charlotte poured herself a cup of coffee and blew on the steaming liquid before she took a sip. As she opened up the donuts, Charlotte looked out the window and saw two of the ladies sitting on a bench facing the lake, though they were too far away for her to see who they were. Whoever they were, they were having a grand old time judging from the muffled hoots and the way their shoulders shook with laughter. Charlotte picked up her coffee and donut and headed outside.

The air was still brisk, though the brightness of the sun washed over Charlotte, providing some respite from the chill. Charlotte squinted as she realized Emma and Karen were the source of the early morning entertainment.

Charlotte tapped Karen on the shoulder and laughed as she wedged herself onto a corner of the bench next to the woman. Karen had dropped last night's multicolored poncho for a pink one, though her eyes were now hidden behind tiny wire-framed sunglasses.

"Well, good morning, sunshine…rough night?" Karen singsonged, though her meaning was clear.

"Ha ha," Charlotte said as she bit into her donut. "Yes, but not why you think. If you must know, I'm a tad bit hungover this morning."

"Oh, oh, oh...lemme guess, a looove hangover!" Karen howled. Emma, her own face obscured by Jackie O sunglasses, quaked with silent laughter.

Charlotte rolled her eyes, exasperated. "You know, Karen, one of the reasons I love you is because your mind is perpetually in the gutter, but you've got it all wrong." Charlotte polished off the donut. "We spent the night talking."

"Honey, in my day we called that *pillow talk*," Emma drawled as Karen slapped her on the thigh, her body hunched over in fits of amusement.

"Oh my gosh! I passed out on the couch." Charlotte poked Karen's ribs. "All right. What else are you guys laughing at?"

Charlotte followed Karen's gaze to the shore of the lake in front of them. David was there, doing sit-ups, his body pumping up and down at a furious pace, oblivious to the fact that he had an audience. Charlotte gulped at the sight of his muscular back, which glistened in the sun, his sinewy muscles flexing with each movement. Charlotte forced some coffee down her throat as a distraction.

"Nice, huh?" Emma said. "I may have a whole new reason to change my Depends today," she said as she nudged Karen, who shrieked.

Charlotte choked on her coffee. "Oh God, Emma, that's disgusting."

Emma shrugged, unapologetic.

Karen turned to Charlotte. "You know, I've been meaning to ask you—when is the last time you got laid, Charlotte? During the Bush administration?"

Charlotte's cheeks flamed with embarrassment, mostly because that *was* the last time she'd gotten laid. She squirmed. "Not here to discuss my sex life, Karen."

"Huh. That long." Karen leaned over to Charlotte. "Listen, girl, if you don't take advantage of the fact that you have *that* under your roof at night, you've got some serious problems."

"Amen," Emma murmured.

Karen looked over at David, who had switched from sit-ups to bending over and touching his toes. The three women paused to take in the sight of David's firm butt pointed right at them. Emma broke the silence with a faint click of her tongue. "My God. If I were ten years younger, he'd be in trouble."

"Emma, you're almost eighty," Charlotte replied.

"Okay—twenty years younger," Emma quipped.

Charlotte put her hand over her face and sighed, "Good Lord," under her breath. "Ladies, please! He's *thirty*! He looks at me like some sort of mother figure, I'm sure. Besides, he can get any woman in the world." Charlotte turned her attention to her nearly empty coffee mug. "Now, will you knock off the comments?"

Before either lady could fling a smart remark in Charlotte's direction, David began to amble toward them, smiling. His face was flushed, and ribbons of sweat cascaded down every inch of his muscular body.

"Morning, beauties! Isn't it a great day?" He winked at Charlotte and headed toward the cabin. Six pairs of eyes followed David and his backside as they both retreated inside.

"Charlotte, how can you stand it?" Karen grinned. "Girlfriend, either you get him drunk and take advantage of him, or I'll do the honors!"

"I already told you I'm too old for him, so stop teasing me," Charlotte snapped. "It's infuriating."

Karen and Emma shot each other a quick look before they stood.

"Well, we're headed to breakfast. Care to join us?" Emma asked.

Charlotte shook her head. "Maybe in a little bit."

Karen bent down and gave Charlotte a hug. "All in fun, dear. You know we love you!"

Emma grabbed Charlotte's arm. "The last time I got any action was during the Bush administration, too, so don't feel bad," she whispered with a reassuring squeeze.

Charlotte rolled her eyes as Emma and Karen trailed off, furtive whispers passing between them before they began to giggle like high school girls. Charlotte let out a deep sigh and let her shoulders slump.

Did that just happen? And which Bush administration was she *talking about?* Charlotte asked herself before she shook her head and headed to the cabin. The shower from David's bathroom was running, and Charlotte went to rinse her coffee cup in the sink. Charlotte heard a yelp come from David's bathroom. Startled, she dropped the mug in the sink and ran toward the door.

Charlotte pressed her ear to the door. "David, are you okay?" she asked.

"Yes—there was a rush of cold water for a sec," came David's muffled reply. "It's okay now, just startled me a bit!"

Charlotte bit her lip, embarrassed, yet relieved he was okay. Turning on the hot water to rinse out the coffee cup had violated shower courtesy; it had been so long since she had lived with someone that she'd forgotten.

The shower stopped. Not wanting to be found lurking outside David's door, Charlotte scurried over to a chair in the living room and began to thumb through a *People* magazine. David walked over to Charlotte, a blotchy green towel wrapped around his waist. His dark hair was slicked back, and the sunlight danced across the muscles of his nearly nude body. Charlotte gulped.

David grinned. "So what's the routine for a little breakfast? I'm starved."

Charlotte gripped the magazine, the glossy pages sticking to her moist fingertips. She licked her lips and tried to stave off the coming heat wave threatening to overtake her. It *had* been such a long time…

Charlotte cleared her throat. "Dining cabin in about five minutes. And I have dish duty today."

"Well, it's been some time since I washed dishes. Should be fun." He turned to leave the room. "Give me a minute; I'll be right out."

As David disappeared into his room, Charlotte slammed the magazine shut and began to fan her face with it. What was wrong with her? She never got this undone by, well...*anything*. She couldn't remember the last time the mere presence of a man had made her swoon like a schoolgirl. Besides... it was like she'd told Karen and Emma, there was no way in the world someone like him, at his age, would *ever* be interested in her. He was just an incredibly sweet person who was being nice to her, repaying his gratitude for helping him hide.

Right?

For what seemed like the millionth time that morning, Charlotte shook her head and resumed leafing through the magazine. A few minutes later, David emerged in a pair of stonewashed jeans and a blue T-shirt, the sleeves of which hugged the width of his biceps. Charlotte bit her lip in an effort to keep from taking a big bite out of him. The scent that had intoxicated her yesterday engulfed the room, and David's green eyes flashed that now-familiar devilish charm.

"Shall we?" David motioned to the door.

Charlotte tossed the magazine to the coffee table and stood. "Sounds good."

David held the door open for Charlotte, and the two stepped outside. In the few moments they'd been in the cabin, the early morning chill had been replaced with gentle, balmy winds. The sun burned bright, and Charlotte made a mental note to herself to pick up some sunglasses in town.

"How's your head this morning?" David smiled.

Charlotte tucked an escaped strand of hair behind her ear. "Better after I had my coffee. Thank you, by the way, for leaving me a fresh pot."

David shrugged. "I figured that'd be the first thing you'd want. Besides a big plate of bacon and eggs. Unless you're a vegetarian."

Charlotte snorted. "Hardly. Or do you not remember me inhaling those meatballs last night?"

David opened the door to the dining cabin for Charlotte. "Ah—that you did."

David and Charlotte had missed most of the breakfast rush, though there were still plenty of carbs to be enjoyed; cheese Danishes, bagels, and donuts were on one side of the table, while a bowl of scrambled eggs and a plate with three lone slices of bacon stood at the other end. The requisite boxes of sensible cereals, cartons of yogurt, and a decimated fruit salad rounded out the middle.

As David and Charlotte perused the breakfast offerings, many of the ladies made a point to stop by to say hello to David, who in turn asked each woman how she was. Even Hendra, on her way out to set up a writing workshop for the day, asked David how he'd slept and if there was anything she could get him. Charlotte bit her tongue over what a difference a night made.

Charlotte picked off the last of the bacon, a cheese Danish, and another cup of coffee. David scooped up the remaining eggs, fruit salad, two yogurts, and a cup of coffee. They sat by themselves at the far end of the table. Still more admirers streamed over to talk to David, eager to hear additional tales of Hollywood and bask in his charisma and good looks. David was gracious and charming with each woman. Charlotte chewed her Danish, watching him. She would have thought a famous actor like David King would be pompous and demanding. However, in less than twenty-four hours with him, Charlotte could tell David was the real deal.

David stood and began to collect his and Charlotte's dishes. "Well, ladies, please excuse me, but I promised Charlotte I'd help with the dishes. I hope we can pick up where we left off later."

The small gathering was duly impressed by David's adoption of domestic duties, and several gave Charlotte winks as they headed out the door.

"Once again you've got the ladies eating out of the palm of your hand," Charlotte said as she filled the sink with suds.

David shrugged and began to scrape the breakfast remnants into the trash. "I enjoy people. Besides, everyone here has been so nice and gracious. Why shouldn't I return the favor?"

Charlotte mulled this over as she gathered a small pile of plates and plunked them into the hot, soapy water.

And they say chivalry is dead, Charlotte marveled to herself while David went back into the dining room to collect the remaining dishes. Charlotte began to scrub the plates and stack them in the adjoining sink. She heard him come back in and motioned with her head toward the dishes. "You're on rinse-and-dry duty."

He nodded. "No problem."

They worked in silence, but before long, Charlotte got the sense that David was looking at her again. It was confirmed when she turned and saw he'd stopped drying a plate. Instead, his head was tilted to the side, a confused look on his face. She brushed a shoulder across her nose, thinking there really was something hanging out of it this time.

"What?" Charlotte dropped her shoulders, exasperated. "You're always looking at me like that. What is it?"

David cleared his throat. "I really want to ask you a question, but you may consider it rude."

"Five foot two if I stand up super straight," she said as she jutted her shoulders back and stood as tall as she could. She smiled and gave him a wink.

David rolled his eyes. "No, no, no. Not how tall you are or how tall you're *not*...though it's another question that's almost as personal." He stopped and looked at her, hoping she'd bail him out. He shifted his feet and looked down at the kitchen tiles. Charlotte gave him a questioning look.

"Okay, you caught me...I'm really a brunette," she teased.

"No, no. Not your hair color, which is gorgeous. It's just...the rudest question you could ask a woman, but it's making me crazy," he whispered and paused for a moment. "How old are you, Charlotte?"

His cheeks turned bright red, and he looked like he wished he could take it back. He resumed drying a fistful of silverware.

Charlotte put down the glass she was washing and leaned against the sink, intrigued. She decided to have a little fun with him. "Well, David, how old do you think I am?" A Cheshire cat grin stretched across her face.

"Thirty-two."

Charlotte stifled a chuckle and shook her head. "Nope, but thanks," she said, still toying with him.

"No?" he asked.

"Forty-four...a week from Saturday," she said nonchalantly.

He paused and smiled. "You don't look it."

"Charming. Are you this way with every woman you meet?"

David wiped the counters, moving around her as she finished the dishes. "You may not believe this, Charlotte...but I'm really not great around women. I'm always wondering if they're spending time with me because they're truly interested in me or hanging out with me because, well, I'm David King. You know what I mean?"

"I've never thought about what that must be like. I'm sure a lot of women you meet are just looking for their fifteen minutes. It must be frustrating." She handed him one last dish to dry. "Do you date a lot? Or is that too personal of a question?" She smirked.

David grinned. "I used to. Date a lot, that is. It got boring after a while. I was always meeting the same type of girl, shallow, plastic bimbos with more matter in their breasts than their brains. When I do red carpets, I like going with someone, but even that got old, so now if I do go, I go alone."

Charlotte drained the sink of dishwater and realized that, for a thirty-year-old, David had a whole slew of problems she'd never had to deal with. It was true; you never knew what other people were going through. Charlotte reminded herself that David was here to relax, not get wound up over his problems. A change of subject was in order.

"Hey, would you please look at the schedule on the fridge and see if I have cooking duty for breakfast tomorrow?"

David took a quick glance and nodded. "Yes, we do. What time do we start?" he asked.

Charlotte grinned at the *we*." "So you're going to help me? Do you even know how to cook?"

"I can scramble an egg and use a toaster."

"Well, that's two things more than me." Charlotte gave the area around the sink one last swipe with the sponge. "We should plan to get in here around seven." She turned to look at David and wiped a few drops of sweat from her forehead with the back of her hand. "I usually go for a walk around the lake about now. Want to join me?"

David hung the now-wet dishtowel over the faucet. "I'd love to."

They headed toward the lake, the sun dancing on the smooth sheet of blue glass. Neither of them spoke; the sound of chirping birds was the only soundtrack to their stroll. David broke the silence. "I'd like to read one of your books. Do you have any copies here?"

Charlotte burst out laughing. "Trust me when I say this; you don't want to read my books. Read Karen's or Hendra's. Not mine. They wouldn't interest you."

David touched Charlotte's arm, stopping her. "Why? You said you write romance novels, right?"

"Yes."

David shaded his eyes with his hand. "Have you ever seen any of my movies? Okay, yes, I have made a few action films, but I've done more love stories than anything."

"Yeah, well, there are love stories and there are *love* stories."

"Oh, come on, Charlotte—I want to read one!" David pouted, demand bubbling up in his voice.

Charlotte resumed walking and shrugged her shoulders. "I'm sorry to disappoint you, but I don't have any copies here. If you really want one... well, you can go back into town and get one!" She grinned and gave him a wink. "Although, I'd like to see you try, considering I have the car keys."

David nodded his head, impressed by this worthy competitor. "So it's like that, eh? All right, then, go into town and get me one."

"Yeah, like I'm going to walk into the local bookstore, where everyone knows me by name, and buy my own book. I don't think so."

David let out a low whistle. "Well, I'm sure I could convince one of the ladies to give me a lift into town." He snapped his fingers. "You know, come to think of it, I *am* running out of toothpaste."

Charlotte gasped. "You wouldn't dare."

"*Hmm.* Maybe not. But you know that as soon as I leave here, I'll read them all," he teased. David turned to look at Charlotte, those green eyes affixed to her mouth. Charlotte licked her lips, nervous. "Have you ever seen any of my movies?" he asked, his voice husky.

Charlotte shoved her hands in her pockets, a chill slicing over her in spite of the sun's warmth.

"A few." She looked down at her feet. "Only one that I liked, though."

"Oh yeah? Which one?"

Charlotte cocked her head to the side. "The one where you and the girl are stuck in a snowstorm and have to screw all night to stay warm." She paused. "Personally, I thought it was Oscar worthy," Charlotte said, her face quivering with corked laughter.

"Well, that does it then. I'm finding a way into town—even if I have to hitchhike—and getting a book." David tapped Charlotte's arm. "I'm sure you must have a chapter or two where your characters need to *stay warm*." He stopped. "Wait. That's the *only* one you liked?"

Charlotte laughed. He didn't need to know that not only had she'd seen all of his movies—some twice—but she also thought he was amazing in all of them. Now back in front of their cabin, Charlotte looked at her watch and saw that her first activity of the day was starting in ten minutes.

Charlotte grabbed a book and a pad of paper out of her purse while David flopped on the couch. "Listen, I've got to head over to one of the other cabins for a few hours. You're sure you can entertain yourself?"

"I've actually got a script that William has been bugging me to read, so I'm going to do that, and no matter how brilliant it is, I'm going to tell him it was dreadful." David winked. "William's a rather easy mark."

Charlotte rolled her eyes and opened the door. "Well…have fun with that."

A famished and spent Charlotte made her way back to the cabin that afternoon. She'd just gotten out of the book club meeting, which was discussing *Madame Bovary*. The conversations had become rather rousing; while they could all agree she was amoral, the group couldn't come to consensus on whether her foolish, fumbling husband, Charles, had driven actions or if she would have wreaked the havoc she had no matter whom she had married. All Charlotte wanted to do for the next few minutes was spend some quality time with a Twinkie.

And David. David. She said his name softly and in spite of herself was thrilled at the thought of finding him waiting for her. Charlotte smoothed back her hair and took a few deep breaths before she opened the door.

She found David in the chair across from the couch, laptop in hand, his feet propped up on the linen trunk that he had pulled over from underneath the window. He was in a trance, his lips moving in silence along with whatever he was reading on the screen. Charlotte closed the door, and David never even flinched. She jangled her keys a bit and made a show of setting her book and papers down on the coffee table. Still nothing. She stood for a moment, hands on hips, watching him, before she tapped him on the foot. He looked up startled and then smiled.

"Oh, hello! Sorry I didn't hear you come in. I was rather engrossed in this." David brought his feet to the floor and placed the laptop on the trunk. "How is everyone?"

Charlotte kicked off her shoes and sat on the couch across from him.

"Good." She placed her head in the palm of her hands. "Must be some script," she said, dying to know if she'd get a peek at the next David King blockbuster.

"Oh. Oh that. I finished that an hour ago." David cast his eyes down and looked up at her through his eyelashes, a wicked smirk on his face. Charlotte wondered how many times he used that look to seduce the panties off women.

Charlotte's eyes narrowed to slits, knowing something was up and also weary from his constant teasing. "Okay, what is it—what's with the face?"

"Nothing," he said in a singsong voice before he leaned toward her, that playful leer dancing on his lips. "Did you know you can download books on the Internet?"

Charlotte's face fell as she realized what he was driving at.

"And, more important, did you know that you can download *your* books on the Internet?" He batted his eyes at her like a ten-year-old trying to charm his way into the cookie jar.

Charlotte turned crimson. "Which one?" she asked, afraid of the answer.

David leaned against the chair and folded his hands in his lap, pleased with his handiwork. "Well, I thought I'd start from the beginning of your series, *Hot Cabo Nights*, and then move on to *Parisian Pleasure*," he said, unable to contain his rich, throaty laughter.

Charlotte popped up from the couch and headed to the kitchen, beyond embarrassed. "I hope you're enjoying yourself," she squeaked. "Can I review your movies now?"

"You already did!" he gasped with laughter. "Oscar worthy—remember?" He was now doubled, practically hyperventilating.

Embarrassed, Charlotte fumbled through the cabinets in search of a Twinkie, but couldn't locate them. Now of all times to not be able to find a Twinkie...

"Charlotte, my dear, you are one naughty girl."

Charlotte found the Twinkie box, but couldn't get it open. She heard David stand and walk over to her.

"I need a cold shower!"

Charlotte ripped open the box and grabbed a snack cake, tearing into the cellophane wrap with her teeth. Her hands were shaking, and she felt like crawling in a hole.

"Hey, look at me," David said as he tugged on Charlotte's shoulder to get her to turn around and face him. Charlotte looked down, but David tilted her chin up and pulled her face toward his. "You are a damn fine writer. I read up on you, and you're well loved by your readers. You should be proud of that."

Charlotte sighed, still flustered over her sensitivity about her vocation. "I don't write great American novels, but they pay the bills." Charlotte felt the beginning of a tear rim one eye and looked up at the ceiling, hoping she could make it glide back to where it came from. David's proximity wasn't helping her frazzled state. He broke away from her and leaned against the counter.

"When did you write your first book?"

Charlotte sat down at the kitchen table, where David joined her. "Twenty-two. I was lucky and got published my first time out of the gate."

"Twenty-two?" he yelped. "You could write that steamy stuff at twenty-two?"

Charlotte shrugged and shoved a finger into the squishy white cream of her Twinkie. "My mother always told me I had an active imagination. All I did was use it for good, not evil."

David put his chin in his hand. "You have nothing to be embarrassed about, Charlotte. I'll give you this, you're good with the written word… You ever thought about screenwriting?"

Charlotte shook her head.

"You might do okay. Of course, the suits would have to tone it down, though, unless you don't object to an X rating."

Charlotte shot daggers in David's direction, and he put his hand on her arm to calm her down. "All right, all right, no more teasing." He stared at her, a serious look on his face. "Friends do tease each other though, Charlotte, and I consider you a friend."

Charlotte's tension slid away, and she felt her breath release. She placed her hand over his, and the two gazed at each other for a moment before Charlotte cleared her throat and polished off the last of the Twinkie.

"Well, I'm glad you think of me as a friend. Now be my best friend and make me a drink."

"More wine?"

"Ugh, no. No wine for a few days. Actually, my drink of choice is a Cape Cod."

David crinkled his nose. "What's that?"

"Vodka and cranberry juice with a twist of lime and lots of ice."

David nodded and stood. "I think I can manage that."

"Thanks."

Charlotte stared out the window while she waited for David to finish making them drinks. He set one down in front of her and waited for her to try it.

"Does it pass inspection?"

Charlotte took a huge gulp, and her eyes grew wide. "Whoa! Little on the strong side." She coughed and plunked the glass down on the table. "Trying to get me drunk, huh?"

David frowned and picked up the glass. "Let me sip." He took a swig and nearly choked. "Wow. Sorry. I don't make my own very often; I am obviously not good at it."

She took both their glasses. "Or too good at it," she said as she went to the fridge to add a little more ice and cranberry juice.

"You know, all the sex aside, *Cabo Nights* is a beautiful story. I'm rather looking forward to reading the next one. What a tragic ending, though. Why do all the good love stories have to have such sad endings?"

Charlotte smiled a little, secretly pleased he had enjoyed her book. She rejoined him at the table. "Not all of them do," she said as she took a sip of her new drink and nodded her approval.

David looked at his watch. "So we've got about an hour before dinner. How about a game of cards?"

Charlotte ran her fingertip along the rim of her glass. "Can I ask you a question?"

"Do you think it will take an hour?"

Charlotte chuckled and shook her head. "No. I was just wondering. Where do you live? Do you have a house or homes? I guess, what I mean is, is there a place you call home?"

"Well, I don't really have a home." He leaned back and drained his drink. "I rented a beach house in L.A. for about a year while I was filming a movie. I haven't had the time to really shop for a home, and honestly I don't know where I would look." David stood to make himself a fresh drink. "I split my time pretty evenly between L.A. and New York, with lots of storage units in between." He sat back down at the table. "You mentioned L.A. earlier. Where in L.A. are you?"

Charlotte didn't realize she was holding her breath. Did he have any idea how beautiful he was? The long, graceful fingers, juicy red lips, and glossy black hair that always seemed to fall into those green eyes at the sexiest of angles. She realized, as usual, he was looking her directly in the eye, hanging, it seemed, on her every word. She straightened up.

"Santa Monica."

What kind of kisser was he? With lips like those, he couldn't be bad. Was he hard and passionate or slow and sexy? Charlotte felt herself start to tingle and took a drink to cool down. She caught a chunk of ice in her mouth.

"Tell me about your parents," she garbled through the ice.

David grew quiet; the only sound was him swirling the ice around in his glass. "Well, my dad, Hugh, died when I was ten."

Charlotte nodded. "I remember you mentioned that at dinner last night. What happened?"

"Heart attack in his sleep." David snapped his fingers. "Just like that. Dead at forty-five."

"That's awful. I'm sorry."

"My mum, Frances, never stopped crying. She was just so sad. She tried to soldier on, but there were too many memories of Dad in England. So she packed me up, and off to New York we went."

"Why New York?"

"She had spent a summer there when she was at university and loved it. It seemed like the perfect place to make a fresh start. We used to call ourselves the 'Two Musketeers,' taking on this brave new world. We had only each other."

"Sounds like you two are close."

David nodded, his eyes misting over. "Were. She died from breast cancer right after my first film came out."

Charlotte reached out and rested her hand on top of David's. He gave it a quick squeeze.

"What do you remember about your dad?" Charlotte asked.

David let out a sigh, his mind shifting back to happier days. "Gosh. There are so many things." David held his chin between his thumb and forefinger. "He used to read me a bedtime story every night. Sometimes we'd share a strawberry jam sandwich and bottle of ginger ale after kicking the football around on Sunday afternoons. Soccer, I guess you call it. One of my favorite memories is going to Piccadilly Circus. You've heard of it?"

Charlotte nodded. "Yes, but I don't know too much about it."

"Well, it's a lot like Times Square in New York, if that helps. People, lights, shops all jammed into one another like bumper cars out of control. Anyway, we'd hop on the Tube every Saturday, and Dad would buy me a little tin of jelly babies from the candy shop inside the station. We'd go into the listening booth of his favorite record shop, and he'd put these massive headphones on me, sound shooting out of each ear and filling up my little body with music. He played me his favorite singers, mostly American soul. Lots of Motown, Otis Redding, Sam Cooke, Aretha Franklin. Oh, gosh, he was mad for her. Funny enough, he wasn't much of a Beatles fan."

"Really? I thought everyone loved the Beatles."

"No, he was much more of a Stones man." He leaned back in his chair and gave her one of his intense gazes. "What about your family?"

Charlotte cleared her throat. "Um, well, both of my parents are also dead. My dad had a series of strokes and was gone within a few months. In less than a year, my mom was gone too. The official ruling was 'natural causes,' but it was of a broken heart, if you ask me."

"That's terrible."

Charlotte gave him a wry grin before she continued. "They were in their seventies, married fifty years. They were told they could never have children, so they were pretty surprised when I came along."

"An *aha*! baby."

"Precisely. They spoiled me rotten, treated me like a total princess. But it was all because they loved me so much, and for that I'm grateful."

"That's tough they went so close together."

"Yes and no. They were extremely devoted to each other—never spent a day apart their entire marriage. They used to joke that when one went, the other one would follow. Every night at dinner, my mom would ask, 'How was your day, Joe?' and he would say "Boy, Marie, it was hard because I sure did miss you.' And she'd always respond, 'And I missed you, too.'" Charlotte chuckled. "It was their little running joke. They had a lot of those. I used to think it was corny, but as I got older, I realized how sweet it was. It's my favorite childhood memory of them."

"It sounds like I would've liked them," David said.

"You would have. Everyone who knew them loved them." Charlotte leaned forward. "Your parents sound amazing. I wish I could have met them." She took another mouthful of ice. "Did your mother ever find love again?"

David shook his head, his voice foggy. "No...she never did. When she got the cancer diagnosis, she was eerily calm. I asked her why she wasn't more upset. I mean, I was ready to tear the doctor's office apart if it meant I'd find a cure. She just told me she would fight it, but that if she lost the battle, at least she could be with my father again. She seemed to miss him more as time went on, though she put on a brave face for me."

"Our parents sound similar," Charlotte said quietly.

"Yeah. Like kindred spirits or something." David swallowed the last of his drink and looked at her glass. "Want another one?"

"Only if I want to show up drunk at dinner."

David took their glasses and rinsed them in the sink. "Good point. Okay, then, let's wait until dinner to have another." They started to walk to the door. "What do you suppose the topic of conversation will be tonight?"

"I don't know. Maybe we could start a topic. If you really want to get them going, we can discuss the pay difference between NBA players and teachers," she giggled.

"Oh no, don't do that. Because then they may bring up overpaid actors, and I rather like being an overpaid actor."

Charlotte laughed.

As they walked to dinner, they met up with Angela and Hendra.

"Well hello, you two," Hendra purred. "Hungry, I hope?"

David smiled. "Indeed. I was so engrossed in reading a script, I skipped lunch completely."

He winked at Charlotte, who just shook her head. David held the door to the dining room open, where only mild chaos was underway. Karen was on dinner duty, which usually resulted in madness of some kind. Women ran back and forth from the kitchen brandishing pots, plates, platters, and glasses.

"Is there anything I can do to help?" David asked.

"Yes, save your energy for afterward. You and Charlotte are on cleanup tonight. After Karen's been in there, who knows what you might find," Angela remarked with a husky chuckle.

Karen had embarked on a hearty coq au vin with a simple green salad and loaves of crispy French bread. They all ladled soup into their bowls and piled their plates high with salad and bread before sitting down. Karen bustled out of the kitchen, her white apron stained with various smears of food and sauce. Her face was flushed, and little wisps of hair were plastered to her neck. She leaned between Charlotte and David. "I'll apologize ahead of time for the kitchen. It's really bad."

Charlotte let out a dramatic gasp. "Really, Karen? I'm shocked. It's not like I wasn't in the kitchen all night cleaning up after you the last time."

"Ha ha," Karen responded. "Listen, when you're creating a masterpiece, it's gonna get a little messy."

"Well, it is delicious," Charlotte allowed. She looked at David. "It's possible we could be in there until tomorrow."

Under the table, Karen pinched Charlotte, who yelped.

Karen turned to David. "Do you know how to do dishes, hon?"

"How about you give me a lesson after dinner?"

"Ha! Not on your life. Nice try."

Karen left to get her own food. The ladies seemed less starstruck by David as conversations centered on more mundane topics such as grandkids and dog-walking services. After a few moments, one of the ladies, Sally, stood and clinked her fork against her wineglass to get everyone's attention. A hush fell over the room as they waited for her to address the group.

"I have a subject to discuss tonight...men, romance, and marriage" Sally stated, a triumphant look on her face.

Murmurs of complaint and even a few loud protests sprang from the room. Sally held up her hands to quiet everyone.

"Now, now. Hear me out," she continued. "We have a man here with us tonight, and although young, maybe he can shed some light on the subject. Perhaps tell us the truth about how men really feel about marriage, romance, and relationships in general."

David's fork was in midair when all eyes turned toward him; it was clear he was caught off guard by Sally's declaration.

"Sally, come on now. That's not fair," Charlotte said. "David's our guest and—"

David held up his hand to stop Charlotte.

"No, no. It's okay. You have all been so nice to me, so I owe you one." David took a sip of water and cleared his throat before he continued. "So how do men feel about romance and marriage? Well, I have never been married, so I can't speak to that, but I can tell you I believe in it. I believe in a partnership in love, life, and romance. I think romance is the battery that keeps the relationship charged, if you will. The reason men act callous about romance is to give the appearance of being manly or macho, but personally I think that, deep inside, men love it, the thrill of being able to make a woman melt. They love the excitement of having a woman make them feel alive. I can't speak for all men, but I know the thought of being *in love* is exciting for me. I personally have never been in love. I've been in *like*...I've been in *lust*, which I had confused for love at one time, but I know now for sure it was lust. The possibility of finding love one day excites me, gives me something to look forward to. Whoever she is, I look forward to getting to know her, and I can't wait to meet her."

Once David finished his speech, smiles beamed on the faces of some women as they gleaned more insight not only about men, but about David. Others looked contemplative as they reflected on their own past loves. The room was silent.

Hendra piped up. "Being that you could probably have any woman you wanted—and probably have..."—a few women tittered, and David chuckled—"how do you know if someone truly loves you? How would you know if she was really there for you or just with you because of who you are?" Hendra asked, genuine concern furrowing her brow.

Charlotte and David stole a quick glance at each other, the memory of their earlier conversation still on both their minds.

"I would hope I could get to know a person well enough to be able to see true love for me in her eyes. I chose this life knowing there would be sacrifices; maybe that's one of the sacrifices. Will I be absolutely sure that the one who says she loves me really does and not for my money or fame? But doesn't *everyone* wonder 'does this person really love *me?*' I just have to hope that I will be blessed to find the person who loves me for me and that I can grow old with and be with her...until the end," David said as he shoved a piece of bread into his mouth.

Karen looked at Charlotte, who was looking at David. She snickered to herself as she picked up her glass of wine. "Well, David dear, I hope you find the person you are looking for. Just make sure you let us know when you do, because we want all the juicy details!"

Emma leaned over and touched David's hand. "Honey, you don't have to look, because I'm sitting right here. My end is coming a lot sooner than yours, but I can promise you that you will enjoy it while it lasts!"

"I have no doubt," David laughed. "You really are too much for me, Emma."

"You don't know the half of it. But if you want to find out"—she winked—"you let me know."

David kissed Emma's hand, and in spite of all her cool come-ons, she blushed.

Charlotte marveled at the scene in front of her and was proud and happy she'd been able to give David this opportunity. Dinner marched on with stories of first dates, bad dates, blind dates, and dates that never should have been. The entire group was in stitches the whole night, and David took his fair share of teasing from the ladies. However, he gave as good as he got, and Charlotte could see that he enjoyed the ladies as much as they enjoyed him.

David's words about love stirred in Charlotte's head as she observed him talking and laughing with everyone. Her insides felt tight, and her breath raced a little. She couldn't fight it; she was falling for him in a big way. The realization made her feel foolish and excited at the same time.

People began to trickle out of the dining room, but not before offering Charlotte and David their condolences on having cleanup duty. They waited until they were alone before venturing to the kitchen.

David poked his head in first and let out a low whistle. "Oh dear. It's like Armageddon in there. Run...Save yourself," David joked.

Charlotte peered around him and gasped. "Holy crap. Let's just burn it down."

Greasy pots and pans and crusty dishes were stacked almost to the ceiling. Food was splattered across the walls and the floor, and it looked like the chicken may well have exploded all over the stove.

Charlotte clamped her hand across her forehead and groaned. "I've never seen it this bad," she muttered. "I mean, this is ridiculous." Her arms dropped to her sides. "I'm not even sure where to start."

David took on the task of filling the sink with hot water, the bubbles from the dishwashing liquid floating up and across the room. "Oh, come on. Teamwork!" He winked. "We'll get it done."

David started to bring dishes over to the sink as Charlotte wearily grabbed a sponge and began to scrub plates.

"Hey." Charlotte turned and saw David taking down an old transistor radio from atop the refrigerator. "I don't remember the last time I saw one of these," he said as he searched for the power button.

Charlotte laughed. "Probably belongs to Hendra. She's quite averse to technology. She's one of those stubborn souls who still uses typewriters."

"Eww."

"Yeah."

David found the knob to turn the radio on, and sound crackled out of the lone, battered speaker like crinkled paper. David frowned and fiddled with the tuner until he came across an oldies station. Martha and the Vandellas struggled to tell them about "Dancing in the Street." David pulled out the antenna and wound it around a few times until the sound pushed through clear as a bell.

"Huh. That doesn't sound half bad," Charlotte muttered, surprised. David started to sing along, and Charlotte was impressed not only that he knew the song, but also by his singing voice, which was actually pretty good.

"Well, that's a little before your time. So you like old songs, huh?" Charlotte asked.

"I like classics," David clarified as he picked up a dish to start drying it. "Like I told you, my dad gave me real appreciation for music. *Good* music."

They continued with their task, the ancient transistor radio spitting out everything from the Beach Boys to Jerry Lee Lewis to Elvis Presley, a lively soundtrack to the drudgery of scouring the kitchen. David knew the lyrics to every song and even provided her with a few bits of trivia. Before long, the kitchen started to sparkle again. What with the abundance of dishes, wine, and music, they were getting a little slaphappy. "The Twist" came on, and David twirled Charlotte's hips from side to side, both in hysterics by this point. Just as they managed to settle down a bit, the unmistakable strains of "You Really Got a Hold on Me" poured through the radio. David yanked Charlotte to him.

"Come on! Dance with me."

Before she knew it, their bodies had melted into one another with ease. His breath, pungent with the tang of wine and chicken, was hot against her ear. Charlotte inhaled his scent, the sheer joy threatening to make her crumple to the floor. Sensing her near collapse, David put one arm around her waist and held her hand against his chest. They began to sway in time to the music, though the truth was the only sound Charlotte could hear was the beating of his heart. She closed her eyes and let him move her around the little kitchen.

"You're very tall," Charlotte whispered.

"And you are not," David replied.

They continued to move, and David was careful to lead her so that her rhythm matched his. She felt the tip of his nose burrow in her hair.

"Strawberries," he said.

"Strawberries," she responded as she ran her hands up and down the length of his arms. The soft skin she felt beneath her fingers belied the massive strength rippling under the surface. The song ended, and David pulled away and bent down to look at her face.

"I think we're done in here," he said, his voice whisper soft.

"Agreed."

David turned the radio off and flipped the switch to the kitchen lights. He grabbed her hand, and she tried to keep her grip light, afraid of scaring him off by squeezing too hard. They arrived at the cabin, and as Charlotte reached into her pocket for the key, David stopped her.

"What? What's wrong?"

David stayed one porch step below Charlotte so they were eye to eye. Fireflies buzzed around David's head like a halo, and the lights from the moon cast a warm glow across his chiseled face.

"Charlotte," David whispered, his finger trailing up her arm, sending a tingle up her spine. She gulped.

"Yes?"

"May I kiss you?" he asked, the words tumbling out like coins dropping into a slot.

Charlotte blinked, certain she hadn't heard that right. Why would he want to kiss her? He was gorgeous, one of the most beautiful creatures of this or any world. Not to mention she was almost fourteen years older than he was and looked *nothing* like those magnificent blonde gazelles she often saw glued to his arm in magazines. She wasn't a great beauty, and she'd always been proud of her age. Now they were both staring her in the face like the drop on a five-hundred-foot-high roller coaster. Suddenly she felt like an awkward, gangly teenager, scared and unsure of herself. God, she hated feeling this way.

"Charlotte," David repeated.

"Why?" she asked.

David recoiled. "What do you mean why?"

"Why do you want to kiss me?" she asked.

"Why *wouldn't* I want to kiss you?" he laughed, puzzled. "You're a beautiful, amazing woman, and I'm dying to know what it feels like to kiss you." He pulled her by the elbows closer to him. "I'll ask you again. May I kiss you?"

Charlotte took a deep breath, her teeth trembling. "Yes. Kiss me."

David slid his hands around Charlotte's face and held them there for what seemed like a lifetime. He began to move toward her, but Charlotte was impatient. She leaned in and took his lips in hers. Their tongues swirled around each other in sexy, dreamy circles. Much like their dance in the kitchen, David slowed Charlotte's movements to match his own as he teased her with long, languid kisses and more sensual nibbles. Charlotte's insides were like runny chocolate oozing out of her toes. She'd forgotten what it was like to feel this way. Had she ever felt this way? David pulled back, his lips shining in the moonlight. Fumbling for the doorknob, Charlotte flung the door open, and David gave her a gentle push inside, planting yet more soft kisses across her lips. They kept the lights out.

"Drink?" he asked.

Charlotte swallowed, various and sordid thoughts bouncing around her head like rogue pinballs. "I don't know. I'm trying to keep my head on straight," she murmured.

David took her hand and traced the lines of her palm with her fingertips. "Drink or not, my head's a little potty as well."

"Your head's what?"

"Ah, potty, *potty*—like loopy, out of sorts." He cupped her face in his hands again. "God, I love kissing you," he said as he drew her into another soulful kiss. Finally he planted a kiss on her forehead and smiled.

Charlotte felt her knees buckle, and as she looked into those perfect emerald eyes, she dissolved into goo. She pulled away from him, her breath ragged. "I need a minute," Charlotte said as she sat down on the couch, her whole body a mass of Jell-O. David joined her.

He reached out and rubbed her shoulder, the gesture sending another shock through Charlotte. "Why don't you turn in and sleep on it, Charlotte? I don't want you to feel uncomfortable about anything. Your friendship is too important to me."

"You kiss all your friends like that?"

"The ones I want to keep."

"You have referred to me as your 'friend' quite a bit these past few days. You really think we'll keep in touch after we leave here?"

As soon as the words slipped out, Charlotte wished she could grab them and stuff them back in her mouth. She sounded like a high school girl who worries that Johnny won't call her after she made out with him in the backseat of his convertible.

David cocked his head to the side, a smile tugging at the corner of his lips. He touched the side of her face. "I knew I made a lifelong friend the minute we met. The fact that you didn't mace me sealed the deal."

They both chuckled before Charlotte resumed her serious tone. "David, I don't want you to get the wrong idea about me. I'm not like the women in my books. I haven't been in a relationship in a while...a long while. I don't consider myself a sexy, steamy lover type."

David put his finger over her mouth to shush her. "I am well aware of who you are," he replied. "Besides, I'm not the suave action guy, go-all-night Romeo you see on the screen. I haven't been in a relationship in quite some time either."

Charlotte looked at him, stunned. "Shut the front door."

"I'm quite serious." He picked up her hand again. "Listen, what I do know about you is that you are a kind, smart, and funny woman who I want to get to know better. I know there is something between us, and I know you feel it too. But if it makes you feel uncomfortable taking it further, we won't."

Charlotte shook her head, still reeling from this turn of events.

"What?" he asked.

"I'm just going to spit this out."

"Go ahead," he replied, unsure of what to expect.

She took a deep breath and plunged in. "David, I'm forty-three. I'm *nothing* like the women you're used to dating. I don't wear sexy lingerie—boxer briefs and tank tops are my preferred sleepwear. Bras irritate me. I snore. I shave my armpits and legs every few days—if I remember. My idea of a romantic evening is to stay home, watch a movie, and be in bed by nine. I don't go to bars; I *don't* sleep around. I find most people your age annoying and spoiled. I'm set in my ways, and never in my wildest dreams did I expect someone like you to show up in my life. If I had known you were coming, I would've dropped a few pounds, and truthfully...I never thought of myself as getting old until I met you. Kissing you excites me to no end and makes me want to run screaming at the same time."

Charlotte realized she was rambling, and she snapped her mouth together to make herself shut up. She looked at David, waiting for a response.

Nothing.

"David?"

He stared at her.

Charlotte's heart jackhammered against her chest. "David? Say something."

More silence. Charlotte realized he'd pressed his mouth into a thin line, and even in the moonlight he looked mad. Furious, in fact.

David unfolded himself from the couch and stood over her, his voice shaking as he spoke in careful, measured tones.

"Most people my age irritate me too. I couldn't care less how old you are. I would bet money I snore ten times louder than you do. Sexy lingerie *is* a huge waste of money because you usually have it on only for a minute or two. And believe it or not, I don't sleep around either. And why would you comment on your weight? Do you think that because I'm an actor I'm only attracted to toothpicks? Most of the actresses I work with look ill. Don't forget the camera adds ten pounds, so can you imagine what I look at all day? Skeletons…who wants to make love to a skeleton? And Charlotte, I don't care if you're fat, skinny, or somewhere in between. I want you because I think you're smart and strong and brave and funny and fun. I hate to think that I may have brought out your insecurities because of who I am. If your appearance and your age didn't bother you before I came around, then I guess you think I'm pretty damn shallow."

David stopped, realizing he was ranting as she had. He took a deep breath and brushed a chunk of hair out of his eyes.

"I need some air," he spat as he turned on his heel and stormed out the door.

"David! David, wait!" Charlotte jumped off the couch and ran after him. But it was too late.

He was gone.

CHAPTER 4

Charlotte stared at herself in the bathroom mirror and sighed. It had been a half hour since David had fled the cabin, and Charlotte was worried and mad at herself. Why had she opened her big mouth anyway? It was a trait that had irritated Ben and had been pointed out by more than one well-meaning friend. As Charlotte halfheartedly brushed her teeth, she realized David was right; deep down she *had* thought he had to be shallow and concerned only with how a woman looked, not who she was. Charlotte pulled her ponytail holder out of her hair and with methodical strokes ran her brush through the liberated curls. Charlotte let out another sigh before she ran a tube of gloss across her lips.

It was the damn age difference that was screwing with her head. It didn't seem to bother him, so why did it bother her? He was acting more grown-up than she was at the moment. Charlotte snorted as she made her way back to the living room. She leaned against the window frame and spotted his moonlit silhouette sitting near the lake. She placed her palm against the cool glass.

"He must be freezing," she murmured to herself. She grabbed two blankets from the couch and opened the door; the contrast between the warm cocoon of the cabin and the frigid night air was like a slap in the face. She had it coming. She walked over and could see goose bumps lining David's arms. Charlotte slipped one of the blankets around his shoulders before she wrapped the other around herself and sat down next to him.

"Thanks," he whispered.

"I'm sorry," Charlotte replied as she put her head on his shoulder.

He draped one arm around her shoulders and kissed the top of her head. "Strawberries," he said.

"Strawberries."

They sat like that for a few moments, enjoying the stillness.

"Just so you know, I can be real a jerk sometimes," Charlotte said.

"I hadn't noticed."

They both laughed and continued to stare out at the water. David rubbed Charlotte's arm, and she shivered. He stood and pulled her up and led her back to the cabin. Once inside, they locked arms around each other and shared more passionate kisses.

"I don't know how I'm going to sleep tonight," Charlotte said as she looked up at him.

"Indeed. You think anyone would notice if I tunneled into your room?"

"Or you could walk through the door."

David drew her close and sniffed her hair again. "What fun would that be?"

"Right, right." Charlotte grinned as she leaned back for another kiss. David obliged, and they held on to each other for a few moments more. He walked her to her bedroom door and played with her hands.

"Is this the part where I say I'll call you tomorrow?"

"Yeah, I think it is. Don't lose my number."

"Oh, don't you worry. It's imprinted on my brain."

Charlotte and David hugged one last time before reluctantly breaking apart.

"Sleep tight," Charlotte said.

"You too."

Charlotte tossed and turned all night, her circuits overloaded with desire. Her feet got into a wrestling match with the covers. The covers lost the battle and landed in a heap on the floor. Around dawn, David's door crept open, and she held her breath, wondering if he would rap on her door. Instead, he passed into the kitchen, and within moments, the smell of fresh coffee wafted into the room. Charlotte heard the front door open and close, and she knew he was headed for his early morning workout. She expelled her breath and lay in bed, contemplating the idea of embarking on a romance with a younger man. And not just any younger man. A younger man who was an international movie star surrounded by beautiful women and—

Charlotte stopped herself. She was doing it again, letting all those insecurities chip away at her self-confidence. She sat up and yawned before she shuffled into the kitchen. She poured herself a cup of coffee and leaned against the counter, the lake visible through the window from the kitchen. She didn't see David, but Karen was sitting on her usual perch by the lake. Charlotte left the coffee on the table and went to slip on a pair of jeans and flip-flops. She came back for her coffee and joined Karen outside.

"Morning, sweetheart." Karen smiled as she folded the newspaper she was reading. "Haven't seen your boyfriend yet this morning."

"He's *not* my *boyfriend*."

"*Psh*! You sure do move slow, girlfriend." Karen turned her attention to the lake. "So how are you?"

"I'm okay. A little tired."

Karen raised an eyebrow, and Charlotte chuckled.

"No, no. Nothing like that. Although…"

"What? Although what?"

Charlotte sipped her coffee. "Well, we did kiss last night."

Karen forgot about the lake and swept back over to Charlotte. "Woo *hoo*! Now we're talkin'! Gimme the dirt, girl."

Charlotte ran her fingers through her hair and sipped her coffee. "So after we plowed through the disaster you left for us last night—"

Karen rolled her eyes and fluttered her hands, indicating Charlotte should keep moving.

"So we danced—"

"Danced to what?"

"Are you going to let me tell this or not?"

Karen bristled. "Go on."

Charlotte related the events of the evening, everything from their sexy kitchen dance all the way to the fight and the lingering kisses.

"And you didn't hit that?" Karen asked, her mouth gaping.

"Jesus Christ, Karen! I just met him. What do you think I am anyway?"

"A dried-up old biscuit."

Charlotte spit out her coffee, spraying the still-dewy grass with a little extra moisture. "Karen!" She wiped her mouth with the sleeve of her flannel nightshirt. "With as much grief as you've been giving me, I have to ask how much sex *you're* having?"

Karen adjusted her sunglasses. "Girlfriend, I'm not one to kiss and tell—no, strike that; I'm *exactly* the type to kiss and tell. Let's just say I have a few rather *well-endowed* gentleman friends who don't mind squiring a hot divorcée such as myself around town."

Charlotte wasn't sure how to respond to that, so she drank her coffee instead.

"All right, so what's the holdup?"

"I—" Charlotte shook her head and put the empty coffee mug down on the bench. "I mean, I'm just…He's so young, and I'm so not…"

Karen flapped the paper down in her lap. "Listen, if you ask me—and I know you didn't, but I'm gonna tell you anyway—you're over*thinking* this. It's not like you're gonna have some great romance with him. Have a fling with him. A little sex never hurt anybody." Karen paused. "I mean *safe* sex."

"Okay, but Karen, you were married to a younger man, and it didn't work out. So you know better than anyone the risks—"

"First of all, my ex was an A1 asshole. Now I haven't been spending the kind of time you have with Mr. Movie Star, but he seems decent enough, so I don't think you'll have that problem. Second, you planning on marrying this guy?"

Charlotte crinkled nose her. "No."

"Okay, then, so what's the big deal? Pull your head out of your ass and go for it. This may be the last time you can say you had a wild and sexy fling with a hot movie star." Karen flicked the newspaper open and started reading. "And then you'll tell all of us about it over dinner next year."

❦

Karen's words of wisdom continued to rattle around inside Charlotte's head as she showered and got ready for the day. What *was* the big deal? She could do this. Maybe all she needed was a sweet and sexy affair to help her get her groove back, and David could be just the guy to do that. The front door opened, and David came bounding through it. He smiled when he saw Charlotte in the kitchen washing out the coffee pot.

"Well hello," he said, eyeing her tight blue jeans and long-sleeved black T-shirt. "I'd hug you, but I'm drenched."

She smiled. "Good workout, huh?"

"Quite. I'm going to hop into the shower, and we can head to breakfast."

Charlotte nodded and sat down on the couch. "See you in a few." The sight of David dripping in sweat gave Charlotte an image of what it would be like for him to be sweating for another reason.

"Huh. Maybe I am like my characters after all," she muttered.

CHAPTER 5

The next few days passed in a tizzy for Charlotte, though she did manage to slip into town and purchase those much-needed sunglasses. The days were filled with book clubs, card games, and a few leisurely writing workshops. The group let David join in on some of the games, and based on the way they all interacted, a casual observer would have thought he was just one of the girls. There was even a David King movie night, as a few of the ladies ventured into town to plunder some of his films from the video store to watch on the DVD in the divorcée cabin.

David and Charlotte spent their nights alone in the cabin, swapping music, sharing Cape Cods, and learning more about each other's backgrounds. They hadn't taken things to the next level; Charlotte had lost her nerve and was still reluctant, but David told her he'd wait as long as it took. They continued to indulge in numerous hot and sexy kisses, with a few roaming hands for good measure.

Charlotte's birthday rolled around, and when she woke up, she saw she'd received some texts from a few far-flung friends. She headed to the kitchen, expecting the usual fresh pot of coffee David would make before his workout. Instead, she found a chocolate cupcake, with one lit candle stuck in the middle, resting on the table. David was making the coffee, and Charlotte burst out laughing.

"What's this?" she asked as she sat down.

"Happy birthday!" David said as he joined her at the table. "Come on. Make a wish."

"This is silly."

"Ah, ah, *ah*. No doubters allowed today. It's a beautiful day, the sun is shining, and today is all about Charlotte."

He motioned for her to blow out the candle. She closed her eyes and thought a moment before she did so.

"What'd you wish for?" David asked.

Charlotte licked the cream off the bottom of the candle. "You know I can't tell you that, or it won't come true."

"Can't have that now, can we?"

Charlotte didn't answer; she licked the chocolate frosting, savoring its rich sweetness as it melted in her mouth.

"Charlotte, do you cook?"

"Define *cook*."

David leaned back in his chair. "I just noticed that whenever you're on breakfast or dinner duty, it's always frozen pizzas and toaster waffles. But no actual cooking."

"Okay, you caught me. I'm a lousy cook. Can barely boil water."

"No kidding," he mused.

"Hey, whoever has kitchen duty after I cook has the easiest cleanup of the bunch."

David chuckled. "Well, I was thinking I'd like to cook you dinner."

"Speaking of frozen pizza."

"No, I'm actually a pretty good cook. My mum taught me."

Charlotte leaned back, surprised. "You never told me you could cook!"

"I said I could scramble an egg and make toast."

"Oh, well, most people can do that."

David lifted his eyebrow.

"All right, except me."

David chuckled and stood to pour them each a cup of coffee.

"So what's on the menu?" she asked.

"Ancient Chinese secret."

"Oh, so it's Chinese." Charlotte beamed.

"Didn't say that."

"Oh. Don't I get a little hint?"

"You'll find out when you get here tonight. Seven p.m. sharp, and don't be late."

Because it was her birthday, Charlotte got out of any kitchen duties for the day. Instead, the ladies presented her with a huge chocolate cake at lunch, but Charlotte was disappointed to see that David wasn't among the well-wishers. They took the rest of the afternoon for a trip to the nail salon for manis and pedis and a quick glass of wine at Jake's, the ladies' favorite bar in Lake Arrowhead. By six thirty they were on the road back to the retreat, and Charlotte was jittery over what David had planned.

At seven, Charlotte turned the key in the lock of the cabin and peered inside.

"Oh my God!" she gasped. David had transformed the space. The room was loaded with huge vases of flowers. Flames from a crackling fire filled the room with a warm orange glow, and the comforting aroma of Italian food hung in the air. Charlotte noticed David had moved the small kitchen table, which was now draped in a white linen tablecloth and adorned with two long red candles, in front of the couch. David popped his head around the corner from the kitchen.

"Punctuality. I love it. I've got a few more things to finish up."

"Can I help?"

David came over and planted a kiss on the tip of her nose. "Nope. You can have a glass of wine."

Charlotte saw that David wore a button-down shirt with his jeans. Suddenly feeling frumpy in her tattered jeans and frayed T-shirt, she decided to change. Back in her room, she examined her clothing—she'd brought so little in the way of dressy clothes. She finally decided on a simple black sweater and a pair of dark-wash jeans. Charlotte pulled her ponytail loose, fluffed her hair, and lined her lips with a pink lip gloss she found marooned at the bottom of her purse.

She stepped out of her bedroom, and her heart stopped when she saw David standing in front of her door. She hoped one of the butterflies flitting around her stomach wouldn't come flying out when she opened her mouth. He smiled and handed her a bunch of daffodils.

"The rest of the flowers are from town. These…picked them myself."

"I never would have guessed," she said as she lifted the bouquet to her nose, inhaling the fragrant scent. She looked back up him. "Thank you. They're beautiful."

"You're welcome," David said as he took Charlotte's hand and led her to the table and pulled out her chair. She was speechless. He took the flowers from her and put them in a glass of water, but not before extracting one and sticking it behind her ear.

"This is amazing," Charlotte said sincerely. "Normally I hate surprises, but this is…this is great." David poured them each a glass of wine. "I'm still wondering how you made all of this happen."

"I pressed Shirley and Hendra into being my coconspirators. I gave them my shopping list last night, and while you were off gorging on chocolate cake and getting your nails done, they smuggled all the food and flowers in."

Charlotte picked up her wineglass. "Oh, so that's why they both cried headache when we went into town." She took a sip of wine. "So they did all the cooking?"

David shook his head. "All me, my dear. I told you I could cook."

Charlotte set her glass down. "You are a man of many talents."

"Come on, let's toast," David said, indicating Charlotte should pick up her glass. "To many more birthdays. Together."

"Cheers," Charlotte said as they clinked glasses, not quite sure what to make of his last word.

David brought two plates and a bottle of wine from the kitchen and carefully set them down on the table. He'd outdone himself. They started with a few bruschetta and a basil, tomato, and mozzarella salad. The main course was baked manicotti, wrapped around layers of gooey cheese and a succulent blend of veal and beef, and topped with a spicy tomato sauce. Each bite melted in Charlotte's mouth, and she still wasn't convinced he'd done it on his own. They spent more time getting to know each other, and they continued the easy, fun banter they'd enjoyed since day one. They both came with new tales to share with each other as she relayed that she and Karen were represented by the same publisher and after meeting at a promotional event had become fast friends.

David filled Charlotte in on how William used to be a struggling actor and the two had crossed paths at various auditions. They became casual acquaintances, and when William decided his real talent was on the business side, he became David's manager. Over the years, the business relationship had grown into a fierce and loyal friendship.

David cleared the dinner dishes while Charlotte poured the last of the red wine into their glasses.

"So not only are our parents similar, our best friends are as well," Charlotte said as she set the bottle down. "This is getting scary."

"What is?"

"How much we have in common. If I didn't know better, I'd start to wonder if we were separated at birth," Charlotte teased.

David chuckled as he came back, brandishing another plate. "Perish the thought. Besides, it's not scary—it's fantastic."

Charlotte smiled when she realized his other surprise for her. "Strawberries," she said.

"Chocolate-covered strawberries," he clarified. He sat down, picked one up, and held it toward Charlotte. She reached out to take it from him, but he pulled it back. "I want to give it to you myself," he whispered.

A slow smile crept over Charlotte's face, and without hesitation, she opened her mouth slightly. David nudged the tip of the strawberry onto the rim of her lip. Charlotte let her tongue slither out and grab the bottom of the fruit while she bit down. A dribble of strawberry juice snaked down her chin, and they both giggled while she lapped up the edge of the strawberry along with a nugget of milk chocolate. David gave her the rest of the strawberry, juice and chocolate bursting in her mouth.

"I must look ridiculous," Charlotte said as she wiped her chin, unable to stop laughing.

"You look sexy," David responded. "You're driving me mad."

Charlotte picked up a strawberry. "I'm not going to be the only one sitting here with food dripping down my face."

David took the strawberry Charlotte offered and surprised her by chomping down on the whole thing and licking her fingertips while he was at it.

"You cheated!" she yelped as she wiped her hands on her napkin.

"It's called being *strategic*," he laughed.

They each had one more strawberry that they fed to themselves before they polished off the wine. After they lingered a bit longer, Charlotte helped David move the table back to the kitchen area. They snuggled on the couch, watching the fire.

"Thank you for giving me the best birthday I've ever had," Charlotte whispered as she leaned into him and rested her head on his shoulder. "I loved it."

"Thanks for giving me a reason to dust off my cooking skills."

"You're sure you didn't have help?" Charlotte cracked. "I mean, that was quite a bit more than scrambling an egg and making toast."

"I swear! My mum was a fabulous cook, and she always had me in the kitchen. She told me that while the quickest way to a man's heart is food, it's an even faster way to a woman's."

"Your mother was a very smart woman," she said as she leaned in for a kiss.

"*Hmmm.*" David pulled back. "I have a present for you," he whispered.

"Oh my gosh, David, you've done enough—the flowers, the amazing dinner—"

David placed two fingers over her lips. "*Shh.* Let me have my moment." He walked over to the mantel and retrieved a small black gift box.

"Something else your coconspirators picked up in town?" she asked.

"No," he said.

"Oh. Something you had delivered?"

"Wrong again." David placed the box in Charlotte's hand and sat down next to her. "What I'm giving you—you will have forever," he breathed.

Her curiosity piqued, Charlotte took the lid off the tiny box. Inside was a small piece of paper folded in two. She took the paper out and unfolded it. As she read it, her eyes filled with tears. Charlotte looked at him, shocked.

David extracted the paper from Charlotte's fingers. "Here, let me read it to you," he said, never taking his eyes from hers. "I love you."

"David, we just met," she whispered.

"You've never heard of love at first sight?" David said as he leaned in for a kiss.

She caressed his face, and he smiled. Without a word he tugged on her arm, and they slid down to the rug in front of the fireplace. They continued their sweet kisses, their hands running all over each other's bodies. Her brain went into overdrive—did this amazing man really see past their age difference? Did he truly love her? What had she done to deserve this—him? She'd been writing about this kind of love and passion for years, but had never fully experienced it.

David dredged his fingers over Charlotte's breast, and moans escaped from them both as her nipple hardened beneath his touch. He moved over to caress the other breast, and Charlotte wrapped one leg around his waist, arching her body toward him. She began to unbutton his shirt, but she was too impatient and ripped the whole thing open. Buttons popped and flew across the room.

David pulled back and laughed. "I knew you were like your characters," he growled.

"I guess so," she panted as she pulled him back into a kiss and pushed his shirt off. Charlotte let her fingers roam over the vast expanse of his smooth chest. She squeezed his pecs and groaned again, the center of her body throbbing. David read her mind and undid the top button of her jeans before he changed his mind and tucked his hand under her sweater instead. He whipped Charlotte's sweater over her head before he undid the clasp of her bra and pulled her firm, full breasts out of their prison. He cast an admiring leer over her unbound breasts.

"My God, your breasts are flawless," he murmured and shook his head in stunned amazement.

"I'm glad you like them."

"Oh, no, no. I love them," he corrected her. "Absolutely love them," he whispered as he lowered his head to flick his tongue over one nipple.

Charlotte cried out as he made contact with her sizzling flesh. He alternated between nibbling on her nipples and lapping at them like a cat with a bowl of milk. David stopped for a moment and finished what he had started with her jeans by lowering the zipper. Charlotte began to wriggle out of her pants as he peeled them down her legs in aching slow motion, his eyes traveling over the lush landscape in front of him.

"You're beautiful," he said as he caught her eye.

Charlotte smiled and ran her hands through his forest of wavy hair, gently stretching him back toward her. Their lips collided again, and this time the kisses intensified, like fiery clashes between them. He continued to stroke her breasts with warm, soft hands while Charlotte licked at the silky, salty skin of David's neck. It felt like an inferno was erupting between Charlotte's legs, and just when she thought she could take no more, David slipped two fingers inside the slippery space. Charlotte wailed with pleasure as he began to pump his fingers inside of her as if she were a well of water. She spread her legs apart even farther and grasped his lips with hers. David stopped and began to drop soft kisses all over her body, which made Charlotte twitch and writhe in exquisite ecstasy.

Charlotte gasped when he buried his head between her legs, probing her folds with soft, light touches before thrusting his tongue deep into her core. Charlotte whimpered, knowing she could hold back no more, feeling the tidal wave rumble deep within her. David clamped his hands on either side of her hips and yanked her even closer to him, showing her no mercy. Charlotte gripped the rug beside her, one nail scratching against the wood floor. Like a speeding bullet, her orgasm ricocheted throughout her body, causing her to convulse and screech out with superb pleasure. Panting and drenched with sweat, Charlotte collapsed back on the floor, her flesh seething. David drummed his fingertips across her belly, and she squealed.

"Don't touch me for, like, two minutes," she wheezed.

"Don't take too long, because I'm not through with you yet." David nuzzled her ear.

Charlotte let out a weak laugh and closed her eyes. "That was amazing."

David planted a kiss on the tip of Charlotte's nose before bringing his lips down to hers. They groped for each other again, when Charlotte broke away and searched David's face.

"I'm almost afraid to ask if there were condoms on that magic grocery list you gave Hendra and Shirley."

David opened his mouth to speak, but then snapped it shut. He sat up slowly and hooked his arm around one knee. Charlotte propped herself up on her elbows.

"Damn," he muttered. "Didn't even think about it." He looked back at her and grinned. "Well, at least you know I didn't set out to seduce you."

Charlotte sat all the way up, and together they leaned back against the couch. "So much for Mr. Smooth Movie Star," she said as she gave him a poke in the ribs. "I hope you don't think I meant anything—"

"Oh, no, no. Of course not. I mean, this is—was—our first time being together. And we're both responsible adults—"

"Very responsible."

"Yes, exactly," David said. "I do hope I get a rain check, though," he said as he stroked her hair.

Charlotte stood up and pulled a blanket from the couch and wrapped herself in it. "I'm holding you to that." She started toward the bedroom. "In the meantime, are you coming to bed?"

David looked at her, perplexed. "But, I thought you said..."

Charlotte raised an eyebrow. "Well, just because we can't *sleep* together doesn't mean we can't *sleep* together." She turned her back and threw him a glance over her shoulder. "Coming?" she repeated.

David scrambled up and ran after her. "Indeed."

Charlotte and David remained intertwined all night long, and though they were tempted to make love, they decided to stick to their vow to wait until all protection was in place. David woke her with a kiss before trotting off to make the coffee and get his workout in. Charlotte decided to wash the dishes and was so inspired by David cooking dinner for her that she decided to share one of her favorite rituals with him. She made a quick call to Hendra and got ready. She scribbled a note for David to meet her at the dining cabin and dashed off.

Twenty minutes later David ambled into the dining room, where Charlotte had packed a picnic lunch into the cooler that normally resided in the big kitchen. David placed a hand on Charlotte's waist and kissed her.

"What's all this?" he asked. "You whisking me away somewhere?"

"Yes. Yes I am." Charlotte beamed.

"Well, can I ask where?" He grinned.

Charlotte shook her head and handed him the cooler. "Nope."

David took the cooler and nodded. "Aha. Giving me a taste of my own medicine, I see."

Charlotte just giggled and grabbed David's hand. They headed down to the lake and a small boathouse where Hendra kept a rowboat. They hauled it out, and Charlotte went in search of the oars.

"So we're going rowing, then?" David yelled after her.

Charlotte emerged from the boathouse, dragging two oars behind her. "Something like that." She smiled. "We're going to spend the day fishing."

David placed his hand over his chest and stumbled back. "My dear Charlotte. How you continue to amaze me."

Charlotte grinned and ducked back into the boathouse to retrieve the fishing rods, while he loaded the boat with the cooler and some bait that

Hendra kept in the freezer. "My dad would take me fishing every spring, so I learned from him."

"I thought you said he treated you like a princess."

"Yes, well, he did always want a boy." Charlotte winked. "Normally, they don't allow public fishing in Lake Arrowhead, but because Hendra is a member of the Lake Association, we're good."

They launched the boat, and when Charlotte started to give David a precursor on how to row, he reminded her that he had had to learn how to row for a movie he had done few years earlier.

It was a beautiful day on the water, and David and Charlotte were joined by a few other hopeful fishermen. Charlotte instructed David where to row, and once they got to a fairly secluded spot, she showed him how to bait the hook. It took him a few tries, as the bait kept slipping off the hook. Finally he was able to get it to stick, and after a few mishaps that Charlotte had to duck, David managed to cast his line in the water. Charlotte explained that fishing was a waiting game; she told David to prepare to sit for a while.

"So what kind of fish is out here?" David asked.

"Catfish, bass, freshwater salmon mostly," Charlotte replied as she cast her own line.

"Sounds like we could open a seafood restaurant," David quipped.

"How about I catch it and you cook it?"

"Deal." He smiled.

They passed the balance of the afternoon with nary a nibble on either line. They left their lines in the water and dug into the peanut butter and jelly sandwiches and potato chips that Charlotte had packed, and David even tried a Twinkie for the first time in his life. He became a convert. The sun was beginning to dip as Charlotte looked at her watch; she thought it might be time to go.

"But we didn't catch anything." David pouted.

Charlotte shrugged. "It happens in fishing sometimes. There were lots of times my dad and I would sit from sunup to sundown and never catch anything more than mosquito bites."

Just then, David's line began to jerk in his hand. They both looked at each other and jumped up, excited.

"Am I catching something?" David asked as he grappled with the fishing rod.

Charlotte nodded, adrenaline pumping. "Yes, yes! Hold on, and grip the rod tight. Now lean back—that's it!"

David bent his knees and lifted his rod out of the water with a huge grunt. Charlotte started to cheer as a gigantic fish emerged, water sluicing down its body, its mouth clenched around David's hook. David maneuvered the fish in and let it slap to the floor of the boat. It flopped around, splashing water all over them. Charlotte threw her arms around David, who gave her a kiss back.

"Oh my God, David, it's enormous!" Charlotte shouted as she looked down at it. "It's a salmon. A big, fat salmon."

"You must be a good-luck charm!"

Charlotte gasped, still not believing David had landed such a massive fish. She and her dad had never caught anything like that in all the years they'd fished.

"What do we do now? Throw it back?" David wondered.

She gave him a playful slap. "No! We cook it!"

"Well, this goes a bit against our arrangement, doesn't it? Seeing as how I caught it." David grinned. "This must mean you have to cook it."

Charlotte scratched the side of her face and shook her head. "You did want to enjoy eating it, right?"

David chuckled. "How about we cook it together?"

"You got it."

David and Charlotte wrestled the fish into the tiny cooler, Charlotte wishing she'd remembered to bring newspaper to wrap it in; of course, she hadn't thought that they'd be bringing any fish back. They rowed to shore and stored the boat, babbling with excitement over their catch. Once they returned to the cabin, they each took quick showers, and David got set up to show Charlotte how to cook a fish. He laid out salt, pepper, olive oil, white wine, and a few cloves of garlic. Charlotte was pulling her hair into a ponytail when she came out to see all the ingredients laid out on the counter.

"Is it too late to rethink this?"

David tugged on her hand and dragged her into the kitchen.

"We're going to keep it very simple. Baked fish and oven potatoes. A little salad."

"We can still order a pizza."

"Come on, Charlotte, it'll be fun."

For the next forty-five minutes, David instructed her in the finer points of how to bake salmon and crispy potatoes. He showed her how to peel garlic by smashing the flat blade of a knife against the clove and then tearing it off. He watched her as she sautéed the garlic in a little butter, and then he had her add wine, salt, and pepper and let it reduce. After cleaning, scaling, and cutting the fish, David had Charlotte slather it in olive oil and generous amounts of salt and pepper, explaining the need to season well before ladling the wine and garlic mixture over it.

After they put it in the oven, they focused on making crispy potatoes. David had Charlotte quarter the potatoes and helped her toss them in olive oil, salt, pepper, and garlic before they went into the toaster oven on the counter. David showed her how to make simple vinaigrette of olive oil and lemon juice, and they tossed it into a bowl of greens. Once everything was done, David spooned fish and potatoes onto two plates, and they dropped into the kitchen chairs, both ravenous.

"I hope this tastes as good as it smells," Charlotte said, eyeing the hunk of fish David had served her.

"It'll be fabulous," David said as he poured the remaining white wine.

Charlotte stuck her fork into the fish and held it up to her lips. "Here goes," she said as she put her fork into her mouth. She moaned and pounded the table. "Oh my God. This is outstanding."

David nodded, having his own culinary orgasm. "Charlotte, this is fantastic." He speared a potato and closed his eyes. "Magnificent."

They barely spoke, forks clinking against plates, wine being slurped, fingers being licked. Satiated, they quickly cleaned the dishes before taking a quick stroll around the lake. They threaded their fingers together, the night air covering them in a slight breeze.

"Convinced I cooked dinner last night by myself?" David teased.

"I'm a believer. I couldn't have done it without you. You're amazing."

"Ah, well, without your expert fishing technique, I couldn't have caught such a delicious fish to begin with."

"I guess we make a pretty good team," Charlotte said.

David stopped and pulled Charlotte toward him. He tilted her face up and took her bottom lip in his teeth. "The best," he whispered.

Charlotte wrapped her arms around David and let him pepper her face with sweet, tender kisses. Charlotte still couldn't believe this was her reality. To think she had almost missed out on this…Life was about taking chances, and she'd almost let her fears chase her from taking the best chance of all. Charlotte traced the outline of David's face with her fingertips, imprinting his features against her fingerprints.

"David," she whispered.

"Yes, Charlotte?"

"I love you, David."

CHAPTER 6

David wiped his forehead with the back of his arm, the early morning sun already beating against him like his body was a punching bag. The heat had caused him to cut his workout a bit short that morning, though he'd still managed to get in his customary two hundred sit-ups. He was on his way back to the cabin when, out of the corner of his eye, he spotted Karen unloading groceries from her car.

"Good morning." He jogged over to help her. "Looks like the early bird caught the worm, eh?"

Karen handed him two bags. "In case you haven't noticed, I'm not much of a people person. Early morning grocery shopping benefits me and the masses."

David chuckled, unsure of how to respond.

"So." Karen slammed the trunk of her SUV. "I never did hear how the big birthday celebration went."

David picked up two more bags, and he and Karen began the walk toward the dining cabin.

"Marvelous. Couldn't have done it without the help of everyone here, what with whisking Charlotte away and such."

Karen maneuvered one of her bags so she could open the door of the cabin. "Uh-huh. And the little fishing excursion. Also fun?"

"Well, nothing stays under wraps around here for long."

Karen shrugged. "No, I'm just nosy. Didn't see Charlotte around yesterday—asked Hendra about where she was."

"Ah," David said as he hoisted two large bags of potatoes onto the counter.

Karen smirked. "Shirley's making pot roast tonight, so lots of potatoes."

"I see." David nodded, and they resumed putting the groceries away in silence. "So," he said as he put away the last of the ice cream that would be the night's dessert, "I get the feeling you don't like me very much."

Karen shook her head. "No, that's not it. I actually like you quite a bit. I can tell you're good people."

David sat on one of the kitchen stools. "Okay, so whatever it is, I want to hear it. I promise my feelings won't be hurt. For an actor, my ego's not all that fragile."

Karen sat down on another stool and steepled her fingers underneath her chin. She was quiet for a moment before she let out a big sigh. "Listen, I think it's one thing to have a fun little fling. Hell, I have several of them on a regular basis. But a serious relationship is quite another. Is that where this is going?"

David glanced down, a shy smile tugging at his lips. "That's my plan."

Karen sliced her gaze into him. "You think you love her, don't you?"

"I *do* love her. I've never felt like this before. I know I've known her only for a short time, but I just...I feel so connected to her. Like I've known her my whole life."

"For all of your thirty years, you mean?" Karen asked, her question wrapped in sarcasm.

In spite of himself, David let out an exasperated sigh. "Why is that such a problem?"

"Well, of course it's not a problem for *you*—you're the younger one, and you're the man!"

"I'm not out just for a good time, Karen, if that's what you're thinking."

"Well I hope not. Listen. Just so you know, I thought it would be good for Charlotte to have a little fun with you. So long as that's all it is. But once you start getting into serious business, well…that's a whole different ball game."

David raised an eyebrow. "What does that mean?"

"Listen, Charlotte likes to play all nonchalant and all that, but I saw her after the whole mess with Ben, and she was a wreck. She couldn't stand to go through that kind of betrayal again." Karen leaned back against her chair. "So all I'm saying is, be sure that you're not just intrigued by the thought of being with an older woman, that you really do care about her the way you say you do. Otherwise, just keep it light and fun."

David crossed his arms. "And what makes you the expert on younger men and older women?"

"My husband was nine years younger than me. Nine years doesn't sound like a big deal, but when you're forty-eight and your thirty-nine-year-old husband changes the deal on you and decides he wants children, and you know you don't want to be a sixty-year-old woman running around after a twelve-year-old, well, that makes me an expert. He's now married to a woman seven years younger than he is, and he's running after kids all day, happy as a pig in mud." Karen stopped and crossed her legs in defiance before she started talking again.

"My ex said he never wanted kids. He had a right to change his mind. And I had a right *not* to change mine. So, okay—you don't have a problem with the age thing, and I have to admit, it makes you a little endearing, but it also makes me wonder if you have any idea what you're getting yourself into."

David was quiet, except for the sound of his fingers drumming against the countertop. "Obviously you feel quite passionate about the subject," he finally said.

"All right, you say you love her. Today. What about tomorrow? Will you always feel this way? Time could change your mind, too." Karen stood and looked at David. "Like I said, I'm a nosy broad, and I hope I haven't crossed a line with you. I guess all I'm saying is…be sure. Be absolutely, positively sure that Charlotte is what you want. Not some Hollywood fantasy."

David smiled and stood to join Karen. "I love to see how much you care about Charlotte, and frankly, if you didn't give me a bit of a hard time, I'd wonder how much of a friend you are."

Karen snorted. "Really?"

David nodded. "She is lucky to have you in her life."

Karen leaned against the counter. "You didn't say whether you want kids."

"Well, truth be told, my biological clock has never jangled so much as a broken note. I like kids, so long as they're other people's. It has honestly never been my thing." David looked down. "I'm sorry your marriage didn't work out, but I can assure you, that will never be an issue with me and Charlotte."

Karen studied his face. "Okay," she said, not entirely convinced.

David glanced at the wall clock. "Well, I'd better get back, or Charlotte might think I've run off." He planted a huge kiss on Karen's cheek. "Thanks for the talk. I appreciate it."

Charlotte gathered her clothes and headed to the divorcee cabin, which housed the washing machine. She stood over her pillowcase, which doubled for a laundry bag, quietly sorting clothes.

"Magnificent."

Charlotte gasped and dropped a pair of jeans. She turned to see David leaning against the doorjamb, grinning.

"Here we go again. How is it that I never hear you sneak up behind me?" Charlotte murmured as David moseyed over for a kiss.

"Even doing laundry you're just so damned sexy."

"Oh yeah—laundry. Every man's aphrodisiac."

David gripped Charlotte around the waist. "I can attest that it's working on me."

They both laughed before going in for another kiss. Charlotte pulled back. "Speaking of laundry, let me throw in a load for you. You couldn't have had much in that backpack."

"Well, I'm not so sure how I feel about you washing my kegs."

"Your what?"

"I believe you Americans call them *underwear*."

Charlotte shook her head. "I feel like I need to go out and buy a British-English dictionary."

"Oh, no worries, love. You'll always have me to translate for you." David planted a kiss on her forehead. "So what's on the agenda for today?"

Charlotte resumed sorting her laundry. "Book club. *Pride and Prejudice*, the ultimate chick lit."

"Oh dear. Sounds fascinating."

"Hey, I could make you sit in on the discussion."

David shuddered. "Not that I don't appreciate good literature, but I've never quite understood the allure of sitting around and discussing it. Probably stems from when I was in school and got called on to give deep, critical analysis, and half the time I hadn't done the assignment."

Charlotte started the machine. "Let me guess. You were one of those kids who charmed and bewitched your way through school."

David laughed. "Hardly. I got my diploma in summer school. Hey, since you're going to be tied up with your book club, do you mind if I borrow your car? I'd like to run into town for some man things."

"What are *man things?*"

"You know…soap, deodorant, razors. That kind of thing."

"And how do you expect to walk around town without being accosted by another mob?"

David licked his lips. "Well, I've got all that figured out. First, if you notice, I haven't shaved yet, so we've got a nice"—he looked at his watch—"ten o'clock shadow going on. Second, I've got a baseball cap and sunglasses and a patented slump that makes me appear about two inches shorter than I am. Finally, if I'm forced to talk to anyone"—he cleared his throat—"I've done several movies in an American accent," he said in a perfectly executed Midwest twang. "I think I'll be okay."

Charlotte giggled. "Sounds like you've got everything covered."

"I thought you'd approve. So how about those car keys?"

All through dinner Charlotte couldn't stop staring at David. He'd caught her a few times and grinned as she busied herself with finishing her salad. After dinner, David and Emma became engaged in a movie trivia one-upmanship game, and so far the older woman was winning. Of course, Charlotte wasn't sure if David was letting her win, but it was fun to watch. She plopped her chin in her hand, her mind shifting to the past few days with David.

During the day, while Charlotte was participating in her retreat activities, David had been burning up the phone lines with William, discussing upcoming location shoots, premieres, and scripts. He continued to teach her kitchen tricks, even helping her prepare a Mexican feast for the ladies the previous night. So far, they'd stuck to the no-sex rule, though there were times Charlotte wanted to just say the hell with it and rip his clothes off.

David and Charlotte were off the hook for cleanup duty that night, so after the games were over, he walked over to her and sat down.

"You've been awfully mysterious tonight," he said as he trailed one finger up her arm.

"Have I? I hadn't noticed."

"Almost like you've got something up your sleeve."

"Sorry to burst your bubble."

David nudged her shoulder. "How about we take a walk around the lake?"

Charlotte nodded her agreement, and after they had said their goodnights to everyone, they set off for a stroll in the breezy night air. David filled her in on his conversations with William, and Charlotte bounced an idea for a new book off him, her embarrassment having finally dissipated around him where her writing was concerned.

Without even realizing it, they were near the boathouse where they'd first gone fishing. Charlotte wrinkled her nose and looked up at the sky, which was filled with patches of purple and indigo, broken up by dark, puffy clouds.

"I think it's going to rain," she muttered.

David looked up. "Oh, I doubt it. We've had beautiful sunny days ever since we got here." He kissed her forehead. "A metaphor, don't you think? Besides, nothing in the forecast said anything about rain."

Charlotte closed her eyes and let the damp wind wash over her face. She shook her head. "Yeah, like the weatherman never gets it wrong—"

Just then a fat, juicy drop of water smacked against Charlotte's bare arm, and it was followed by a rapid succession of raindrops. Sheets of rain began to cascade against them in short order, followed by furious crackles of thunder and quick snaps of lightning.

"I'll never doubt you again," David yelled as he grabbed Charlotte's hand and they dashed through the downpour to the boathouse. Fortunately, it was unlocked, and they managed to duck inside.

"Woo!" Charlotte yelped as she flung water from her hands. She and David looked at each other and burst out laughing.

"Well, you're certainly a better predictor of the weather than I realized," David laughed.

"Now you know, from now on, to listen to every word I say."

David cupped Charlotte's face in his hands, her face slick with rainwater. "Every word," he whispered as he drew her in for a kiss.

Charlotte's teeth began to chatter, and she held him close.

"Cold?" he asked. Charlotte nodded, and David wrapped his arms around her. "Here...better?"

Charlotte tilted her face up to David, the tiniest sliver of moonlight from the boathouse's lone window illuminating his flawless features. The rain beat against the outside, raw and primal like a tribal drum. She ran her hands up and down the length of his arms and shivered.

"Do you remember when I made fun of you about that movie you made where you had to screw all night to stay warm?" she breathed.

He pushed her hair back from her face and looked deep into her eyes. "How could I forget?"

"I think I'd like to give it a try now."

Without a word, David smashed his lips against Charlotte's. She moaned and shucked his wet T-shirt from his body, her hands traipsing across his chest. He responded by flipping her T-shirt over her head and yanking the straps of her bra down in one frenetic motion. His hot tongue melted one of her icy nipples, and Charlotte began to groan softly as she pushed her fingers through the thick brush of his hair. He began to gnaw at her other breast, greedy with lust for her. David grunted and bent down to lift Charlotte from behind her knees, which elicited a surprised gasp from her. He set her down on the floor, and she whimpered.

"What's wrong?" David pulled back.

"Find a tarp...something, anything to put down on the ground."

David moaned and looked around furiously. He spotted a shiny blue tarp wedged inside one of the boats. He looked up and saw a worn blanket hanging from a hook on the wall. He grabbed that as well, and threw them down on the rough concrete. Charlotte wriggled on top of them, getting comfortable. David pounced and ripped the zipper of her jeans open, anxious to get them off her. Her cotton panties were soaked, and David let his finger linger over the moist material for just a second before he pulled them off. He drove his face in between her legs, which caused Charlotte to cry out just as a raucous slap of thunder shook the boathouse. Charlotte screamed as he devoured her like a sumptuous feast. Just when she thought she would explode, he stopped. He looked at her, his body heaving.

"I have a confession to make."

Charlotte's heart lurched. "What?"

"You remember when I went to town to get 'man things' the other day?"

Charlotte nodded, struggling to catch her breath. "Yes."

David pulled his wallet out of his jeans and extracted a condom. "I bought a box and put one in my wallet, in case, well, you know, you never know where you might be..."

Charlotte laughed and pulled David's face to hers, and they greedily tore each other's lips off. Finally they broke away, and together they slashed open the condom wrapper before Charlotte helped David out of his jeans. She gulped when he took off his boxers, and her hand fluttered to her throat.

"Wow, *this* is what I've been missing out on all this time?" She shook her head at the rock-hard mound of flesh pointing straight at her. "Goodness— I'm glad I'm not a virgin."

David grinned. "Oh, I would have enjoyed deflowering you."

"I think you're deflowering me now," she said as she let her fingertips meld into him.

David closed his eyes and let out a soft sigh at Charlotte's touch. She took the condom from between his fingers and rolled it down his shaft. They resumed their passionate kisses, intoxicated by each other. David pushed her breasts together, forming one giant nipple, and began to suck relentlessly. Charlotte panted and writhed beneath him, clamoring to feel him inside her. She clutched his shoulders, beseeching him to fulfill her unspoken request. His head bobbed up and down, his tongue swirling all over her nipples as though they were tiny lollipops. Charlotte flung one leg around David's waist, on the verge of tears from wanting him so bad.

Without warning, he plunged deep into Charlotte, causing her eyes to pop open in shock and she emitted a guttural growl. Charlotte flopped back against the blanket, rapture flooding every pore of her body. David lifted her bottom and pressed himself against her.

"My God, woman…" David gasped as he moved in and out of Charlotte.

Her only response was to gyrate her hips to meet his thrusts, her mind focused only on the incredible waves of passion rolling through her. Charlotte began to mewl and thrash her head against the slick tarp. Her mouth dropped open, and she squeezed her eyes shut.

"Oh God," she moaned. "Oh, I don't want to come. I want it to go on forever."

"No, no, no," he murmured. "You have to come, because I want you to come like you've never come before."

"Oh God, oh God," she bleated.

The rain continued to pound against the roof as David and Charlotte thumped against each other with unfettered abandon. Finally, Charlotte could hold back no more, and she gave in to the climax she'd been holding off for so long. Charlotte grabbed David's arm as she shot straight up and let out a long, piercing scream of pleasure. She clenched around him, her core still pulsating around his thickness, which continued to pound away inside of her. Charlotte collapsed onto her back, her body convulsing as David clasped his hands around her hips.

"Oh, sweetheart," David chattered. "My God, I'm about to burst!"

David pumped away, picking up speed as he dropped deeper inside her. Charlotte felt him tense up, and she held him as he let out a cry. He wobbled inside her, and for a moment, all he could do was hold himself above her, his face contorted like a crying newborn. Finally he collapsed on her, his sweat dripping onto her chest and shoulders. The rain had stopped, and now only occasional flashes of lightning were the lone clues to the ferocious thunderstorm. Charlotte delivered soft, gentle kisses all over David's face as he ran his fingers along the outside of her thigh.

"God, that feels so good," he whispered.

"*You* feel so good," she breathed into his ear before she flicked her tongue over the succulent lobe for a brief second. A rumble of pleasure fled from his lips before he finally rolled off her, removed the condom, and fell onto his back. Charlotte stared up at the ceiling and placed her hand over the thud of her heart in an attempt to regain her equilibrium. David pulled her over to him and engulfed her in his arms. She burrowed her head into his embrace, content.

"Well, that was certainly worth the wait," David said.

Charlotte let out a soft laugh. "Yes, it was."

He rubbed her arm. "You're amazing, Charlotte."

"Well, you get some of the credit."

He chuckled. "You're so kind."

"Aren't I?"

David kissed the top of her forehead. "Indeed."

"You know what? If we don't go now, I may fall asleep here," she murmured. "We should head back to the cabin."

David gave her a quick squeeze. "What? You don't want to stay here all night on top of this lovely tarp?"

"Oh yeah—that's all we need. Some fisherman walking in on us in the morning naked as jaybirds. Besides, you're supposed to be hiding out, remember?"

Charlotte sat up. David grinned and put his hands behind his head.

"What a lovely view. I could look at it all day."

Charlotte giggled and planted a quick kiss on his lips. "Flattery will get you everywhere," she quipped before she went around in the dark in search of her clothes. David hoisted himself up and joined her.

Finally dressed, they crept out of the boathouse and headed to the cabin. The air smelled fresh and clean, and now only a light mist fell across their rejuvenated bodies.

"I will now have a whole new appreciation for rain," David said.

"Better than an umbrella," Charlotte said as she opened the door of the cabin, the warmth rushing to greet them.

"Indeed."

They locked their arms around each other and kissed once more as David kicked the front door closed with his foot. Never letting go of each other, they made their way back toward the bedrooms.

"Your place or mine?" David asked.

Charlotte grabbed David by the collar of his T-shirt and pulled him into her room as passion overtook them yet again. David pushed Charlotte onto the bed and pulled down her pants. He slowly removed her gray Jockey panties and hooked the elastic waistband around his finger.

"Thought you said you didn't like sexy knickers," he said, the mischievous twinkle that drove her mad all over his face.

Charlotte frowned, confused. "I thought you called them kegs?"

"Knickers are women's undies; kegs are for men," he said matter-of-factly.

She grabbed them from him and threw them across the room.

"Well, whatever they are, I couldn't care less. Now shut up and kiss me."

The toasty slices of sun that filtered through the bedroom window the next morning held no evidence of the downpour from the night before. David blinked several times and held up his wrist to check his watch. He let out a soft grunt and smiled as he rolled over to look at Charlotte, who was hunched in the fetal position. He watched her for a few moments, drinking in the wonder of her. The way those unruly auburn curls swathed themselves across her porcelain skin, the soft curve of her hip jutting up from beneath the rumpled bedsheet, the smooth arch of her bare shoulder inviting him to take a bite. He spooned around her, nuzzling into her neck.

"Charlotte."

She didn't stir, so he blew gently into her ear before he dotted the back of her neck with light kisses. Finally she moaned and brushed her hair out of her face. She turned to look at him, one eye propped open.

"A girl could get used to waking up like this."

"I hope you'll let me spoil you."

Charlotte grinned, and David moved in to kiss her on the lips. She clamped her hand against her mouth and shook her head.

"Oh, come on," David laughed. "I've seen you naked. I can kiss you with morning breath."

Charlotte jumped out of bed and ran toward the bathroom. "I refuse to kiss you until I've brushed my teeth," she yelled out.

David sat up and hooked his elbows around his knees. "Well, hurry up, because I need to kiss you!"

"Hey, what time is it?" she called out.

David looked at his watch again. "A little after ten."

Charlotte spit out her toothpaste and squeaked. "Damn it!"

"What's wrong?"

Charlotte bolted out of the bathroom. "We missed breakfast."

"Uh-oh," David said. "How about this? We'll say the storm knocked the power out."

"In one cabin?" Charlotte asked sarcastically.

"Okay, bad excuse."

Charlotte flopped back onto the bed. "Ten. I haven't slept in until ten in—" She stopped to think. "I've *never* slept in until ten."

"Never? Ever in your life?"

"What can I say? I'm a morning person."

"Oh dear." David slapped his hands together and hopped out of bed. "All right, since we've missed breakfast, how about I brew up some coffee, and we'll nosh on some of those cupcake things you're so fond of?"

Charlotte giggled. "Sounds great. While you're doing that, I'll be in the shower."

David moaned and pulled Charlotte into that near-forgotten kiss. "Want some company?"

"Believe it or not, I'm going to shave my legs, but I will take a rain check."

"Don't say *rain* around me, woman. Drives me bonkers." They both laughed, and David gave Charlotte a teasing slap on her bum as she scooted off to the shower. David raked on his jeans and T-shirt from the night before and headed into the kitchen to make the coffee. As he waited for it to brew, he noticed a small, neatly folded white piece of paper shoved under the door.

David wrinkled his brow; he went to pick it up and read it.

Open the door, it read.

Not sure whether to laugh or be afraid, David eased the door open and looked down to see a basket covered with a red cloth napkin. He grabbed the basket and shut the door; he gently lifted the napkin and took a peek underneath. It was filled with bananas, some muffins, and a few cartons of yogurt, along with a note in looped and swirling letters.

"To keep up your strength," he read aloud and chuckled. David set the basket on the kitchen table and tore into a blueberry muffin, suddenly starving. He had to hand it to the ladies. They were quite a perceptive bunch.

A few moments later, Charlotte emerged from the bedroom in a worn pair of jeans and tight white T-shirt, her hair pulled back in its habitual ponytail. David's heart stopped at how gorgeous she was: a sexy, curvy body, sparkling eyes, and skin so flawless that it was hard to tell if she was even wearing makeup. However, knowing Charlotte as he did, it was all her. And he loved it.

David pulled a muffin out for Charlotte. "Here you go."

Charlotte frowned at the muffin. "What the hell is all this?" she asked, pointing to the basket.

David handed her the note, which she glanced at.

"Oh God," she groaned. "We will *definitely* be the topic at dinner tonight."

David and Charlotte lingered over coffee for a few hours before they decided to venture out for lunch. They walked hand in hand toward the dining cabin, their nerves palpable.

"How bad do you think it'll be?" David asked.

"They're going to razz us pretty bad," Charlotte snorted. "At least lunch is a short meal," she muttered under her breath.

As they reached the dining cabin, David gave her hand a quick squeeze. "Now or never," he said.

"Right."

David opened the door for Charlotte, and they both walked in, trepidation all over their faces. Charlotte scanned the room; it seemed like business as usual. Some of the ladies were preparing lunch, a few said hello, and the rest were reading the paper or chitchatting.

Charlotte took a deep breath. "Afternoon," she said to Angela, who was filling in a crossword puzzle. David also gave her a brief nod.

"Hello," she responded cheerfully.

As David and Charlotte made their way to the food table, where grilled cheese and tomato soup awaited, a few more people called out hello. They shot each other a quick look, unprepared for the nonreaction of the group. David and Charlotte grabbed their food and sat by themselves at the far end of the table.

"Hey David," Shirley yelled from the opposite end of the table.

He looked up, startled, his soupspoon clattering to the table. "Yes?"

Shirley looked back down at her newspaper. "Are you a baseball guy or a football guy?"

A slow smile full of surprise and relief spread across David's face. "I like both. Why?"

Shirley kept her gaze glued to her paper and shook her head. "Just wondering," she replied.

David and Charlotte looked at each other again as the room filled once more with the sounds of easy conversation and eating.

"David dear," Emma said as she casually flipped the pages of the magazine splayed in front of her on the table. Charlotte rolled her eyes, and David took another bite of his sandwich.

"Yes, Emma?"

"I hope you wrapped your rascal last night," she drawled, cool as ice. The entire room burst into laughter, David nearly choked on his grilled cheese, and Charlotte turned as red as her tomato soup before she dropped her forehead into the palm of one hand.

David took a sip of iced tea and cleared his throat. "Come now, ladies. A gentleman never kisses and tells."

Angela let out a wolf whistle. "Well, girls, I think we have our answer."

※

"I wondered when you'd emerge from the love shack," Karen chirped as she joined Charlotte on the bench by the lake.

Charlotte looked up from her notepad, where she was scribbling notes for an outline she owed to her publisher. She chuckled. "Publisher's been calling me, hounding me for my next title, so I'm working on some stuff to placate them."

"Huh. I guess that's why they keep calling me, too. Of course, I just pretend like I can't get cell reception up here."

"Remind me again why they keep you around?"

"'Cause I sell books, honey, and lots of them."

"Ah, right," Charlotte said as she set her notepad down and picked up the bottle of water at her feet.

"So what's Mr. Wonderful up to?"

"Taking a jog around the lake. I don't think he's missed a day since we've been here."

"He is dedicated; I'll give him that." Karen whipped out her newspaper. "Speaking of, did he tell you about our little chat?"

Charlotte lowered the water bottle. "Dare I ask?"

"I just wanted to see what his intentions were."

"What are you, my father?"

"He seems pretty devoted to you."

Charlotte cocked an eyebrow. "*Seems?*"

"Just want to make sure he's not harboring some Mrs. Robinson fantasy or something."

Charlotte let out an exasperated sigh. "Karen, where is this coming from? First you tell me to go for it, and now you're telling me to be careful. I'm dizzy from trying to keep up."

"All I'm saying is know what you're getting yourself into." Karen flicked the paper open again. "That's basically what I told him, and now I've told you."

Charlotte opened her mouth to say something else, but then thought better of it. She took another sip of water.

"Thanks for the advice."

"Do you keep a calendar?"

"*Hmmm?*"

"A calendar—you know, for appointments?"

It was nighttime, and David and Charlotte were laid out on the couch, her feet perched in his lap while she continued to add notes to her outline. He had been thumbing through a script when he stopped to query her about calendars.

Charlotte set her notepad down. "I'm sorry, what are you asking me about calendars for?"

"Where do you keep yours? On your phone?"

"No way. I'm old school. I tote a big old bulky agenda around with me everywhere I go. Why?"

David tossed the script onto the table and pulled his BlackBerry out of his pocket. He frowned for a moment before he opened his calendar. "Do me a favor and grab your agenda."

Charlotte heaved an annoyed sigh and went to retrieve her agenda from her purse. She flopped back down on the couch and looked at him.

"Okay, now what?"

David's face was screwed up in concentration as he tapped buttons on his BlackBerry.

"We are coordinating schedules so we can plan out when we can see each other," he said casually.

"Ah, I see. Does that mean you're not sick of me yet?"

"Never, sweetheart. Now, I have to be in Vancouver at the end of the month. What are you doing?"

Charlotte perused the pages. "My publisher is due to send me back my current manuscript for a little bit of editing." She looked back at him. "Why?"

"Well, I have to be in Vancouver for a week or so doing some reshoots for a film. After that I've got to jet off to New York for a premiere." David gave her a sidelong glance. "And I want you to come with me."

Charlotte gulped. "You want me to do what?"

"Allow me to whisk you away for some bona fide movie star business." David streamed his fingers up her arm. "Seriously, all jokes aside, I want you with me. Besides, your job allows you to go wherever, be wherever."

Charlotte swallowed again, trying to comprehend everything he was throwing at her. "Wow. Premiere. With all those photographers and everything?" Charlotte shook her head. "That's not really me. I'm not so sure I want to do that."

"Listen...I understand if the thought of walking the red carpet makes you nervous." He started to play with her fingers. "I made the commitment, so I have to be there. But if you're really not keen on it, you don't have to actually walk the red carpet with me. So long as I can stash you somewhere nearby."

Charlotte smiled and cocked her head to the side. "And what do you plan to do with me once you've stashed me?"

"Well, for starters, let me show you New York. We can see a show, see the sights. See it all." He threw the BlackBerry down and began to crawl toward her with that glint in his eye that Charlotte had come to know and love in very short order. "Of course, I already have the sight I want to see every day right here in front of me," he said as he ran his hands over one of her nipples, which hardened beneath her T-shirt.

A moan slipped from Charlotte's lips as David began to stroke her neck with his tongue. "Do I at least get some time to think it over, or do I have to book the flight right now?"

David pulled Charlotte's shirt up and began to nip at her breasts through her bra. "You can think it over all you want, but you know you can't stand the thought of being without me." He paused. "So, you know you'll be going with me."

Charlotte ran the sole of her foot against David's leg. "You are *awfully* demanding, Mr. King," she purred. "Must be the movie star ego."

Before David could answer, his phone vibrated on the table. "Just ignore it," he murmured as he started to kiss her. Within the space of three minutes, the phone vibrated five more times. Charlotte stopped and held his face in her hands.

"Sounds like an emergency," she said. "Maybe you should answer it."

David let out a frustrated sigh and picked up the phone. He looked at the caller ID and got the same disturbed look on his face he'd had when he had pulled the phone out of his pocket to look at his calendar. He hit the ignore button before he turned the phone off altogether.

"Is everything okay?" Charlotte asked.

David nodded. "Oh yeah. Everything's fine." He gave her a devilish grin. "Now, where was I?"

Charlotte snaked her hands around his neck and pulled him to her. "I think right about here." They kissed again, and before Charlotte knew what was happening, David swooped her up and over his shoulder and carried her to his bedroom. She squealed, and David laughed.

"You Tarzan, me Jane?" she asked.

"I'll have to remember to pick up a loincloth."

"You won't need it," Charlotte whispered as she jerked his jeans down.

David stepped out of his jeans, and then he bent down to his knees, cupping Charlotte's face in the palm of one hand. She ran her fingertips along the edges of his face, getting lost in the luscious green fields of his eyes.

"Charlotte," he whispered.

Charlotte leaned back against the bed and spread her legs, inviting him to come in.

He didn't waste any time.

Charlotte's hand dropped into the empty space beside her. She ran her hands up and down the cool sheets in search of David's body. She opened her eyes and propped herself up on her elbows. She took a big sniff, expecting the customary scent of coffee to fill her nostrils.

Nothing.

"Hmm." Charlotte frowned. "That's not like him," she muttered to herself as she swung her legs over the side of the bed. She stood and felt like she might topple over. She and David had made love no less than six times over the past few days, and it was starting to catch up with her. Her body wanted to know what was up. In spite of the sore muscles, she'd never felt more alive; even through the pain, her body tingled with desire for David. Charlotte wandered out to the kitchen to make coffee. While she waited for it to start, she looked out the window and saw David by the lake. His back was to her, and he was on the phone. Charlotte crossed her arms and watched him. Whoever he was on the phone with had him highly agitated. He paced back and forth a bit before she saw him punch his index finger in the air in an angry stabbing motion. Charlotte ran her tongue across her teeth, curious. She watched him for a few moments more before she poured a fresh cup of coffee. She busied herself with leafing through her outline, but after a while, it was clear David wasn't getting off the phone anytime soon. Charlotte drained her coffee and headed to the shower.

The hot water was a salve for the knots in her muscles as she melted underneath the steam. Charlotte scrubbed herself clean before dumping a glob of shampoo into her hand and lathering it through her tangle of curls. As she rinsed the shampoo from her hair, she saw David's form through the frosted shower door. She slid the door open and poked her head out.

He stood before her wearing nothing but a naughty grin. Her breath caught in her throat as her eyes traveled up and down his finely sculpted work of art. She shivered inside.

"Hi," she said softly. "You okay?"

He nodded. "Oh yeah. I'm fantastic."

"That seemed like a pretty intense phone call. Want to talk about it?"

"*Psshh*. Oh, that. That was nothing." He narrowed his eyes. "Mind if I join you?"

"Are you sure?"

"About getting in the shower with you?"

"No, no. About the phone call. Everything's okay?"

David nodded. "Yes. Absolutely. Now, we were negotiating showering together?"

Charlotte bit her lip, hoping he wouldn't pick up on her hesitation. It was one thing to be flirty and fun under the covers. It was quite another to be standing in the stark light of day, where there was no hiding the stretch marks or cellulite. She took a deep breath and admonished herself for acting so silly after everything they'd been through.

"Of course," she finally said as she stepped aside to make room for him.

He reached around her and grabbed for the body wash, which he squirted on her shoulder. He began to soap her up.

"I've already washed myself."

David lathered up her breasts from behind. "Are you sure? I'll do it again just in case."

"I'm starting to wonder if I should have let you in here."

"Oh, I wasn't going to take no for an answer," he said as he flipped her around and continued to whip frothy bubbles up and down her body. He leered at her.

"You ever done it in a shower?" he asked.

"I can honestly say that's one I've never tried," she giggled.

He plastered himself against her. "Well, there is a first time for everything, isn't there?"

"So I've heard." She smiled.

David stood staring at her for a few moments, shaking his head in awe.

"What?" she asked.

"It's just that…you make me happy. Dizzy, crazy, silly happy."

Charlotte snaked her arms around his neck. "I do? How?"

He groped the air for the words. "Just by being who you are…funny, smart, and passionate. *Compassionate*." He leaned back. "Most important, you think I'm funny and smart."

They both laughed. "Of course that's *the* most important thing," Charlotte said.

"Indeed."

Charlotte put the bottom of her chin on David's chest as she gazed up at him. "Don't ever change, okay?"

He grinned. "You either. Now, about that doing it in the shower bit…"

David's phone continued to ring off the hook all day. Mostly he ignored it, though there were a few times he stepped outside to take the calls. Each time that Charlotte would query him, he would brush it off. As they were walking to dinner, his phone rang again. David looked ready to throw it in the lake, and told Charlotte he'd have to take the call, but that he would meet up with her at dinner. Of course, everyone asked where David was, and Charlotte was nonchalant as she told them he had some business to take care of. He never showed for dinner, and as Angela helped Charlotte with the dishes, she was starting to worry something was truly wrong.

On her way back to the cabin, Charlotte chewed on the nail of her index finger, her nerves unraveling. Her overactive imagination was running rampant with all sorts of terrible scenarios—scenarios she didn't dare voice.

When she opened the door, David was sitting on the couch, his shoulders hunched up around his ears, his hands wound together. Charlotte's heart stopped when she noticed his backpack loaded and ready to go. He gave Charlotte an uneasy look. She cleared her throat and shut the door.

"Um, we still have a few more days here. Do you have to go to Vancouver sooner than you thought?" she asked, her voice low and soft like a shy little girl.

He patted the spot next to him on the sofa. She waited a moment before joining him. He took her hand in both of his and kissed it repeatedly. He focused in on her eyes.

"I'm afraid I have to cut our time a little short. I've had something come up that I have to take care of. I'll need to leave first thing in the morning."

"Oh," Charlotte said, taken aback. "I see. What is it? Does it have to do with all those phone calls you've been getting?"

David let out a deep breath. "Yes, it does, but I...I can't get into it right now."

Charlotte nodded, her heart racing with dread. "Sure. I understand. Things to take care of. I get it."

"I've just got to deal with something. Won't take more than a day or two at the most."

Charlotte felt tears spring to her eyes. Not wanting him to see her cry, she jumped off the couch in search of a doughnut. "David, its fine." She found the doughnut box and ripped into it. "Besides, I need a few days to myself anyway. You know, get home, water the plants, check my mail—that sort of thing. You go and do whatever it is you need to do."

David sighed and stood up. "Charlotte, it's not what you're thinking—"

"What am I thinking?" she cut him off as she tore off a chunk of doughnut.

David's shoulders slumped. "Listen, it's just something I need to tend to. I'll meet up with you back in L.A., and we'll finish planning our trip."

"Oh yeah, right, our trip," Charlotte said.

David sighed. "Come on, Charlotte. Stop acting like this. You're scaring me."

"I just don't understand what the big secret is and why you can't tell me. God knows we've told each other just about everything since we've been here." She paused. "Haven't we?"

"Yes, yes, of course, but this is...It's just something I need to do, okay? Please, I'm asking you to just give me a few days."

Charlotte took a deep breath and put the doughnut on the counter. She shook her head. "I'm sorry. It's just with the phone calls, and something you obviously don't want to talk about, and now this..." Her voice trailed off. "It's just all very mysterious and weird, and I'm just not sure what to make of it."

David drew her into his arms. "Sweetheart, I swear—just a few days." He kissed the top of her head before he looked deep into her eyes. "You trust me?"

Charlotte stared at him a moment before pressing her lips against his. Finally, she pulled back and nodded. "Yes. I do."

That night David and Charlotte made love with zealous intensity. No words were spoken. No double entendres. No jokes. Just mad, passionate love. The next morning, they woke early, as Charlotte had agreed to take David into town to rent a car to drive back to L.A. for his mysterious mission. They kept conversation to light topics before they set off. Charlotte turned the oldies station on, and they both listened to the radio, not saying much. Charlotte pulled up to the rental agency and turned off the car. They sat in silence.

"So I'll call you in a few days, and I'll meet you at your place."

Charlotte nodded, afraid to speak for fear of her voice squeaking.

David turned to Charlotte and traced the outline of her jaw with the tip of his index finger. He smiled. "The next few days will be torture, being away from you."

Charlotte managed a feeble smile. "Right."

David leaned over and gave Charlotte a kiss, and she swore she felt her heart fracture into a million pieces right in her chest. They broke away from each other, and Charlotte looked down.

"Guess it's time to pick up the car," David said.

Charlotte touched his hand. "David, please drive carefully," she whispered.

David grabbed the back of Charlotte's neck and looked into her eyes. "I will. I promise. Charlotte clamped her hand around David's wrist and nodded, not sure how much longer she'd be able to keep her steely resolve.

David opened the door of the Jeep and looked down at her. "I love you," he said.

She nodded.

With one last look, David gave her a small wave before he headed inside. Charlotte sat there for a moment, stunned. A single tear slid down her cheek, and she started the car.

She cried all the way back to the cabin.

CHAPTER 7

Charlotte put on a brave face for the ladies over the next two days. She told them that David had some business to tend to, but was vague about the details. They seemed to sense she didn't want to talk about it, so they let her be.

Memories of him—his scent, his taste, the way he would double over whenever he found something particularly funny, the way he moved inside her when they made love—were all stuck on repeat inside her head. He'd pleaded with her to trust him that everything would be okay, and Charlotte was holding on to that slim hope, slippery though it was between her fingers. If only he'd told her what was going on…

On the last day, Charlotte halfheartedly packed in preparation for the trip back to L.A. There was a knock on the door. Charlotte's heart leaped.

"David," she whispered as she ran to the door, all sins, real or imagined, forgiven.

She threw the door open and tried to hide her disappointment when she saw Karen and Hendra standing there.

"Oh, hey guys," she said with forced enthusiasm.

"Jeez, you'd think we showed up with a batch of cholera to pass on to her," Karen snorted, her hand on her hip.

"Karen and I were wondering if you'd take a walk with us before you got on the road," Hendra said.

Charlotte twirled a strand of hair around her finger. "Well, I've got a lot of packing to—"

Karen rolled her eyes and yanked Charlotte outside. She yelped and was barely able to close the door behind her before the forced stroll.

"What's this all about?" Charlotte asked, annoyed.

"What's going on with you and Mr. Wonderful? Where did he run off to?" Karen demanded.

"I already told you. He had to head back to L.A. for some business."

Hendra shook her head. "Seems a little abrupt. I mean, you two seemed to be getting on quite well, like you'd known each other for years. In fact, he seems pretty crazy about you."

The trio came upon some benches near the boathouse. Charlotte winced and tried not to let memories of that rainy night flood her brain. They sat down.

"So are you meeting up in L.A. or what?" Karen demanded.

Charlotte swallowed and nodded. "Yeah, in a few days, once he's done with his business. And he wants me to go to Canada with him for a movie shoot and then to New York for a premiere."

Did he still?

Hendra let out a low sigh, and Karen clucked her tongue. Charlotte crossed her arms in a defensive gesture. She wouldn't have been in the mood for this, no matter what the circumstances.

"All right, Karen, whatever it is you have to say, spill it."

"Listen. You know I was all for you gettin' your groove on, though it seems it's gone a little past that." Karen stole a quick glance at Hendra. "And like she said, it seems like the guy is pretty crazy about you. But now you're headed out into the real world."

"And?"

Karen shifted in her seat. "And so now it's a whole different ball game. When this man gets a haircut, it's in the paper. Every time he does a film, the tabloids wag that he's screwing everyone on the set. Are you ready to be a part of that? People being in your business all the time?"

Charlotte was silent, deciding to let Karen continue with her rant.

"Do you know how you're going to react when someone says you're old enough to be his mother? Or call you a cradle robber, or a leopard?"

"Cougar," Charlotte and Hendra corrected her in unison.

"Fine, cougar, whatever...You've never had to deal with this before. People are going to crawl up your ass with a flashlight. You got a mild taste of it in town, and it bothered you so much you brought him here to hide out."

Silence fell over the group. Tears began to roll down Charlotte's face.

"What is it?" Hendra asked.

"Do I look like a fool?"

Hendra took Charlotte's hand. "No, dear. The heart wants what it wants. You shouldn't have to defend it. Unfortunately, you both will have to."

Charlotte sniffed. She was afraid to tell them she was already questioning her involvement with David. She decided it would keep. She wiped her nose with the back of her sleeve and stood.

"Well, I appreciate you ladies showing so much concern, but I'll be fine."

One way or another.

Hendra stood and gave Charlotte a fierce hug. "You know how much we love you, right?"

"Even Karen?" Charlotte joked.

Karen joined the hug. "Only on my good days."

Charlotte let out a groan as she got out of the Jeep and stretched her cramped limbs. It had been a difficult drive between an unexpected patch of traffic on the 10 and memories of David brought on by the oldies station; Charlotte was ready to stick a fork in the day. She frowned as she looked at the droopy multicolored flowers that filled the small, fenced-in front yard. She unlocked the black door to her white one-story bungalow with blue shutters and sighed. She knew that she should do some gardening to keep her mind off David, but the truth was that all she wanted to do was fall into bed with a pint of rocky road.

Charlotte spent the next hour going through mail, unpacking, and changing the sheets on her bed before submerging herself in a bath filled with jasmine-scented bubbles. She kept her cell phone perched on the bathroom counter, her ear trained for a ring. It had already been nearly three days since she'd dropped David off at the rental place, and he'd promised it wouldn't be more than a day before he called. She sighed as she examined her breasts beneath the soapy cobwebs. He'd thought them flawless. Charlotte closed her eyes and leaned her head back against the slippery tile, trying not to succumb to the tears shimmering just below the surface of her eyelids.

Suddenly, the shrill pierce of her cell phone punched the air. She jerked up and scurried out of the tub, bubbles floating through the air, water sloshing over the sides and onto the rug. She grabbed it, hoping it hadn't gone to voice mail. She didn't even bother to look at the caller ID.

"Hello?" she shouted.

"Charlotte? It's Karen. Just wanted to make sure you got back to L.A. okay."

Her bottom lip began to quiver, but Charlotte composed herself. "Oh, yeah, about an hour or so ago. Did you make it back to San Francisco yet?"

"Got a few more hours ahead of me. Listen, you seemed a little out of it before you left. I just wanted to check on you, see how you were."

Charlotte leaned against the counter, soap bubbles dripping down her body to the floor, goose bumps beginning to sprout all over her legs and arms. "Oh, I'm fine. You know, I think just the emotion of everything got to me a little bit. But I'm okay. Really."

"You heard from David?"

"Um, no, not yet, but I will," Charlotte said more for herself than Karen.

Karen didn't say anything, and Charlotte knew she was holding her tongue. "Okay. Well, have a good night, and talk to you soon."

"Thanks, Karen."

Charlotte hung up and drained the bathtub. She hadn't gotten much relaxation out of it anyway.

Nighttime droned on in a long, gaping maw. Charlotte found an old Lean Cuisine pasta dinner hiding in the back of her freezer, and pain stabbed at her heart at the flash of remembrance over the dinner David had prepared for her birthday. She wasn't normally a TV person, but she comforted herself with reruns of *Friends*, unable to cope with the eerie quiet of her house. She downed a few glasses of wine and obsessively checked her cell phone every few minutes, willing it to ring.

At midnight, an exhausted Charlotte trudged off to bed. She brought her phone with her, something she had never done, and set it on the nightstand, careful to position it as close to her ear as possible. She flopped down on her stomach, afraid of the tears she knew were coming.

There was no stopping the deluge.

The first thing Charlotte did the next morning was check her phone. No missed calls—no voice mails. She let out a heavy sigh and wearily got out of bed. She would lick this. She'd licked worse. Charlotte would outsmart this pit of despair gnawing at her insides. It had been a delicious fantasy. Maybe she'd turn it into a book one day. That thought cheered Charlotte up slightly as she set about getting her house back in order after having been gone for a month. Fortified by two cups of coffee, she paid bills, scrubbed her house from top to bottom, and made out her grocery list. She'd even decided to spend some time gardening that afternoon.

By the time Charlotte left for the store, she was humming. The sun was out, the sky was blue and brilliant, and the birds were chirping. It would be a glorious day. She'd make sure of it.

Because it was the middle of the day, the grocery store was practically empty except for a few elderly women doing their daily shopping, and some moms with kids going cuckoo for Cocoa Puffs. Ignoring them all, Charlotte set out to fill her cart with all sorts of goodies that she never used to buy: exotic cheeses, fresh pasta, hunks of salmon, bulbs of garlic, and stalks of firm green asparagus. After an hour, when she was ready to check out, she pulled up behind a frazzled mom who kept finding items in her cart that her two kids had dumped in when she hadn't been looking. Charlotte didn't even let it bother her as she casually scanned the items in her own cart, pleased with her purchases.

While she was humming to herself, her eye fell upon the magazines in the rack next to her, the usual trash. And then her eyes got wide as she saw David with a tall, skinny blonde on the cover of one. She felt the color drain from her face as she read the headline, which screamed out at her in bold yellow block letters: REUNITED! DAVID KING AND OLIVIA HUDSON REKINDLE ROMANCE!

Charlotte snatched the paper and stared at the photo. There was David with one arm around the waist of starlet Olivia Hudson, the other raised to shield his eyes from the paparazzi's flashes. Olivia wore a broad smile and faced the cameras directly, her porcelain white teeth gleaming beneath her pale pink lipstick. Trembling, Charlotte tossed the rag on top of her groceries and gripped the edge of the shopping cart in order to keep herself upright. She licked her lips and felt the salt of her tears begin to sting her eyes.

"Ma'am? Are you ready?"

Charlotte blinked at the checker, who stood there staring at her, waiting for Charlotte to unload her cart.

"Oh, yeah, sorry," Charlotte said as she started to dump her food onto the conveyer belt. Charlotte mechanically wrote a check and refused assistance out to her car. Once locked inside her Jeep, Charlotte struggled to keep it together until she got back to her house; that's when she would read the article. She arrived home by rote and quickly grabbed her bags and dropped them on the counter before she started digging through them in search of the tabloid. She yanked it out and flipped to the page with the story about David and Olivia. Plump tears poured from her eyes, blurring the newsprint. She forced herself to read the article:

Hunky David King, star of the forthcoming rom-com To Have and To Hold, *was holding on tight to his ex, super-sexy Olivia Hudson, who just signed on for the female lead in the action flick* Black Knight, Dark Knight, *after a romantic weekend at the Beverly Wilshire. Sources say Hudson checked in Friday afternoon and that King joined her later that night and that the canoodling couple didn't come up for air until early Monday morning.*

The rest of the article detailed their six-month "torrid romance" and "dramatic breakup" and "romantic reconciliation." By the time Charlotte finished reading, she was hyperventilating.

"Oh God," she whispered as she scrunched up the paper and threw it in the trash. Charlotte sat hunched over her kitchen table for the better part of an hour, sobbing until her insides were scraped raw. She felt like she had the world's biggest "Kick Me" sign on her back. She couldn't believe how stupid she'd been to believe in David, to have allowed herself to be swept off her feet by his undeniable charm. Charlotte finally stood and went to splash cold water on her face from the kitchen sink. She threw her groceries in the fridge, not bothering to take them out of the bags. Charlotte draped herself across her bed and cried the rest of the day.

CHAPTER 8

Charlotte's bedroom was shrouded in darkness. She unglued her eyes from the deep slumber she'd fallen into after crying herself to sleep. Charlotte inhaled and rolled over on her back. She lay there for a moment, her hand splayed across her stomach, the hushed sounds of the house enveloping her. The afternoon's events came flooding back, stabbing at her chest. David. The tabloid. His ex. Charlotte squeezed her eyes shut, willing the images to disappear. She glanced at the clock on her nightstand and saw she'd been asleep since the early afternoon.

Charlotte slowly raised herself and lumbered out of bed, her body aching from both the positions she'd twisted herself into and the sobs that had shredded her insides. She stumbled to the bathroom to splash some cold water on her face, and she took a long look at herself in the mirror. Her face was puffy from her crying jag, and the wrinkles of sleep lay across one cheek. Charlotte heaved a big sigh and shuffled to her kitchen, it, too, cloaked in night.

She noticed her cell phone on the counter, the red light blinking furiously, indicating she had messages. Charlotte picked it up and scrolled through to see that she had several voice mails from Hendra and five texts, all from Karen, inquiring about David. Disgusted and in no mood to deal with anyone, Charlotte tossed the phone back on the counter and opened her fridge in search of a bottle of wine. She poured a glass and carried it and the bottle to the living room, where she plopped down on the couch.

She took long, slow swallows and stared in front of her, her gulps the lone sound in the room.

She almost didn't hear the faint tap. Charlotte ignored it, certain it was a branch or something scratching against a window in the house. The knocking grew louder and more persistent before Charlotte realized it was definitely someone rapping on her door. Charlotte swallowed, afraid. Who would be knocking on her door at this time of night?

Without a word, she set her wineglass on the coffee table and tiptoed over to the door, her heart pounding. There was one more knock, and now Charlotte looked around frantically in search of a weapon before she let her shoulders drop and shook her head.

"Would a murderer knock, Charlotte?" she whispered to herself before she flipped on the hall light and looked out the peephole. She could see a dark figure huddled over, but couldn't make out anything else.

"Who is it?" she yelled out.

"It's David," came the muffled reply.

Charlotte stood rooted, her feet mired in cement. Her mouth filled with cotton. She licked her lips, unsure of what to do.

"Charlotte, please open the door and let me explain everything."

Charlotte blinked and found her voice. "There's nothing to explain," she shouted. "You got back with your ex. I read all about it. Now go away."

"I'm not leaving until you let me tell you my side."

"Why should I listen?"

"Because, Charlotte, I know you're a fair person. All I'm asking is that you listen to what I have to say. And if, after you hear me out, you still want to send me away and never have me darken your doorstep again, I won't."

Charlotte groaned and placed her forehead against the door. What was that old saying about giving people an inch and they'd take a mile? Then again, she was curious to hear what he had to say...

Curiosity won out, and Charlotte undid the latch and opened the door. She trembled at the sight of David, his green eyes cloudy, worry and fear creasing his handsome features. His normally lush dark hair was limp and stringy, and it looked like he was carrying about twelve suitcases under each eye. Charlotte looked down and gestured for him to come in. David obliged, and Charlotte shut the door, still unable to look him in the eye. She crossed her arms and leaned against the wall.

"Well, you look like hell," she said.

"How can you tell? You've barely looked at me. Not that I blame you."

"I can tell."

David shoved his hands in his pockets before he took a glance toward the living room behind him. "Nice place," he said.

"I'm sure you didn't come here to talk about my decor, David."

David gave her a wry grin and shifted his feet. "No. No, I didn't." He sighed. "Can we sit?"

Charlotte pushed herself off the wall and brushed past David, into the living room, where she resumed her place on the couch. David followed and started to sit next to Charlotte before he thought better of it and took a seat on the overstuffed navy blue chair opposite her. He sat perched on the edge, his shoulders bunched up around his ears, and he rubbed his hands together uneasily. Charlotte picked up her wineglass and waited.

David sighed. "I'm trying to think of where to start."

"The beginning is usually a good place," Charlotte responded as she sipped her wine.

"Yes, I suppose it is." David clasped his hands together. "Olivia."

Charlotte tensed up at the sound of her name. "Yes," she said coolly. "Olivia."

David hung his head for a moment before he continued. "I met Olivia about two years ago at some movie premiere party. I can't even remember which one it was now. She was there with her agent; I was there with William. We just started talking, hit it off. I'll admit, my head was turned by how she looked—blonde hair, blue eyes, all that stereotypical nonsense. We exchanged numbers, met up a few days later for coffee. It started off as just being fun. She was just fun to be around, up for almost anything, understood the industry. Sweet." David let out a snort. "On the surface anyway."

Charlotte watched David and waited for him to continue.

"So we dated, and for me it was just…casual, you know? Someone to hang out with, go to premieres with, have dinner with once in a while. About three months in, I realized that she's just…that she's just an awful person. Clingy. Desperate. Manipulative. That the reason she's the life of the party is because she's got nothing else going on. No depth, no real personality beyond what you see on the screen. Half the time Olivia doesn't know where Olivia begins and whatever character she's playing at the moment ends." David leaned back against the chair before he continued. "And then I found out she's a total cokehead. I mean a straight-on-would-sell-her-mother-for-a-line-then-sell-herself cokehead. Caught her doing lines in my bathroom one day. So I told her to get out," David said matter-of-factly. "And she starts crying, begging me to let her stay…she loves me so much, she'll change, blah, blah, blah."

Charlotte gripped her wineglass. "So then what?"

"She promised she would change, and I told her I would stick by her until she got clean. Which was my first mistake, because she used it to try to keep the relationship going. Always finding a reason to call me—she didn't get the movie she was up for and might do a line. She broke a nail; she might do a line." David shook his head. "But I felt sorry for her. She has no one else. Not one friend, not one family member she can turn to for anything. No one wants anything to do with her."

Charlotte looked down into her wine. "And you're the only person she can turn to," she said sarcastically.

David sighed. "Unfortunately, yes. Anyway, I just got to a point where I couldn't do it anymore. I cut off all contact, got a new cell phone number, and picked up and disappeared to New York for a few months. You can be a lot more anonymous there than you can out here."

Charlotte let out a small exhale. "What about the other day—at the lake?"

David dropped his chin into the palm of one hand. "I saw her number come up—I'd know it anywhere, unfortunately—and I knew right away it was her. She'd wrangled my number out of a mutual acquaintance. I figured if I ignored it, she'd get the hint and stop calling me. But as you saw, she just kept on. Turns out the studio for her next film got wind of some rumors about her using and ordered her to take a drug test. If she failed, it meant they couldn't insure her for the movie and she'd be fired. Then a big scandal, so on and so forth. Not to mention her salary was going to be bigger than Donald Trump's ego, and she didn't want to lose out on that."

"So she called you."

David nodded. "Yeah. Begged me to help get her into a rapid detox because she knew it was just a matter of time before she got random tested. That's why she kept calling me—she was running out of time. Sure enough, they tested her last night."

"And?"

David shook his head bitterly. "And she passed."

Charlotte drained the last of the wine, her head starting to float above her. "Since when does detox take place at the Beverly Wilshire?"

"Ah, yes...the romantic getaway at the Beverly Wilshire. Her agent planted that story. Trying to buy Olivia some time to get clean. I was furious when I found out about it. The truth is, all three of us were holed up at his house in the Hills with a doctor who specializes in rapid detox. I promise you, I was never anywhere near the Beverly Wilshire."

"I thought you said she didn't have anyone. If you were at her agent's house…"

David stood and began to pace the room. "Only because I made him. Truth is, he's ready to drop her. Of course, I had to remind him that if she didn't do the movie, he wouldn't get his cut of her salary. After that, he was all too happy to put up his house. Then he repays me by planting that stupid story." David shook his head. "Lousy son of a bitch," he muttered under his breath.

"But the picture…"

"What picture?"

"The one on the cover of the magazine. You had your hand around her waist."

"What was I wearing?"

Charlotte blinked, caught off guard. "What were you wearing?" she repeated.

"What was I wearing in the picture?"

"I…I don't know, jeans and a T-shirt probably."

"May I see it?"

Charlotte narrowed her eyes at him for a moment before she stalked into the kitchen in search of the rumpled tabloid she had tossed into the trash earlier. She extracted it from the bin and brought it into the living room, clicking on the lamp next to the couch. She smoothed the paper out on the coffee table.

"See?" Charlotte thumped her finger against the table. "You've got your hands all over her."

David tried to contain his grin. "First of all, it's one hand around her waist. Second, that picture is over a year old." He leaned forward and pointed to the hand that was around Olivia. "Look, do you see that? A big bandage on my hand. Slashed it doing a stunt on the movie I was filming at the time." David held up both his hands and flipped them back and forth to show they were unblemished and bandage free. "So if this picture was taken a few days ago, how do you explain this?"

Charlotte bit her bottom lip to keep from laughing and crying all at the same time. She straightened up.

"Okay, so, you were helping her. I don't understand why you had to stay with her the whole time—I mean, her agent stepped up when push came to shove."

David's eyes pierced Charlotte's face. "Do you remember what you told me about your husband's girlfriend when she died?"

Charlotte's breath caught in her throat, and she looked down at her lap. David sat on the couch next to her and hooked his index finger underneath her chin, forcing her to look at him.

"You said she was all alone and what were you supposed to do—leave her?"

Charlotte sniffed, an impending downpour of tears threatening to break free. One escaped and trickled down her face. She wiped it away with her hand.

"And you couldn't leave Olivia," Charlotte whispered.

David took her face in both hands. "Sweetheart, believe me when I tell you, you absolutely, one hundred percent, have nothing to worry about from her or any woman. What did I tell you on your birthday?"

Charlotte laughed in spite of herself and wiped away another tear. "What is this, a walk down memory lane?"

David chuckled and rubbed her tear away with his thumb. "Something like that. Come on now—don't leave me hanging. What did I tell you?"

Charlotte's bottom lip trembled, and she then sniffed again. "You told me you love me."

"I meant it then, and I mean it now." David searched Charlotte's eyes. "I love you," he whispered.

Charlotte couldn't help it; the waterworks burst forth, and nothing could stop them. David folded her into his arms and rocked her gently while she sobbed into his chest. Finally, Charlotte pulled back and laughed.

"You look like you've been in another rainstorm," she said as she wiped her nose.

David looked down at the front of his shirt, which was soaked, and smiled. "I think you just said the magic word."

Charlotte didn't say anything; she just fingered the hem of his shirt. David's hand found hers, and their fingers intertwined. He moved closer and dragged the tip of his tongue along Charlotte's bottom lip before gently sucking on it. Charlotte responded by pulling him into a full-on kiss, which they both melted into. Charlotte unlocked her hand from David's and let the fingers of both hands trickle underneath his shirt. She pushed his shirt up underneath his arms and bent back down to his belly button, letting her tongue trail up his chest. David groaned and affixed his hands underneath her armpits and hauled her toward him until they were eye level.

"My God, Charlotte. I..." he breathed.

"*Shhh*," Charlotte said, placing her fingers over his lips. She kissed him and ran her hands all over his face. David rubbed her bottom before he slipped his hands inside the waistband of her pants and pressed her against him with urgent intensity.

"Where's the bedroom?" he whispered.

Charlotte jumped up and pulled David by both hands toward her room. He laughed when he saw her bed, which ran from one end of the room to the other.

"Wow," he said as Charlotte went to kiss him again. "What is this, two king beds? Do you ever get lost in this thing? It's huge!"

"Sometimes. I always thought small beds were silly. You spend a lot of your life in bed; you might as well make it comfy. It's a deluxe California king."

David moaned and fastened his hands around Charlotte's waist. "How about I king you right now?"

"I was hoping you'd say that," Charlotte said as she yanked David's pants open and pushed them to the floor. David stepped out of his shoes and pants, and Charlotte flopped back against the bed. David dropped down on top of her and pulled her T-shirt over her head before cupping her breasts with both hands.

"Do you have any idea how much I've missed you?" he whispered.

"I think I do," Charlotte said, already feeling the rumbling between her legs.

David went to work on kissing her breasts with tender intensity. His fingers slipped inside her, and Charlotte let out a small yelp and began to thrust toward him. As he swirled his fingers around inside of her, Charlotte fondled his hardness, aching to feel it pumping inside her. She hooked one leg around David and pushed his fingers in deeper.

"Well, look at you." David chuckled. "Is it fair to say you missed me too?"

Charlotte nodded frantically. "Yes, yes—I want you inside me in the worst way."

David stopped his frenetic motion, and Charlotte positioned herself, waiting for him to enter her. Nothing happened, and Charlotte opened her eyes to see David grinning at her.

"What? Come on, why aren't you...you know..."

"I just love seeing that look on your face, that anticipation, the pleasure." David took the tip of his index finger and traced a figure eight pattern around Charlotte's nipple. "I love to pleasure you, you know."

Charlotte grasped David's forearm. "All I know is that right now it feels like you're torturing me."

David laughed and resumed his outline of Charlotte's nipple. "You know what they say...Good things come to those who wait," he said as he bent down next to Charlotte's feet, which were dangling over the side of the bed. He picked one up and kissed the top of it.

Charlotte screwed up her face. "Are you kissing my feet?"

David nodded and flicked his tongue around her ankle bone, all while caressing her instep with his fingers. With slow and sure movements, he alternated light, supple kisses with twirls of his tongue all up and down Charlotte's legs. She shivered at the exquisite sensation coursing through her and lay back against the bed, giving every fiber of herself over to David. He continued his ascent up her body, taking great care to nibble at the soft skin behind her knees. David continued upward, sucking and kissing her thighs as Charlotte began to shake with desire. He paused briefly between her legs to blow on her, which caused Charlotte to jump up and cry out. David merely eased Charlotte back down on the bed, and she continued to writhe underneath his delicious touches and teases. He swept his tongue across her stomach, careful to dip into every crevice and curve. By now Charlotte was weeping; it felt so good. When he got to her nipples, he licked and then blew on them, the cool rushes of air sending her body into shock as she began to quiver. Without warning, David planted his knees and plummeted inside her. Charlotte gasped, and within seconds, she exploded around him. She dug her fingers into his back before she grabbed a pillow next to her and screamed into it—her entire body tingled, like a million feathers were brushing over her skin at once. She stayed clenched around David, who stopped, his sweat dripping onto her shoulder.

"You all right?" David asked from somewhere far away.

Charlotte kept the pillow mashed over her face and shook her head. David chuckled and moved inside her once more. Charlotte squealed, and her head began to spin before she burst into a fit of giggles. David pulled the pillow off her face, where she launched into full-on guffaws.

"What is going on with you?" David asked, his own laughter creeping into his voice.

"I don't know," Charlotte panted. "This has never happened before." She looked at him. "What in the hell are you doing to me?"

David leaned down and resumed his thrusts. "Pleasuring you."

Charlotte dropped her head back, and David's movements became faster and deeper. It wasn't long before his own guttural howl roared from beneath his lips and he collapsed on top of Charlotte. They lay there, drenched in sweat, neither willing to move or speak.

Finally, Charlotte's leg began to sting with sleep, and she tapped David on the shoulder so she could roll over on her side. David plastered himself against her and nestled his nose within the tangles of her hair.

"Strawberries," he murmured.

"Strawberries," she whispered.

Charlotte rolled over, expecting to run into David as she did so. She propped one eye open and saw that his side of the bed was empty. She gasped and sat up, panicked. She swung her legs over the side of the bed and grimaced. They'd made love twice more before nodding off to a symphony of their own snores. She tripped over David's shoes, which he'd kicked off the night before. Charlotte bent down and laughed before she moved the shoes underneath her nightstand. She pulled her pink terrycloth bathrobe from the hook on the back of the door and tied it around her waist as she went in search of David.

She found him in her living room, clad only in his boxer briefs, standing in front of her floor-to-ceiling bookshelves. He was lost in perusing her shelves crammed full of CDs, books, and photos. She crept up behind him and slipped her arms around his torso.

"See anything you want to borrow?" she mumbled into his back.

David chuckled and whipped around to kiss her. "You know, there was a time when you wouldn't let me kiss you unless you'd brushed your teeth." He leaned back. "You better not be getting bored with me."

Charlotte gripped him tighter. "Never."

"Good," David said as he kissed the top of her head. "How about some eggs? I'm famished."

Charlotte nodded, and David grabbed her and led her to the kitchen. He busied himself with pulling out his ingredients along with pans and spatulas.

"Looks like you've already been nosing around my kitchen," she said as she perched on a barstool.

David dumped a pat of butter into the frying pan. "Well, I figured I'd be here lots of mornings, so I'd better get acquainted." He looked at her sheepishly. "At least that's what I was hoping, anyway."

Charlotte twisted a lock of hair and looked at her hands. "I'm sorry I didn't trust you," she said quietly. "I'm sorry that I automatically assumed the worst."

David continued to scramble the eggs. "I'm not going to kid you, Charlotte. When you date someone like me, the tabloids are a way of life. Someone will always be fabricating a story, dredging through the garbage—all kinds of things. It's not going to be easy." He sprinkled some cheese on top of the eggs. "You sure you don't want to cut and run?"

"Why? You trying to get rid of me?"

David grinned and shook his head. "Not a chance." He slid some eggs onto a plate in front of Charlotte. "To be fair, I should have just told you right away what was going on. I guess, in my foolhardy, misguided way, I was trying to protect you."

Charlotte doodled on the bar with her finger. "Can we make a pact?"

"What's that?"

"That we're honest with each other. Even if we think the other person can't handle it. No secrets."

David put some eggs for himself on another plate and smiled at Charlotte. "Deal."

Charlotte picked up her fork and grinned. "Good," she said as she scooped up a forkful of fluffy eggs. "You know, I have to say...there's something about the sight of you cooking in my kitchen in your kegs that's rather sexy."

"Aha! You remembered!"

Charlotte giggled and swallowed her eggs. "At least you know I listen to what you say."

"Greatly appreciated." David scooped up the last of his eggs. "So... what's on the agenda for the day?"

"Ugh, well, I really do need to buckle down and do some actual work."

David sucked in his breath. "That's too bad."

Charlotte frowned. "Why?"

"I planned to get lost in that big, fantastic bed with you."

Charlotte threw down her fork and stood. "Race you to the bedroom."

It was early afternoon before Charlotte slipped out of bed and into the shower. She hated to leave David, but she knew she'd better get going on her work. She had cordoned herself off in her office, and within moments there were papers scattered everywhere, and at least two pencils were sticking out of Charlotte's hair. She was tapping away on her laptop when she felt David's arms around her. She jumped, and David planted a kiss on her neck.

"Admit it; you missed having me sneak up on you when you least expect it."

"Oh yeah, it was my favorite part of the day."

"I almost put my eye out on those pencils."

"Oh, those," Charlotte said sheepishly as her hands flew to her head to extricate them from her hair. "Sometimes I forget and have been known to walk around all day with a pencil here, a pencil there…"

"Good thing you work from home."

"Tell me about it," Charlotte snorted as David stuck a yellow sticky note on her chest. "What's this?" Charlotte pulled the note off her T-shirt and saw an e-mail address.

"You need to e-mail William your info for the Vancouver trip so he can make all the arrangements. We leave day after tomorrow."

"Ah, right. Vancouver," Charlotte said as she leaned back in her chair.

"You still want to go, don't you?"

"Oh yes, yes. Of course. I'm sorry. I guess with everything going on I completely forgot."

"It'll be fun. Promise." David searched Charlotte's face. "What is it?"

Charlotte waved her hand. "Oh, well, this…this sounds so silly, but… what, uh…what have you told William about…us?"

David knelt down until he was eye level with Charlotte. "That you make me deliriously happy. He thinks it's funny how we met."

"*Hmmm.* I see, and uh, did you tell him that I'm a couple of years *younger* than you?" she said sarcastically. "I want him to know before he meets me so that he doesn't faint in front of me."

David rolled his eyes. "Oh, here we go."

Charlotte laughed. "Okay, okay, sorry. I'll stop. And I'll e-mail William."

"Excellent. While you do that, I'm going to hop in the shower."

"I set out some towels for you on the counter in the bathroom."

"Thanks, love," David said as he stood and went to leave the room. When he reached the door, he turned to look back at Charlotte.

She glanced up. "Yeah?"

David smiled. "For everything."

CHAPTER 9

"Remind me again why our flight is at four in the morning?" Charlotte yawned and dropped her head back against the headrest of the limo William had sent to Charlotte's house to ferry them to the airport.

"The earlier it is, the less people," David responded. "Cheer up. We're flying first class, and you can sleep on the plane. I'll even let you drool on my shoulder."

"Well, gee, with an offer like that," Charlotte muttered. "Just wake me up if I start to snore."

David chuckled and sipped his coffee. "Only if I'm not snoring myself. So, you ever flown first class before?"

"A few times. My publisher actually springs for it when I do big, big book tours or conferences. Which has happened only about a handful of times. Still, it was nice."

"Stick with me, love; everything for you will be first class."

Before Charlotte could respond, they'd pulled up to LAX. The driver unloaded their luggage, and a pair of guards came over to whisk them away to the security checkpoint. As they sailed past the small line of people standing in general boarding, Charlotte couldn't help but feel a bit woozy over the preferential treatment. Everyone looked bleary-eyed and hardly alert, so no one took notice of the handsome movie star and his mystery companion gliding through security. People were mostly busy slurping on coffee or scrolling away on their BlackBerrys, and Charlotte was relieved no one held up their phones to snap David. They were the first people seated on the plane, and shortly after takeoff, Charlotte kept her word and conked out on David's shoulder; he followed suit a short time later.

Just before they landed, David tapped Charlotte on the thigh to wake her up. "Sleep all right?" he asked.

Charlotte stretched. "Amazingly well. I usually can't sleep on planes. Must be first-class flying."

"And here I thought it was me."

"Oh, well, that too." Charlotte sat up. "So is William meeting us at the airport? I'm dying to meet him."

David rubbed his hands together. "Yes," he said, drawing the word out. "And there may also be some paparazzi."

"Oh." Charlotte took a deep breath. "But William will help us out though, right?"

"Absolutely. I just wanted to give you a heads-up. Just remember to stay close to me and hold my hand."

Charlotte pulled her compact out of her purse, glossed her lips, and ran a smidge of powder across her nose. "I think I can manage that." She smiled as she smoothed her hair back and popped a mint.

"Just be prepared...for anything."

"You make them sound scary," she laughed nervously.

"They can be at times. I've met some really nice guys and some monsters. You just never know who is going to be there. Like I said, just stay close to me because I move pretty fast."

"I'm glad I have you to help me navigate the madness."

David smiled and kissed Charlotte's hand. The plane descended and touched down in a matter of minutes. David and Charlotte were first off the plane, and David pulled a baseball cap out of his carry-on while Charlotte slipped on her sunglasses. David grasped Charlotte's hand before they stepped into the airport.

"Ready?" he asked.

Charlotte squeezed his hand back. "Ready."

They stepped through the door where two large security guards were waiting. They nodded at David and Charlotte.

"Mr. King? Follow us."

Before Charlotte knew what was happening, they were on a fast track through the airport. David wasn't kidding—he moved at the speed of light, his long legs crossing over giant patches of floor at a dizzying pace. Charlotte had to run to keep up with him, and she was a little out of breath. Within seconds they were outside and being hustled into the backseat of a large black town car. Charlotte barely even noticed what the weather was like in Vancouver.

"You okay?" David asked.

Charlotte nodded and exhaled. "Yes, that was…different."

For the first time, Charlotte noticed the dapper gentleman with sandy blond hair in an expensive-looking charcoal gray suit with a pink silk handkerchief peeking out of the breast pocket. He was reclining against the plush seats.

"Don't worry, kid," he said. "My assistant will pick up your bags and bring them to the hotel."

"William." Charlotte smiled.

William winked. "The one, the only," he said as the car pulled out of the airport.

Charlotte sized him up. She pegged him to be in his early forties, and there were streaks of gray at his temples. His loafers shimmered like mirrors, and his socks looked to be silk. She noticed that his gold cuff links were emblazoned with big *W*s, and his gold watch flashed in the sunlight.

Charlotte extended her hand. "I'm Charlotte, although I guess you knew that already."

They shook hands, and William chuckled. "Based on what David said, I'd know you anywhere."

Charlotte twisted around to look at David. "Really? And just what has he been saying about me?"

"That he's nuts about you, although I have to say, you're far prettier than David described."

"William!" David scolded.

William waved his hand and clucked his tongue. "She knows I'm joking, right, Charlotte?" He winked as he looked at Charlotte, who giggled. "All kidding aside, he's been e-mailing me about you nonstop, and I'm so glad you came with him." William leaned back and crossed one leg over the other. "You're gonna love Vancouver."

Charlotte looked out the window. "It looks beautiful so far. David told me you used to be an actor, right?" Charlotte asked.

"Ha! Yeah, you could say that. Mostly bit parts, supporting roles, dime-store stuff. I managed to squeak out a decent enough living, but I'll tell ya, kid, the real money's on the business side."

"Oh, I do all right." David grinned.

William chuckled. "That you do, my friend. No, I'm much better at managing and producing than I ever was at acting. Oh, and running after this one all the time," he said, pointing at David.

Charlotte looked back and forth between the two. "Seems like you guys make a pretty good team," she said.

William grinned. "I guess we do, huh?"

"Yes, well, as long as William's able to make his tennis lessons, he stays quite productive."

The car slowed in front of a lavish hotel that easily took up one city block. They turned the corner and stopped in the back, next to some dumpsters. The driver opened the door, and the trio exited the limo. Charlotte put her hand over her nose.

"Anyone who says the movie star life is a glamorous one should trade places with me right now," Charlotte muttered.

William held a service door open for David and Charlotte. "Sorry, kiddo, but we go through the front and it'll be a brigade of camera phones and a stealth paparazzo or two."

Charlotte nodded as David grabbed her other hand and followed William through the dark and dank loading dock, which reeked of yet more garbage. A security guard met them at the entrance to the kitchen and hustled them onto the service elevator. They all rode silently to the fiftieth floor, where security walked them right to their room. Charlotte saw William slip the guy some money before he whipped out the room key and showed them inside.

"Your home away from home for the next week," William said as Charlotte slowly walked in.

"Whoa," she whispered as she drank in the luxurious accommodations. It was a four-room suite complete with a master bedroom, a smaller guest room, living room, kitchen, and two bathrooms. The scent of fresh-cut flowers eradicated the stench of garbage from Charlotte's memory, and the entire room was ablaze with the sunshine that poured in from the floor-to-ceiling windows that took up one wall. Oversized graphic artwork dominated many of the walls, which were wrapped in pale beige wallpaper with flecks of gold. She could hear David and William murmuring to each other as she walked over to the window and pressed her forehead against the glass and looked down. People scurried around on the street below like ants at a picnic.

"Charlotte?"

She turned at the sound of her name, still dizzy from the room. "Yes?"

William was standing by the door. "I'm taking off. Great to meet you, and I'll schedule you in for a drink so we can talk smack about David behind his back."

David jabbed William on the shoulder while Charlotte laughed and waved. "See you soon."

William closed the door, and Charlotte stood in the center of the room, her jaw still on the floor.

"God, I feel like Julia Roberts in *Pretty Woman.* Except for the hooker thing." Charlotte continued to explore the suite. "I mean, this room is really something—I think it's bigger than my entire house," she yelled from the guest room.

David grinned as he sat on the edge of the couch and watched her. "Even though it was a pain to get here, right?"

Charlotte walked to David and threw her arms around his neck. "Yeah, well, except for that." She kissed his nose. David dove down and picked up Charlotte behind her knees. In spite of herself, she squealed as he ran toward the master bedroom and dropped her on the bed. She closed her eyes as she sank into the down comforter.

"My God, it's like falling into a cloud," she said as she spread her arms and legs out to either side of her. She yawned and closed her eyes and felt David lie down next to her. He began to trace her lips with his finger.

"Tired?" he whispered.

"You're not?"

"I'm beyond tired, and I have to be up at dawn."

Charlotte's eyes flicked open. "Dawn?"

David leaned his head against the palm of his hand. "You don't have to go with me. You can stay here and enjoy the hotel or take the car and driver and see some sights. Or"—David leaned down and pelted her face with kisses—"you can go with me and sleep in my trailer. That way I could come and see you on my breaks and wake you up with my lips." He nibbled on her ear.

"Do you want my answer now?" she purred.

He moved from her ear to her lips. "*Mmmm...*" he moaned.

She held his face in her hands. "Sleep now, trailer tomorrow."

He grinned. "Excellent."

Charlotte gave him one last kiss before she rolled over to assume her sleep position. David spooned around her. Within minutes they were both snoring away.

Charlotte and David had woken up long enough to order room service and call down to have their luggage sent up before drifting back to sleep. Their wake-up call the next day came at four in the morning, and they stumbled around the room, trying to get ready to head to the set. While David read through his script in the back of the limo, Charlotte dozed on his shoulder. When they arrived on set, David whisked her away to his trailer before having a production assistant load up a plate of fruit from the craft services table and get them both steaming mugs of coffee. After they devoured their food, Charlotte helped David run his lines before he got called to the set. Charlotte forced herself not to avail herself of the bed in the back by going back to sleep and decided to take advantage of the quiet time by continuing work on her new manuscript. She got herself a bottle of water from the mini-fridge and waited for her computer to boot up. Her home page was a news site, and as she did every morning, she scanned the various headlines. She saw David's name in the top of a group of headlines under the entertainment section. She leaned forward to read it and gasped.

"David King Playing in a Cougar's Den," Charlotte murmured. "Oh jeez." She paused for a moment, contemplating if she should click on the link and read the story.

Oh, what the hell, she decided and clicked on the link. A photo of them getting out of the limo at LAX popped up, and Charlotte groaned before she read the blurb:

Looks like mega heartthrob David King's short-lived reconciliation with Olivia Hudson is kaput, as he and a mystery cougar boarded a flight to Vancouver early Wednesday morning, where King is doing some reshoots on the upcoming thriller Claim. *Could it be that twenty-six-year-old Hudson was just a tad too young for King? Stay tuned.*

Charlotte winced. Cougar...just like her friends had warned her.

The trailer of the door swung open, and David stepped inside. "Hey, love," he said. "Lighting problem, so thought I'd come hang out with you for a few moments." He looked over her shoulder and saw what she was reading. "Bad?" he asked.

"I don't know about bad, but definitely not good."

David read it and shook his head. "Charlotte, you're too smart to let this get you down. I could be five years younger than you and it would say the same stupid thing." David flopped down on the couch across from her. "Personally, I don't see what the big deal is. My dad was twelve years older than my mum, and nobody ever said a word. I really don't get why it's such a big deal for the woman to be older. After all, it's not like we're the first couple—and won't be the last, I might add—who are like this." He shrugged and stretched out on the couch. "I find it bloody fascinating that people would find this scandalous or strange."

Charlotte cocked her head and looked at him, still amazed over his nonchalance over their age difference. "How'd you get to be so wise?" she asked.

"Years of practice." He grinned.

"You really are an old soul, you know that?"

"So I've been told." He nodded toward her laptop. "I hope you were actually going to do some work and not just surf the Web all day reading tacky tabloid articles."

"No, no, no. I really am planning to do some work on my new book."

David sat up and stood over her. "Oh yeah? What's this one about?"

Charlotte ran her hand up David's thigh until it landed on his butt cheek. "Can't tell you yet, although I do need some inspiration."

He pulled Charlotte into a kiss. "It'll probably be about an hour before they get that lighting thing resolved," he breathed.

Charlotte chuckled and began to undo the buttons of his shirt. "Good. Maybe you can inspire me twice."

"Indeed. Just don't smear my makeup," David said as he picked up a giggling Charlotte and carried her to the back of the trailer.

It was late afternoon when Charlotte looked up from her laptop and rubbed her eyes. The words were starting to blend into each other, which was her cue to take a break. Charlotte stood and stretched before she stepped outside for some fresh air. Even though the sun shone, it did little to warm the crisp, cool air. Charlotte shivered a bit as she made her way to the one of the director's chairs just outside David's trailer. She peeled her eyes for David, but all she could see were cranes and lights and cameras and a bunch of people running around like chickens freed from the coop. Charlotte closed her eyes and let the chilly wind wash over her face for a moment. She took a big inhale and opened her eyes in time to see William decked out in yet another impeccable suit, walking toward her. She smiled and waved.

"How's everything?" she asked.

William nodded and dragged a nearby director's chair and planted it next to Charlotte's. "Everything's on schedule, and who knows? We may even get out of here a day early. And you?"

Charlotte nodded. "Good. Just taking a break."

"Ah, yes. The books, right? David told me about that. He's determined to read them all, you know." William snapped his fingers. "Hey, maybe we can option some."

Charlotte shook her head. "If my books were made into movies, they'd be the kind you show on cable at three in the morning."

"Hey, don't knock it. There's a market for just about everything."

Charlotte grinned. "True."

William shifted in his seat to face her. "There's something else I wanted to talk to you about."

"Okay. Shoot."

"I know from here you guys are heading to New York for a premiere."

Charlotte nodded. "Right, except I'm meeting David *after* the red carpet."

William rubbed his earlobe and looked down at his lap. "Listen, he would never say this because he's a selfless son of a bitch—which, as you know, gets him into trouble—but it would mean a lot to him if you *were* there."

Charlotte straightened up a little in her seat. "Really?"

"You better believe it. And hey, it might not be a bad idea. You know, just get the photo ops out of the way and be done with it. Then maybe the press will move on. Otherwise they'll just—"

"Crawl up our asses with flashlights and never leave us alone," Charlotte cut him off as she remembered Karen's declarations.

William chuckled. "Yeah, that's about the size of it, kid."

Charlotte spun a lock of hair around her fingers, mulling over what William had said. "I mean, what you're saying makes sense, but…"

"But what?"

"Well, I don't have—"

William nodded, understanding. "A dress. Got it. I'll take care of everything. You tell David that tomorrow you're taking a little 'me' time, and he can hang out in that drafty trailer by himself."

Charlotte giggled in spite of herself. "You got it. What time should I be ready?"

William stood. "Be downstairs at ten a.m."

The next morning Charlotte was downstairs in the circular driveway in front of the hotel at ten sharp. David had struggled out of bed at five and had given her a quick peck before he trudged off to the set. Charlotte didn't tell David, but she was actually glad not to drag herself out of bed at an ungodly hour.

She looked around now for William, but didn't see him. The limo they'd been riding around in pulled up in front of her, and the hotel doorman opened the door for her. The driver started to pull away.

"Oh, no. We can't leave yet," she called out. "I'm waiting for—"

"I'm to take you to Holt Renfrew this morning, where everything will be taken care of." The driver smiled.

Charlotte leaned back. "Oh." She wrinkled her nose. "What's Holt Renfrew?"

"Finest department store in Vancouver."

Charlotte's cell phone trilled inside her purse. She didn't recognize the number, but answered anyway. "Hello?"

"Good morning, Char, how are you?" William asked.

"I'm fine, except I'm a little confused. I thought you were coming with me."

"Oh no, no. Sorry to have mixed you up. I've got to be on set all day, but when you get to Holt Renfrew, head up to the fourth-floor women's department, personal shopping—ask for Evelyn."

Charlotte breathed a sigh of relief. Shopping wasn't her strong suit, but at least she'd have some help.

"Thanks, William," she said. "It seems you've thought of everything."

"Always do. See you later, sweetheart. And have fun!"

Charlotte smiled and hung up, a little nervous and a little excited.

Charlotte twirled a piece of hair around her fingers as she stepped off the escalator on the fourth floor. Impeccably attired mannequins loomed above her as she walked past racks of expensive clothes in search of her destination. She was more comfortable among the jean-laden tables of the Gap or Old Navy than in a high-end department store like this one. She looked for the floor signage directing her to Personal Shopping and within a matter of moments located the elegant suite awash in soft, soothing shades of taupe tucked into the back of the floor. The young redheaded girl sitting behind the desk smiled when Charlotte walked up.

"May I help you?"

Charlotte bit her lip and looked around, now a little uncertain. "Yes, hi, um...I have an appointment with Evelyn."

"And your name?"

"Charlotte. Charlotte Taylor."

"Ah yes, Miss Taylor. We've been expecting you." She came from behind the desk and ushered Charlotte over to two plush, oversized chairs decorated in alternating shiny and matte taupe stripes. "Have a seat, and I'll let Evelyn know you're here. Can I get you some water?"

"Yes, please. Thank you."

The woman walked back to a small table near the desk, where there was a glass pitcher filled with water next to a set of small crystal glasses. She filled one with water and brought it over to Charlotte.

"Here you go. Be right back."

Charlotte sipped the water and detected the faint taste of cucumber. *Okay, this is my new favorite thing.* Charlotte chuckled to herself before she finished the whole glass.

A tall, toothpick-thin woman emerged from the back. She was adorned in a cloud of perfume along with black-and-white houndstooth jacket trimmed with bits of fringe at the wrist, along the bottom hem, and up and down the lapel. She also wore a knee-length black wool skirt, and her sheer black pantyhose swished as she moved. Her jet-black hair was pulled back into a French twist, and her lips were lined in bright red, a brilliant contrast against the alabaster veneer of her skin.

"Miss Taylor?" she inquired in a nasal voice curiously devoid of a Canadian accent.

"Uh, yes, that's me. I'm Charlotte Taylor," she stammered.

The woman smiled, a surprisingly warm and welcoming smile considering the high pitch of her voice and sophisticated appearance. Charlotte decided she probably wasn't all that different from Hendra—tough-looking on the outside and a marshmallow on the inside.

"I'm Evelyn, and I'll be assisting you today." When Evelyn clasped her hands, Charlotte noticed that her nails were lacquered in a shade matching her lipstick. Charlotte shoved the ratty cuticles of her own hands into the pockets of her jeans. "So I understand we have a special event coming up in New York. Walking the red carpet?"

"Yes, so I'll need a dress for that."

"Uh-huh. I see," Evelyn said as she began to circle Charlotte, sizing her up. She put a hand on her hip and leaned back as she continued her appraisal of Charlotte. "Probably going to dinner, see some shows too, I would imagine."

Charlotte paused. She hadn't thought about that, but Evelyn was probably right. "Yes, that too."

"Right, right." Evelyn tapped her long, tapered fingers together and inhaled. "Well, dear, I have some absolutely fabulous things to show you. Don't you worry." She smiled.

Charlotte nodded and returned Evelyn's smile. "Okay. Oh! I should probably give you my size—"

"Already know it, dear." Evelyn winked. "Your advance man, as it were, gave us an estimate. And I have to say he got it pretty well on the mark. Must know his way around a woman's body," Evelyn muttered as she signaled to Charlotte to follow her to the back and the dressing suites, where a rack of dresses in every conceivable color and style waited for them. Evelyn began to riffle through the dresses, her face screwed up in concentration.

"Now," she said more to herself than Charlotte. "Let's see. Oh, yes, this one—let's try this one on first," she muttered as she extracted a dress from the rack and held it up for Charlotte's inspection. "You can never go wrong with the classic little black dress. As Coco said, we should all have one. And black is very slimming."

Charlotte winced. "Whatever you think is best," she said meekly.

Evelyn rolled her eyes. "Oh, for heaven's sake, dear, don't get offended. First off, you have an absolutely lovely figure. Second, even the skinniest of girls should wear black. It does wonders for us all." She thrust the dress at Charlotte. "Go on now, dear. Try it on."

Charlotte stepped into the dressing room to try on the sequined cocktail dress with a scooped neckline and a full skirt that flared at the bottom. Charlotte inspected herself in the mirror, not crazy about the way it looked on her. Of course, she thought everything looked bad on her. She'd let Evelyn be the judge. Evelyn frowned when Charlotte stepped out of the dressing room and dove back into the rack for another dress. Charlotte tried on dress after dress, and there was something just a little bit off about each of them—too short, too long, wrong color, wrong fit. Charlotte was growing frustrated over not being able to find the right one. She wanted it to be perfect so she wouldn't embarrass David on the red carpet. Or herself.

Evelyn finally brought out a simple floor-length black sheath dress with an Empire bodice, square neckline, and small slit up the back. Charlotte held her breath when she zipped it up and looked in the mirror. She gasped and ran out of the dressing room, where Evelyn was standing over her rack of dresses, giving them a disapproving stare.

"My dear, I just can't—" She looked up as Charlotte came out. "My goodness." Evelyn beamed. "It's lovely. Absolutely lovely." She walked around Charlotte, giving her the once-over, her approval evident.

"Yes?" Charlotte asked, her excitement bubbling up inside her.

Evelyn nodded and put her hand on her hip. "Dear, you're a vision."

Charlotte let out a round of giddy applause, and Evelyn joined in her laughter. "Okay, now that we've got that nailed down, let's move on to the rest of the trip!"

Fortunately, the rest of the shopping was a breeze as Evelyn helped Charlotte find two more outfits appropriate for going out on the town in New York on the arm of a famous actor, even picking out the right accessories and shoes. Charlotte, overwhelmed, felt like Cinderella. She never spent this much time on herself, but she was surprised to find she actually enjoyed it. Evelyn's assistant rang up the purchases and told Charlotte she'd have everything delivered to the hotel later that afternoon. On impulse, Charlotte hugged a startled Evelyn.

"Oh my *dear*. What was that for?"

"To thank you for helping me today. I wouldn't have had clue one about how to do this."

Evelyn patted Charlotte on the arm. "Well, dear, the tabloids are merciless. Can't have you winding up on the 'What Was She Thinking?' list."

Charlotte giggled.

Evelyn pulled Charlotte to the side. "You know, dear," she spoke in hushed tones, "it might not be a bad idea to visit our salon—sixth floor. You know, a little manicure, a little pedicure. The tabloids are relentless. Even a tiny little hair out of place, and *quelle catastrophe*." Evelyn straightened up. "Not saying you have to change who you are. Just saying a little freshening up never hurt anybody."

Charlotte broke out into a smile and cocked her head to the side. "You know, that might not be such a bad idea."

"I'll call up for you, if you like."

Charlotte nodded. "That would be nice, Evelyn. Thank you."

Evelyn winked and walked over to the phone on the front desk. "You're welcome, and good luck, dear."

Charlotte waved good-bye and headed toward the escalator to the salon. She laughed and shook her head. "This really is like *Pretty Woman*," she whispered to herself.

※

Three hours later, Charlotte emerged from the Holt Renfrew salon with a new pale-pink manicure and matching pedicure. They'd even washed and conditioned her hair for her, and her curls seemed to have an extra bounce. Never in her life had she ever done either of those things, and once again Charlotte was amazed to discover it wasn't as torturous or unnecessary as she'd always thought. Maybe she'd make a habit out of it.

The driver had told her to call him when she was ready to be picked up, and just as she pulled out her phone, she passed by the makeup counter. Charlotte slowed as she scanned the displays, lit up like Christmas trees with an assortment of shiny ornaments and glossy-colored packages underneath. Charlotte stood in front of one counter, mesmerized. Images of the Internet story about her being a "cougar" echoed in Charlotte's head, and she suddenly pictured the young and firm Olivia, with her silky smooth skin and freakishly long legs. Charlotte wiped her hand down her face to erase the pictures from her head. She looked back at the bottles and potions and grimaced.

"Good lord, there must be twenty different brands to choose from," she whispered to herself.

Behind each counter were young, overly coiffed, overly done girls, goopy lipstick painted over their lips, powder and foundation shellacked over their faces, shimmering eye shadow smeared across their lids, eyebrows plucked almost to oblivion. Charlotte meandered past a counter in the corner that was staffed by one such girl. She looked like she was in her midthirties, though Charlotte secretly hoped that she was pushing fifty and that all the jars and tubes laid out beautifully in front of her actually did perform miracles. Charlotte cast her eyes down at the products behind the display case, the images blurring into a pool of pink.

"Hi! I'm Liz," the woman chirped in a perky voice, and Charlotte smiled. There was the Canadian accent she'd been waiting for. "What can I do for you?"

Charlotte screwed up her mouth. "I'm not sure," she replied.

"Well, was there something specific you were looking for, or is there something you normally use that you're out of?"

"Um, well, I don't get my makeup here." Charlotte lowered her voice.

"Oh? Do you shop at another department store?"

"Not exactly. More like I pick up what I need from the drugstore," Charlotte said with an embarrassed little smile.

Liz grimaced and shook her head. "Oh no, no, no, *no*. No—that just won't do."

Charlotte sighed. "Well, okay. Let me start with some wrinkle cream."

Liz held up a forefinger and bent over several display cases, plucking jars from their plastic holders. "Preventative measures are a *great* idea. I mean, if you wait until your forties"—Liz made a slicing motion across her neck—"you're in the danger zone."

Charlotte raised an eyebrow. "Well, I'm forty-four. Should I call the crypt keeper now?"

Liz gasped. "No!" she said as she whipped her head around before she leaned toward Charlotte. "Who do you use?" Liz tugged at the corner of one eye.

Charlotte looked at her, not understanding at first, before she burst into laughter. "Oh God, no. No, I've never had any work done. Truth be told, I don't really use anything."

Liz narrowed her eyes and shook her head. "My God, you're lucky. Good genes, huh?"

Charlotte shrugged. "I guess. But you know, you're right. Preventative measures are a good thing. So maybe show me what you have?"

Liz smiled. "Absolutely!" she squeaked as she began to slather various creams and liquids across Charlotte's hands. Charlotte's head was swimming from all the choices as she tried to keep up with Liz's explanations about eye creams, wrinkle serums, scrubs, tranquility lotions, and the difference between oil-based and water-based moisturizers. Liz delighted in piling up as many tubes and jars as she could locate behind the counter in front of Charlotte. Two hundred dollars and an hour later, Liz handed Charlotte a plastic bag the size of a postcard with a triumphant smile.

"Well, it sure was a pleasure helping you today," Liz said. "And I just know you're going to love the products. I mean, doesn't your skin feel amazing?"

Charlotte nodded weakly, her head throbbing. "Oh yes," she said, eager to get back to the hotel and recover from the sensory overload. "Thanks for all your help."

"My pleasure!" Liz cocked her head to the side. "You look exhausted. You should get home and get some rest. It makes such a difference. Can't expect good genes and moisturizers to do all the work, right?" She winked.

Charlotte plastered on a smile. "Right. Right. I'll go ahead and do that."

Liz waved, and Charlotte made her way outside to wait for the car.

"Screw rest," Charlotte muttered to herself. "I need a drink."

The week in Vancouver flew by. Besides completing a good solid chunk of her manuscript, Charlotte managed to do a little sightseeing while David was on set. And one night after David passed out from exhaustion, she and William spent a riotous night in the hotel bar having dinner and drinks. William was the life of the party, and it struck Charlotte that he was a good contrast to David's more reserved nature.

By week's end, they pushed off to New York, duplicating the same manic schedule they'd employed in L.A.—fly out before dawn had a chance to crack, bolt off the plane, and cram into a limo at breakneck speed. Charlotte had followed David's lead and had purchased a hat to plunk down on her head. She made a point of keeping her eyes down as they sped through the airport—just in case any photographers, amateur or otherwise, were lurking around.

They checked into the Mandarin Oriental, which had stunning views of Central Park. Charlotte had been to New York only a handful of times, and always for work, never for pleasure. She was excited to see the city through David's eyes.

Preparations for the night commenced in a flurry. Charlotte showered while David and William spoke on the phone every thirty seconds, figuring out logistics. Afterward, she wrapped herself in one of the hotel's plush white bathrobes, pulled out the dress she'd bought in Vancouver, and hung it up on the back of the bedroom door to stare at it. David came up behind her and slid his arms around her.

"I can't wait to see you in that dress. More important, I can't wait to see it on the floor at the end of the night."

Charlotte gave him a cheerful slap. "I'll have you know this dress is going right back on the hanger. It's too beautiful to get tossed on the floor."

"All right, all right, I'll be sure to take the time to hang it up very carefully in the closet." David chuckled and gave her a quick smack across her bottom. "Car'll be here by six, so we've got a few hours..." David's voice trailed off.

Charlotte shook her head. "Okay, this may be the one time I turn you down. I just showered, and I have to figure out something to do with my hair."

"*Psssh*. Just wear it up. That's what all the actresses do."

"In case you haven't noticed, I'm not an actress," Charlotte said as someone knocked on the door.

"Which is why I love you," David said as he went to open the door. "Must be William," he murmured as he went to look out the peephole.

William bustled into the room, still wearing his suit from earlier. "Okay, you, out." He pointed at David. "I've got hair and makeup on the way up."

Charlotte's hand flew to her throat. "Oh my gosh, William, I—"

William shushed her and went in search of David's tux. "We'll see you downstairs at six." He winked at Charlotte. "Have fun, kid."

Charlotte hugged William and smiled. "Thank you," she whispered.

David gave Charlotte a quick kiss and grabbed his tux. "See you downstairs."

Charlotte nodded and sent them on their way. Within minutes there was another knock at the door, and a hair stylist and makeup artist, both clad in black from head to toe, breezed in and began to cluck over her, wanting to know what her dress looked like, what shoes and jewelry she planned to wear. Charlotte estimated they weighed about a hundred pounds total between the two of them. The "team" set to work on getting her red carpet ready.

Renee, the stylist, a redhead from Kentucky, maneuvered product through her hair before blowing it out. The makeup artist, Jackie, fluffed brushes and pads over her face for the better part of twenty minutes. She wasn't used to being fussed over, but just as she had felt that day in Vancouver, she discovered she didn't hate it.

Renee helped her into her dress, and Charlotte slipped her new high-heeled, strappy black leather sandals on, which she'd been practicing walking in for the past few days. Charlotte clamped the cuff bracelet dripping in crystals around her wrist, while Renee fastened the matching necklace around her throat. She took Charlotte by the shoulders and marched her over to the full-length mirror in the bedroom.

"Okay," Renee drawled in her Southern accent, "time for the big reveal."

Charlotte took a deep breath, opened her eyes, and gasped. She didn't recognize herself—in a good way. Her formerly unruly curls had been blown out into delicate sheets of glass, and her skin was luminous—like she had a little uplight tucked under her chin. Tears rimmed Charlotte's eyes as she took a good look at herself.

Renee's face fell. "You don't like it?"

Charlotte shook her head, her nose starting to run. "No, no, I love it. I just...I...I feel so beautiful," she whispered, her tears threatening to ruin the makeup job.

Jackie tsk-tsked. "All right now, girl, don't go messing with my masterpiece," he said as he dabbed Charlotte's face with a tissue. "Here, let me touch you up."

"Okay, let me just blow my nose," Charlotte laughed. "God, this is so embarrassing."

Renee and Jackie both shook their heads. "Don't feel bad, honey," Jackie said as he refreshed Charlotte's face. "We princesses always cry when we look fierce."

Charlotte giggled and smoothed down her hair. "Good to know."

Jackie and Renee put Charlotte back together before they each hugged her and told her to have fun. Charlotte filled the little red satin clutch that she'd bought in Vancouver with Tic Tacs, her phone, powder, and the lipstick, liner, and gloss Jackie had left for her. She took another deep breath and gave herself one last look in the mirror.

"Okay." She exhaled. "Here goes."

Charlotte walked out to the elevator and rode down to the lobby. She spotted David pacing near the front door, and her breath caught in her throat. She'd never seen him in anything fancier than jeans. The man was made to wear a tux. She stood for a moment, until she knew his gaze would find her. When it did, she cocked her head to the side and gave him a small smile. David stopped his march and looked at Charlotte, transfixed. She walked toward him.

"My God, Charlotte." David gulped and shook his head. "You're...my God! I don't even have the words."

"You mean I've left you speechless?"

"You may as well have ripped out my voice box," he said as he bent down to kiss her.

Charlotte ducked away from him. "Forget it," she warned. "It took a village to do this, and they already had to rebuild me once." She lowered her voice. "By the way, you don't look so bad yourself."

"So I clean up good, eh?"

"Oh yeah."

David grasped her hand. "Well, I'm just happy that I'll be walking the red carpet with the most gorgeous woman in the world."

Charlotte blushed. "Careful, Mr. King, you're going to spoil me."

"That's the whole idea," he said before he stole a quick peck on her cheek. Charlotte glared at him, and David merely winked.

"Where's William?" Charlotte asked as they slid into the limo.

"He's already there. We'll see him inside."

As the limo pulled into early evening Manhattan traffic, Charlotte tried to keep her composure, but she was getting nervous.

"Would you like a little champagne? Settle you down a bit?" David asked.

"Uh-uh. I don't want it to come back up." Charlotte looked down at her lap. "I guess this is our official debut, huh?"

David turned to face her. "Charlotte, I'm ready to show you off to the world." He grabbed her hand. "It's going to be fine, and over before you know it."

"Ha! Easy for you to say. You do this all the time."

The limo continued its stops and starts toward its final destination. Charlotte stared at the lights of Manhattan while David pointed out various landmarks and points of interest. The limo finally came to a stop, and the door swung open. Charlotte took a deep breath and waited for David to exit. As he did, a flood of noise invaded the car, and she saw the flashes of many cameras, along with people yelling and cheering; a few people screamed David's name. Charlotte felt her stomach tighten, and she took a deep breath. David reached in to help her out of the car, and she was blinded by the wall of light as she stepped onto the red carpet. Another wave of cheers and screams went up as David took her hand and began to lead her down the carpet. Charlotte's hand was clammy inside David's, and the hot sensation of nausea washed across her body. She swept her hair out of her eyes and squinted at all the ruckus around her. Photographers began to yell for David, demanding he pose for them. David obliged, making sure his hand stayed clasped around Charlotte's waist. They began to ease down the red carpet and pose for more pictures. Or David posed while Charlotte tried to concentrate on which camera to look at.

"Hey, David, let us get a couple of you by yourself," someone called out.

Charlotte started to step away, but David held firm. "Sorry, fellas, it's both of us or neither of us." He smiled.

"Who's the lovely lady, David?" someone from the throng bellowed.

"Charlotte Taylor, my girlfriend," David responded.

Some of the entertainment reporters camped near the door thrust their microphones in David's face, all wanting the scoop on Charlotte.

"David, what can you tell us about your date?" one blonde Amazon with huge brown eyes and a dazzling white sequined dress inquired.

"This is my girlfriend, Charlotte Taylor. She's a writer."

The woman nodded. "That's fantastic. What do you write?" she said, jutting her microphone in Charlotte's face.

Charlotte took a deep breath. "I'm a novelist," she blurted.

Before the reporter could ask another question, David smiled and thanked her before he steered Charlotte inside. Spotlights crisscrossed the entire room, and the thumps of the DJ's spins fought for prominence over the din of the crowd. David and Charlotte wound their way through the swarm of tanned and bejeweled men and women. They located William by the bar, deep in conversation with a leggy brunette, who excused herself. His eyes popped out of his head when he spotted Charlotte, who smiled and did a little twirl for him. He grabbed her by the elbows and planted a huge kiss on her cheek.

"Well, hello, gorgeous," he shouted. "You look fantastic. Not that you didn't already."

"I couldn't have done it without your help," Charlotte said. "I should start calling you my fairy godfather!"

William winked. "Only for people I like."

Charlotte grinned. "Glad to be a part of the chosen few."

David's fingers grazed Charlotte's elbow. "If you can tear yourself away from my girlfriend, we've got to be pushing on," he said.

William released Charlotte. "Right, of course." He gave Charlotte a kiss on her other cheek. "Great to see you, and have fun tonight."

Charlotte waved good-bye, slightly confused, as David pulled her away. They made a quick round-robin of the room, where he introduced her to a few people before cutting the conversations short. About twenty minutes later, David led Charlotte to a nearby exit door.

"Wait." Charlotte tugged on David's hand when she saw their limo waiting outside. "What are we doing?" she asked.

"Ditching this place. William will tell us if the movie was any good."

"You mean we're not staying?"

David shook his head, his eyes twinkling. "I'm going to waste how fabulous you look on these people." He encircled Charlotte's waist in his hands. "We've got other plans."

❧

The limo inched down Broadway before coming to a stop in front of another hotel.

"Well, here we are," David said.

"And where is *here*, exactly?" Charlotte asked.

"You know, you're really quite terrible with surprises."

Before Charlotte could protest, a doorman from the hotel descended upon the car and whisked the door open.

"Good evening, ma'am." He smiled at Charlotte as he helped her out of the limo. He merely nodded at David before averting his eyes, trained not to make eye contact with celebrities. David smiled at the guy and patted him on the shoulder before he grabbed Charlotte's hand.

Charlotte craned her neck as she drank in the sights and sounds of Times Square. Though it was nighttime, the neighborhood was lit up as bright as if it had been high noon instead of nearly eight in the evening. David tugged on her hand and led her inside the hotel. They stepped onto an elevator, and David punched forty-seven on the panel. Charlotte opened her mouth again to ask David what he was up to, but sensing her questions, David planted a kiss on her lips instead. The elevator glided to a stop; the doors slid open. A man in a black suit, white shirt, and burgundy tie with a matching pocket square and a lush mane of silver hair greeted them as they stepped off the elevator.

"Good evening, and welcome to The View," he said as he ushered them into the restaurant. It took Charlotte a moment to realize the room was spinning ever so slowly.

"What is this place?" she gasped, laughing.

"New York City's only revolving rooftop restaurant," the maître d' answered as he began to lead them toward their table.

Charlotte licked her lips and looked around the cavernous space, noting it was empty except for a few waiters and chefs who stood at attention. The maître d' seated them at their table, which was next to one of the floor-to-ceiling windows that doubled as the walls of the restaurant. Charlotte waited until he left before bowing her head near David's.

"This place can't be that good," she whispered. "There's nobody here."

David burst out laughing before he grabbed a confused Charlotte's hand and kissed it. "Don't ever change, love."

Charlotte wrinkled her nose. "David, it's just that I don't want you wasting your money on someplace that must be pretty bad if no one's here on a Friday night."

David roared with more laughter and leaned toward Charlotte. "This is one of the most renowned and popular restaurants in New York City. And the reason no one is here"—David picked up Charlotte's hand again—"is because I rented it out for the night. It's all ours until the fat lady sings."

Charlotte's cheeks flamed red at her naïveté. She plunked her forehead down into the palm of her free hand. "I'm such an idiot." She shook her head.

"You really do need to get out more, love," David laughed.

"You sound like Karen."

David nodded his head toward one of the waitstaff, who smiled and immediately planted himself next to the table. He presented Charlotte with a menu, and her eyes widened when she noticed her and David's names were printed across the top. She peered at David over the top.

"What did you do?" she asked.

David grinned. "You should really learn to go with the flow, love."

Charlotte gave David a knowing look before she scanned the menu, which looked to be a smaller version of the restaurant's standard menu. Charlotte hadn't realized how hungry she was until she laid eyes on the still-plentiful selection of food David had chosen.

"Would it be bad if I got steak?" she whispered.

David chuckled. "Why would that be bad?"

Charlotte shrugged and went back to the perusing the menu. "I should have the salmon," she reasoned. She flicked the menu down. "But I really want the filet," she giggled.

David took a sip from his water glass. "Then you shall have it."

Charlotte nodded, satisfied. "Then I will."

The waiter came to take their order and to deliver two ice-cold cosmopolitans with curlicued lime rinds floating in the middle.

"A little twist on your favorite," David said.

"Huh?"

"Cape Cods. A cosmopolitan is just another way of making a Cape Cod, right?"

Charlotte shook her head and picked up her glass. "Seriously, I can't keep up tonight. Did you slip me something?"

"I plan on slipping you something later."

"Mr. King!" Charlotte feigned indignation. "What kind of girl do you think I am?"

"I know exactly the kind of girl you are." David leered as he picked up his glass and motioned for Charlotte to do the same. Charlotte complied, and David licked his lips and stared at Charlotte for a moment. "To you. For saving me. In more ways than one." David clinked his glass with Charlotte's. "I love you."

Charlotte smiled and sipped her drink. "The feeling is mutual, Mr. King." She let out a soft groan as the cosmo slid down her throat. "Oh man, this is good."

"Much better than my heavy-handed attempts, eh?"

"Let's just say you should stick with moviemaking and leave the bartending to someone else."

"Indeed."

Charlotte took another sip of her drink, her gaze moving over to the window and the New York City skyline as it crept past her.

"This view is amazing," she murmured. "I never knew New York could look so incredible."

David put his chin in the palm of his hand and joined Charlotte in enjoying the scene.

"William first brought me here. It was to celebrate me getting my first lead in a movie. He said I should feel like I was on top of the world. And he was right." David turned back to Charlotte. "Up here, you feel like nothing bad could ever happen to you."

Charlotte reached for David's hand, and they stared out into the night, never saying a word, but comforted by each other's presence. Members of the waitstaff broke their reverie by first bringing goat cheese salads followed by dinner: the filet for Charlotte and rack of lamb for David. They each dug in with gusto, surprised by how ravenous they were. As they indulged in their gourmet meals, soft music spilled forth from some unseen corner of the candlelit room. Charlotte crinkled her nose and cocked her ear toward the sound. Her jaw dropped open in warm surprise as she realized a DJ had been spinning the same tunes from the night she and David had cleaned the kitchen at Lake Arrowhead. She set her fork down on her plate and smiled at David.

"Okay, you really have thought of everything, haven't you?"

David shrugged and grinned as he popped a bite of lamb into his mouth.

"I'm trying to impress you."

"Oh, I'm impressed, Mr. King."

"I hope that means I'll get lucky later."

Charlotte resumed eating. "Maybe." She winked.

More cosmopolitans magically appeared, and before long, David and Charlotte were giggling about the party they'd left and speculating as to how William had made out with the brunette giraffe. The dinner dishes were cleared, and two thick slabs of cheesecake slathered in marinated strawberries materialized. Charlotte laughed and speared a strawberry with her fork and held it up to David.

"Strawberries," she whispered.

"Strawberries." David smiled as he bit down on Charlotte's offering. After they lapped up their cheesecake, David held out his hand to Charlotte.

"Dance with me, love?"

Charlotte took his hand and allowed David to lead her to the dance floor, where they slow danced to "You Really Got a Hold on Me," which they'd first danced to in Lake Arrowhead. Charlotte sighed happily and laid her head on David's shoulder.

"This sounds a lot better with a professional DJ than it did coming out of Hendra's ancient radio," she said.

"I should hope so. But we won't tell her that."

"Oh, no, of *course* not," Charlotte whispered and closed her eyes as David spun her around the dance floor. Just as when they made love, their bodies fit together with ease, responding instinctively to each other's rhythm. The DJ continued to play all the oldies they'd listened to before, and Charlotte was impressed by David's stellar memory, though she guessed she shouldn't have been all that surprised since he memorized words for a living.

Charlotte turned to look out the window at the skyline. "You know what's sad? The only building I recognize is the Empire State Building." She shook her head. "I gotta get out of L.A. more."

David rolled Charlotte around so her back was against him. They swayed together in time to the music. "What do you want to know?" he whispered in her ear.

Charlotte leaned back against David. "That's the Chrysler Building, right?" She pointed to a building as it came into view.

David nuzzled his chin into Charlotte's neck. "Yes, that is the Chrysler Building."

"Right, right..." Charlotte said. "Hmmm...we've already established the Empire State Building. What about that one?"

"New York Times Building. And over there is Manhattan Plaza."

"You're really good at this." Charlotte grinned.

"I told you, I'm trying to impress you," David murmured. "Okay, now we're facing New Jersey. Doesn't the Hudson River look magnificent?"

Charlotte just gave a contented sigh and continued to let David point out various buildings: Carnegie Tower, the Time-Life Building, Rockefeller Center.

"Do you feel sufficiently versed on New York City architecture now?" David teased.

"Oh yes. I feel quite smart now."

David chuckled and kissed her neck. "Glad I could help," he said as he turned her back to face him. Charlotte draped her arms around his neck, and David caressed her cheek.

"What are you thinking about?" she asked.

"You."

Charlotte looked down. "You know, I didn't think anything could top my birthday, but"—Charlotte swallowed and shook her head—"you did. And then some." She shifted her eyes back up to meet David's. "Thank you."

"I love doing things for you. It makes me delirious."

"Ah, so you're saying I make you crazy?" Charlotte teased.

"Crazy in love." David leaned back. "How's that?"

Charlotte leaned in for a kiss. "Perfect," she whispered as their lips met. David's hands roamed the length of Charlotte's torso, and she moaned.

"Sounds like it's time for me to whisk you back to the hotel and have my way with you," David said as he and Charlotte walked back to the table so she could retrieve her purse and one of the menus as a keepsake. David winked at the DJ, who made an "okay" sign with his fingers, patted his jacket pocket, and smiled. The waitstaff also beamed, and Charlotte figured William must have given them all big fat envelopes of cash before they got there. The maître d' met David and Charlotte up front.

"I trust everything was to your and the lady's liking?"

David nodded. "Everything was fantastic."

"Will you be needing anything else this evening?"

David shook his head and smiled. "Oh no. We're all set."

"Very good, sir." The maître d' nodded at Charlotte. "Good night, ma'am."

Charlotte murmured a good-night, and she and David stepped into the waiting elevator. Charlotte threaded her fingers with David's and leaned against the mirrored wall.

"It's going to be hard to go home in a few days," Charlotte sighed and closed her eyes. "I'm just glad you'll be there with me."

David was a silent a moment before he tapped Charlotte on the shoulder. "Did you just ask me to move in with you, love?"

Charlotte's eyes flew open, and she saw David standing in front of her, a huge grin on his face. "What?"

David leaned down over her. "Did you…just ask me…to move in… with you?" he repeated, his eyes twinkling.

As the elevator came to a stop, Charlotte gulped. *Had* she just asked David to move in with her? She stayed silent as they made their way outside to their limo, which the maître d' had called down for. Charlotte waited until they were tucked safely inside before she turned to David.

"*Did* I just ask you to move in with me?" She echoed his earlier question.

David grinned. "I think you did."

Charlotte fell back against the plush interior of the limo. "I guess I did," she mumbled to herself, still swimming in the three cosmos she'd had. Charlotte snapped her head up and looked at David. "Yes. Yes, I want you to move in with me."

"You're sure?"

Charlotte slowly nodded her head, wondering why it had taken her so long to come up with the idea. *Of course* David should move in with her. "Yes, one hundred percent sure." She held David's face in her hands. "I don't want to be without you. If that's okay with you."

David smiled. "I thought you'd never ask."

Loving David

❦

The next two days flew as David showed Charlotte his New York. She got to don some of the outfits she'd picked up in Vancouver and was thankful once again for Evelyn's foresight in making sure she had New York City appropriate attire. As they scurried around the city, Charlotte noticed David seemed freer and more alive than he had at any other time. He chalked it up to the nervous energy the city gave him, as well as the ability to be more anonymous there than when he was in L.A. He showed her the old brownstone he'd lived in as a kid, and they played on the swings at the park his mom used to take him to. They took long walks in Central Park, and David introduced Charlotte to the joys of chewy, salty New York City street vendor pretzels dripping in mustard.

Their last night in town, they took in a Broadway show and had dinner at the famed Elaine's. The whole trip had been tinged with magic and wonder, but truth be told, Charlotte was ready to head home to L.A. It was time to start their new life together.

And she couldn't have been happier.

CHAPTER 10

"I thought you said you didn't have that much stuff!"

"I don't. I mean, it's not like I'm lugging around a box of Oscars."

Charlotte hoisted up a People's Choice Award for Favorite Actor. "Only a box of these."

David shrugged and smiled. "Ah, well, what can I say? The people love me."

Charlotte rolled her eyes and continued unpacking a box of David's memorabilia and lining them up along her mantel. A few days after returning from New York, they'd emptied David's storage unit and had spent the last week merging all of his stuff into her place. It was fascinating to see some of what he had collected over the length of his relatively short career, including various movie scripts, a letter box full of the ticket stubs from his movies, the suit he wore in his first romantic comedy, a smattering of awards, and a few autographed pictures from the sets of some of his movies. What Charlotte didn't relish was the seemingly endless supply of plaid shirts and jeans that burst from one bulging box after another. She was ready to haul them out to the curb and be done with it.

"Not too late to change your mind, love," David said.

"Very funny," Charlotte muttered as she opened another box of plaid shirts. "Honestly, David, how many plaid shirts do you need? Grunge is dead."

"How many T-shirts do you need?" he countered.

Charlotte's mouth gaped before she closed it and the top flap of the box. "*Touché*."

David laughed and stood up from his cramped position on the floor. "You have to admit—we've been making pretty good progress since yesterday. I predict we'll be done before the day's out."

"*Hmmm*. From your lips…" Charlotte's voice trailed off as she opened another box for inspection.

They continued unpacking boxes, making "To Keep" and "To Toss" piles, and slowly brought order to chaos. Charlotte was stunned to discover that David's prediction had come through: they had indeed finished by nightfall.

David took a shower while Charlotte sprawled across the couch, admiring their handiwork. Her cell phone buzzed at her from the coffee table. She looked at the caller ID and groaned a little. She took a deep breath and steeled herself.

"Hi, Karen."

"Well you've sure taken your sweet time filling me in on any details about all your globe-trotting."

Charlotte sat up. "I've been meaning to call you. I *have*. It's just that things have been insane the past few weeks."

"So what happened? Last I knew, his ex was in, you were out, and I was pissed."

Charlotte played with a piece of her hair. "Don't believe everything you read, Karen."

"All right, all right…So how did Mr. Wonderful go from being a son of a bitch to being Mr. Wonderful again?"

Charlotte heaved a sigh and stepped out onto the small porch in her backyard and detailed the past few weeks to Karen, including Olivia, her and David's reconciliation, and their current living situation. She didn't want David to step out of the shower and overhear her conversation. Karen would interject a snide comment here and there or let out an incredulous snort. Charlotte tried to ignore it, but it was starting to hurt her feelings.

"So now you're all caught up on the craziness that has been my life."

Karen was silent on the other end of the line. Charlotte frowned. Karen was never silent. *"Helloooo?* Are you there?"

Karen stuttered a bit before falling quiet once more. Finally she could hold her opinion in no more. "I'm sorry, Charlotte, but what the hell are you doing?"

Charlotte's heart pounded from a mixture of fear and nerves. "What do you mean?"

"Exactly what I asked. What the *hell* are you doing? I mean, this guy's got you traipsing all over the world after him, pulling you through kitchens, hanging out in trailers all day—I mean, Charlotte, what about *your* life?"

"Karen, it's not like that. We were spending time together, and he was giving me a glimpse into his world. And now we're home." Charlotte couldn't help but smile at the thought of being home with David.

"Charlotte, I think you're letting yourself get caught up in some crazy fantasy world, and you're not being realistic. Furthermore—"

"Stop...Stop!" Charlotte started to pace the deck. "Just stop it! Why can't you be happy for me? Why is that so hard?" Karen didn't say anything, so Charlotte resumed talking. "I'm happier than I've ever been in my whole life. I can't explain it, but David makes me *happy*."

"So, what, I can't be worried now?"

"Of course you can be worried, but enough is enough. I just—" Charlotte searched for the words. "I appreciate your concern, I do, but I'm tired of you coming down on me—on us. We're in love, and I just can't worry about tomorrow or the next day or the day after that. All I can do is focus on today, and today David makes me feel more alive and amazing than I've ever felt. And I'm not ready to let go of that. And if it doesn't work out, at least I took a chance. Isn't that what you're always telling me to do?"

Charlotte heard only static on the other end, and she feared she may have gone too far. "You still there?"

Karen cleared her throat. "Well, I guess for the first time in my life, I'll keep my opinions to myself."

The phone went dead.

"Karen? Karen!"

Nothing.

Charlotte sighed and clicked her phone off. She opened the patio door and found David sitting on the couch, leafing through a magazine. He peered at her.

"Who was that? You seemed rather perturbed."

Charlotte flopped down on the couch next to him and laid her head on his shoulder. "Karen. We had a disagreement."

"About me, huh?"

"How'd you guess?"

"Well, she hasn't exactly been crazy about the idea of us as a canoodling twosome." David planted a kiss on Charlotte's head. "I'm sorry."

"Don't worry about it. I'll call her in a few days."

David nodded. "Good...good. How about, in the meantime, I whip us up a little dinner?"

"I thought you'd never ask."

It was nearly ten the next morning when Charlotte rolled over to David's side of the bed and saw a note on the pillow. She yawned, rubbed her eyes, and read:

I had to run an errand, and when I get back, I'm taking you out. Jeans required, which shouldn't be a problem, right? ☺. *Love you, David.*

Charlotte giggled to herself. "How on earth is he going to top New York?" She couldn't wait to find out and hopped out of bed and into the shower. She got dressed and slicked her hair back into a ponytail. She found David hunched over a cup of coffee in the kitchen, dressed in his standard disguise of jeans, T-shirt, and baseball cap.

"Good morning." She gave him a kiss on the cheek and went in search of a mug, which she filled halfway with coffee.

"Good morning to you, love. I'd ask how you slept, but I know you didn't get much."

Charlotte stuck her tongue out at him and took the stool next to him. "You know, I wanted to tell you that while I admire your efforts to hide how sexy you are"—she took a sip of coffee—"you're not fooling anybody."

"No? Not even a little?"

"Hardly. Like trying to make Halle Berry look like a hag." Charlotte sipped her coffee. "I would ask what the big surprise is, but I get the feeling you're not going to tell me."

"Finally! She understands the method to my madness." David put his coffee mug down on the counter. "It took you long enough."

"I'm a slow learner."

"Indeed."

"Can I get a little hint at least?"

David drained his coffee. "Okay. Um...we'll be in motion."

"I thought you said we were going out?"

"Oh, we'll be upright, love."

"All right, I give up."

"We're going bike riding."

"Bike riding? Wow...I haven't been on a bike in who knows how long. Not to mention, I don't have a bike." She looked at him. "How's this going to work exactly?"

David gave her a mischievous grin. "Don't you know by now I have my ways? Now come on, drink up so we can get going."

"Aye, aye, Captain," Charlotte hurried to finish her coffee. She grabbed her sunglasses before David dragged her outside. Parked in the driveway was a shiny black motorcycle with two gleaming helmets dangling from the handlebars.

"Like I said, a bike ride." David beamed, obviously pleased with himself.

"Where'd this come from?"

"Buddy of mine who owns a bike shop has been holding it for me. I had him drop it off at the gas station around the corner."

Charlotte gulped. "I'll let you in on a little secret. I've never been on a motorcycle before, and I don't feel like changing that status."

David picked up a helmet and crooked it under his arm. "Oh, come on now. It'll be fun."

"Do you even know how to ride one of these things?"

"Of course!" David laughed. "It wouldn't be here if I didn't. I had to learn how to ride one for this TV show I did about a million years ago, and after that I was hooked. Been riding ever since."

"Funny...you never mentioned that."

"Sweetheart, you have nothing to worry about. You'll be completely safe with me. Besides, I know I've got precious cargo."

Charlotte wasn't convinced. "I don't know. They scare me quite a bit. When you said *bike ride*, I thought you meant a bicycle built for two."

"You won't try it?"

Charlotte sighed, struck by the note of disappointment in David's voice. She tucked a loose strand of hair behind her ear. "What'd you have in mind?"

David looked around. "Well, it's shaping up to be such a beautiful day, I thought a ride along the coast would be fun. Maybe grab a bite to eat."

Charlotte twisted her lips around in deep thought, her sense of adventure and curiosity piqued.

"Okay." Charlotte couldn't help but laugh as David perked up. "You're right—that does sound fun."

A giddy David handed Charlotte the extra helmet and went over a few basics with her. He climbed aboard the bike, and Charlotte slid into the seat behind him, her arms Velcroed around his waist. David gave her a thumbs-up, while Charlotte squeezed her eyes shut and braced herself. The engine roared to life, and Charlotte yelped beneath her helmet. David revved the engine a few times before he backed out of the driveway. He gave Charlotte another thumbs-up before he peeled off down the street.

The tiny window of her helmet misted over with the breath of her squeals as they zoomed out of her neighborhood, toward Pacific Coast Highway. They headed south out of Los Angeles to Orange County, and after a few minutes of deathly terror, Charlotte began to enjoy the ride. David maneuvered in and out of traffic with the skill of an expert, and Charlotte enjoyed having her arms around him as the scenery of Southern California whooshed past them. She decided it was much more fun to deal with PCH on a motorcycle than in a car. Not that she ever wanted to be the one in control of the handlebars.

They rode past countless beaches before arriving in Newport Beach. David slowed and coasted to a stop near one of the city's less-populated beaches. Charlotte's ears were ringing as she removed her helmet, and it felt as though her body were still racing down the highway. David whipped his helmet off and looked over his shoulder at Charlotte.

"Well? What'd you think?"

Charlotte laughed, once again caught up in his glee. "I hate to admit it, but I loved it."

David slapped his hands together. "Ha! I knew it. I knew once I got you on the bike you'd understand why I love it so much."

David helped Charlotte off the bike, and she adjusted her jeans and shirt. "I have to say it's a pretty incredible feeling. It's like you and the open road. It's awesome."

David nodded, his eyes shining. "Exactly! It's just this amazing sense of freedom, a rush like no other." David grunted a little. "I love it!" He locked the bike and grabbed Charlotte's hand as they made their way down the beach. Even though it was a little before noon, there weren't many people on the beach: a few scattered surfers in search of better waves than the Pacific was offering and a few random suntanners sprawled out on the sand. Charlotte's stomach grumbled and she pointed out a small pizza stand with a walk-up window tucked back away from the surf.

"I wonder if anyone will recognize you," Charlotte muttered as they walked over to order a few slices.

David pulled his baseball cap from the back pocket of his jeans, pushed it down on his head, and adjusted his sunglasses. "Here's hoping."

A thin, wiry woman with dark, wavy hair and a white "I ♥ NY" T-shirt with old pizza sauce stains around the collar smiled at them.

"Can I take your order?" she asked in a raspy New York accent as David got Charlotte's order.

"Two slices of pepperoni, please," David said in his cleanest American dialect.

The woman went to write the order down, when she looked up and peered at David. "Hey, wait a minute...You're that guy—David King!"

David smiled and shook his head. "Sorry. I get confused with him all the time."

The woman shook her head and laughed, not letting David get out so easy. "Oh no. I'd know you anywhere. I just saw you on *Entertainment Tonight* last night. They were talking about your new movie. What is it, *To Have and To Hold*? It's you!"

David grinned and slipped back into his regular voice. "Guilty."

The woman pounded the counter in triumph. "Ha! I knew it. You're David King! I'm Paula." She snapped her fingers. "Oh, hey, do you mind if I take a picture with you? The bunco girls will die."

"Sure, okay."

The woman squealed and implored Charlotte and David to sit tight while she grabbed her camera. She came running out seconds later, brandishing her phone, which she waved at Charlotte.

"Do you mind? Taking our picture, I mean."

Charlotte took the camera while the woman went to put her arm around David and to pose in front of the window. "Um, how about we get the beach in the background instead?"

The woman thumped the side of her head. "Even better."

David and Charlotte gave each other amused looks as Paula got into position. Charlotte snapped a few pictures from a couple of different angles, to Paula's delight.

"Oh my *God*. The girls will absolutely, one hundred percent, die," she gushed as she scrolled through the pictures. She snapped her fingers again. "Oh, hey...could I get your autograph?"

"On one condition."

"Oh, anything. Anything at all."

David glanced around and leaned toward Paula, his voice a conspiratorial whisper. "Don't tell anyone we're here. Not until after we leave, that is."

Paula patted David's shoulder, thrilled to be in on the secret. "Oh, hon… it's between you and me. *Swear.*"

David smiled. "Do you have a pen?"

"Do I have a pen?" Paula chuckled as she plucked one from behind her ear like a magician pulling a rabbit from a hat. She reached into the pizza window and grabbed a napkin. He signed it, *To Paula, love, David*, with a flourish. Paula let out a howl and impulsively hugged David and Charlotte, and then she insisted on giving them their slices and Cokes on the house. She thanked them profusely as they made their way down the pier with their food.

They parked themselves against some boulders to watch the now-robust waves crash against the shore as they munched on their pizza and guzzled their Cokes.

"So how would you compare this date to dinner and dancing in a revolving restaurant?"

Charlotte licked a drip of grease that was starting to wiggle its way down her hand. "Honestly, it doesn't matter to me where we are." Charlotte sipped her Coke. "Red carpet…Lake Arrowhead…Newport Beach, chomping on pizza…I'm just happy we're together."

David picked a piece of pepperoni off his pizza. "You know, if you wanted me to, I would give it all up for you. Today, if you wanted."

Charlotte frowned. "Where'd that come from?"

"I understand that I'm asking a lot from you, I mean, with this crazy lifestyle I lead. Dashing through airports, ducking and running and hiding. You never asked for any of this."

"So…you'd give it all up for me. Tomorrow?"

"Today."

Charlotte mulled this over.

"I see, and what would you do?"

"Farmer."

Charlotte contained her giggles. "Farmer. Really? And do you actually know anything about farming?"

"Nope, but I'm a quick study."

Charlotte laughed. "Thanks, but no thanks. I'm not interested in being the Yoko to your movie career."

"Charlotte, I get paid a lot of money for what I do, and I don't spend a dime. We could really just disappear."

Charlotte put the last bit of pizza crust in her mouth and chewed while she contemplated her words. "David, I love you for making this offer, but…I know how much you love what you do. I could see it in Vancouver. I could even see it in New York, on the red carpet, with everyone screaming your name and the cameras flashing away. You were made to do this."

David looked down sheepishly. "I just want to make you happy."

"Babe, you being happy is what makes me happy. Don't ever forget that."

David smiled. "Well then, I guess that's all I can ask for, huh?"

Charlotte took David's chin between her thumb and forefinger. "I guess so." She leaned in for a kiss.

David laughed. "You taste like pepperoni."

"What do you think you taste like?"

"Um…strawberries?"

Charlotte swatted David's leg and took another sip of her Coke.

"I hope you're feeling better," David said, rattling the ice in his Styrofoam cup.

"What?"

"After last night. Your fight with Karen."

"Oh. That. It wasn't really a fight. More like a difference of opinion."

"Still, she's your best friend. Can't be easy to be at cross-purposes with each other."

Charlotte traced a pattern in the sand with the toe of her tennis shoe. "No, it's not." She looked up. "Is that what today was? To take my mind off Karen?"

David looked out at the water. "Did it work?"

"Wonders."

They turned their attention to the surfers and boogie boarders bobbing in the crystalline blue water. The beach started to fill up with more people, which made David nervous. Charlotte squeezed his knee.

"Do you want to leave?"

David rubbed his hands together and looked around. Charlotte could see him getting more and more agitated.

"We'd better. We might have a full-scale war on our hands otherwise."

They jumped up and made their way to the bike. A couple of girls whom Charlotte pegged to be in college noticed David and couldn't contain their giggles as they asked for pictures. Once again, Charlotte played photographer and snapped several shots for the girls to have in their gallery. As soon as they were done posing, they jumped on their phones to text everyone under the sun about their encounter with *the* David King.

"You don't always have to take the pictures, Charlotte," David said as he handed her a helmet.

"Ah, but the more pictures I take, the less I'm in!" she sang. "Besides, people don't want to see me—they want to see *you*. Plus, they seemed like nice girls, and you obviously just made their day."

David got on the motorcycle. "Well, how about we head home so I can keep making your day?"

Without a word, Charlotte leaped onto the bike, but instead of getting behind him, she got on in front, facing him, which sent them both into fits of laughter.

"What are you doing?" he gasped in between laughs.

"I want to ride home like this, with me facing you, kissing you the entire time."

"The whole idea is to make it home in one piece, you know."

Charlotte hopped off and picked up her helmet. "Okay, okay...next time."

David blew her a kiss, and Charlotte assumed her position on the back of the bike. As she went to pull her helmet on, she noticed a few people across the street snapping pictures of them with their phones.

David sighed. "We'd better take off." He shook his head. "You know, it's not too late to take me up on my offer to give it all up. I could even get plastic surgery."

"Ach! Don't you dare touch that gorgeous face!" Charlotte hugged his waist. "And stop apologizing. Nothing, and no one, can ruin this day."

David winked at Charlotte before he flipped his visor down. She followed suit before he took off in the direction of home.

༺☙༻

"How do you feel about going to a movie this afternoon?"

Charlotte slapped the top of the metro section down to peer at David. "What'd you have in mind?"

"Well, it says here that *Breakfast at Tiffany's* is playing at the art cinema downtown. I haven't seen it in ages."

"Would you believe I've never seen it?"

"And you call yourself a romance writer."

"I know, I know. I always wanted to see it, but never got around to it."

"Show starts at two p.m., so now's your chance."

"You know we've never seen a movie together?"

"Well, we'll have to do this right then. Jumbo bucket of salty, buttery popcorn, dump a box of Raisinets in there, a kidney buster of Coke." David grinned. "My mouth's watering just thinking about it."

"Raisinets in the popcorn? You're kidding. That is my absolute favorite way to eat popcorn."

"And yet another reason I adore you."

They smiled at each other for a moment before going back to reading their respective sections of the paper. It was Saturday morning, and Charlotte and David were perched in what had become their favorite spot in the bedroom other than the bed—the reading nook by the window populated with two periwinkle blue overstuffed chairs with a little white shabby chic occasional table between them. They often read the paper together, or Charlotte read books or magazines while David pored over new scripts.

The weeks had passed in a dizzy, happy daze as David and Charlotte settled into an easy domesticity. During the day, Charlotte wrote while David went on with the business of being a movie star. It was much more involved than Charlotte ever realized. There were production meetings, photo shoots, media interviews, looping work. David treated being an actor like a business; he said it was because he didn't want to work forever.

Every night David came home and cooked one delicious meal after the next for Charlotte: steaks, chicken, pasta, seafood, salads that went beyond the shreds of iceberg lettuce drenched in Thousand Island dressing that Charlotte had eaten before David came into her life. She joked that he was making her as fat as a house, and he shooed her away, saying that cooking for her made him happy.

During the weekends they escaped the city on David's motorcycle, browsed farmer's markets and bookstores in deep disguise, or met William and his latest conquest for quiet dinners in out-of-the-way locales. They made love every night, their passion for each other still as ferocious as it had been during those heady times in Lake Arrowhead.

"So you're in?"

"Won't it be hard? I mean, trying to go to a movie. Won't you get mobbed?"

David shrugged. "It's the middle of the day at an art house cinema in L.A. I think we'll be okay."

Charlotte was quiet for a moment. "You're right." She resumed reading the paper. "It'll be a great day."

Charlotte always loved the smell of movie theaters, the aroma of fresh-popped popcorn filling every crevice, the sweet, syrupy scent of Coca-Cola. Even the hot dogs and nachos with fake cheese smelled good. There was a hush over the theater as David ducked inside while Charlotte took on the task of loading up on goodies for the show.

Charlotte found David seated in the middle of the middle row; they were the only ones in the theater. She handed him the popcorn and drinks as she ripped into the Raisinets and poured a few into her hand.

"Hey! That's for the popcorn!" David protested as he went to grab the box from Charlotte.

"Sorry...couldn't resist."

David twisted around. "It's a shame more people aren't here."

Charlotte scoffed as she dove into the popcorn. "You actually *want* more people around you?"

"No, it's just, this is such a great movie. I would have thought a few more people would have been here."

Charlotte shrugged as the lights lowered and music blared out of the speakers, indicating the movie was starting. David draped his arm across Charlotte's shoulder as they took turns rooting around in the popcorn and making sure they were mixing salty and sweet with each bite.

"So what'd you think?" David asked as "The End" flashed across the screen.

Charlotte sighed and popped one more Raisinet in her mouth. "I absolutely loved it. They just don't make them like Audrey Hepburn anymore. Or George Peppard, for that matter."

"Kind of makes you forget that whole *A-Team* thing, huh?"

"I'm happy to say I never had the pleasure." Charlotte was picking up her purse when David touched her arm.

"Do you mind? I love watching credits."

"Oh. I thought all the credits were at the beginning," Charlotte said, a bit surprised as she leaned back against the chair.

Just then, in bold white letters, "Marry me, Charlotte" blazed down at her. Charlotte gasped and blinked, certain she hadn't seen right. She looked again, and sure enough, the words were still there in all their unmistakable glory. She turned to David, her jaw open. David shook a box of Cracker Jack at her before squeezing down on one knee.

"What are you doing?" she whispered.

"You didn't open the Cracker Jacks. You know there's a prize in each box." He gestured to the screen. "Just like in the movie, we can take it to Tiffany's to be engraved if you want."

Charlotte looked down and slowly took the box from David, her eyes brimming with tears. She fumbled to get it open and thrust her hand deep inside the sticky kernels in search of the prize David wanted her to find. Her fingertips grazed the corner of the paper envelope and yanked it out.

"Well, don't leave me in suspense. Open it."

With trembling fingers, Charlotte ripped open the small, bulging envelope and extracted a platinum diamond eternity band. Tears tumbled out of Charlotte's eyes, and she was grateful no one was around to see her blubbering. David took the ring and looked at her.

"You know that we belong together, right?"

"David," was all Charlotte could say.

"I've never been more sure of anything in my life than I am of wanting to be with you for the *rest* of my life." He slipped the ring on her finger and continued looking deep into her eyes. "Marry me."

"But David, it's been only..."

"I know. Mere months. It doesn't matter. When you know, you know."

"David, people will think you're nuts."

"I already told you. I am crazy—about us."

She took a deep breath and looked at the ring. It was one thing to play house, but this...this was more than Charlotte ever imagined.

David searched her face. "Charlotte, answer me."

"David, you know how much I love you and our life together..."

"What? Say it."

"In, let's say"—she looked up at the ceiling, her tears now falling for a different reason—"twenty years. Twenty years from now, when I need help getting around because my knees are bad and it's time to start stocking up on Depends and denture cream, you'll be only fifty, and I'll be..."

David held up his hand, disgusted. "Stop right there." He licked his lips and focused his gaze on her. "My God, I thought we were over this. Listen to me, because I want to say this only once since I don't plan to waste another moment of breath on this. I don't care that you're older than me.

There are no rules about the age of the person you love. The only rule I can think of is you need to be eighteen before you marry, and I think we've got that covered."

Charlotte laughed in spite of herself. "Yeah, we've definitely got that one covered." She looked at him, her eyes shining. "You always know how to make me laugh."

"Charlotte, nowhere does it say you have to marry within a certain age bracket. Why would you let someone else's opinion determine your happiness or mine? You're always saying you don't care what other people think. Put those words into action."

Charlotte looked down where her hands lay folded in her lap. What the hell was wrong with her? This man loved her, wanted to spend the rest of his life with her. She thought about the age difference all the time, and why? David was right. It mattered only what they, and no one else, thought.

Charlotte flipped her head up and locked eyes with David. "I'll marry you," she said.

David's own tears began to shimmer along the bottom of his eyelids. "Seriously?" His voice quivered.

"Yes." Charlotte nodded as David let out a triumphant yelp and struggled to extricate himself from beneath the seats and draw Charlotte into a kiss.

"I love you so much, Charlotte. I can't even express how much."

Charlotte cupped David's face with one hand. "Same goes for me, Mr. King."

CHAPTER 11

Charlotte decided to make the morning coffee for a change, and every time her eye caught the sparkle of her ring she broke into a smile so big that she thought her face would crack. The ring was perfect for her—simple and elegant and not at all flashy. It was startling how well David knew her after a relatively short time. She sighed happily as she dumped a mound of coffee grounds into the filter and started the machine. The front door opened, and Charlotte could hear David's heavy breathing from his workout. She smiled again, waiting from him to come up behind her and plant a kiss on her neck as he always did whenever he came home from being out.

"Morning, love," he said as he followed through with his morning ritual. "How does it feel to be engaged all of"—he looked at his watch—"sixteen hours?"

"Fantastic," she said as she pulled down two mugs. "So I was just leafing through the entertainment section of the paper, and you know what I discovered?"

David sat down on a kitchen stool. "What's that?"

"*Breakfast at Tiffany's* was never playing at the theater."

"Really? You don't say?"

"Yeah, how about that?"

David laughed. "Okay, you caught me. I asked them to show it especially for us."

"And how did you get the ring inside a Cracker Jack box?"

"I'm entitled to some secrets, aren't I?"

Charlotte poured coffee. "Only a few."

"So how about we set a date? I was thinking next week."

Charlotte sputtered her coffee. "Next week? Slow down there, cowboy."

"Like I told you, when you know, you know, and I don't want to wait."

"Okay, well, I've been thinking about a date, and how do you feel about"—Charlotte put down her coffee mug—"the lake, next year. Nice and quiet. Romantic."

David was silent for a moment, a broad grin on his face. "I love it. It's perfect."

Charlotte smiled. "Good. I was hoping you'd say that. I just hope you feel the same way about me in a year," she teased.

"Oh, I can guarantee I won't feel the same way about you next year."

"Excuse me?"

David chuckled and kissed her nose. "I won't feel the same way in a year because—I'll love you more."

Charlotte twisted her ring around her finger and stared at her cell phone on the counter. David had gone to William's house for tennis and to share the news about the engagement. Charlotte had declined, saying she had a few things she wanted to get done around the house. The truth was that she wanted to try Karen one more time. Charlotte had reached out to her multiple times since their last phone call, but Karen kept blowing her off. Charlotte was determined not to give up, even if it meant driving to San Francisco and camping out on her best friend's doorstep. Charlotte snapped her fingers and sent Karen a text expressing that exact sentiment. She put the phone back down on the counter and waited, toes tapping, fingertips drumming. About a minute later, her phone dinged.

It was Karen.

Okay. Call me.

Charlotte grabbed the phone and dialed Karen. After three rings, she picked up.

"I was starting to think maybe you died."

"No such luck. I'm starting to think I'm like Cher and the cockroaches."

Charlotte took a deep breath. "Well, I wanted to share some news with you."

Karen was silent, so Charlotte plunged in. "David asked me to marry him yesterday, and I said yes."

Karen still didn't say anything, and Charlotte cleared her throat. "We're thinking about getting married at the lake. You know, since that's where it all started."

Charlotte waited for a response and was about to erupt into tears when Karen finally spoke. "I'm happy for you, Charlotte. And I really mean that."

Relief washed over Charlotte as the tears came forth after all, though they were tears of joy. "I can't tell you how much that means to me, Karen."

"Well, I'm glad my opinion counts for something."

Charlotte reached for a paper towel to catch the drips from her nose. "It does."

"So when's the big day?"

"Um, well, we haven't set a firm date yet, but we're thinking next year. Probably spring, but maybe sooner, maybe later. Don't know."

"A springtime wedding is always nice. Birds and flowers and all that."

Charlotte took another deep breath. "I'd like you to be my matron of honor."

Karen scoffed. "I know I'm old, but I just hate the way *matron* sounds. Can't I be a maid? Or better yet, how about diva of honor? And I don't have to wear an ugly dress, do I? I mean, I love you, but not that much."

Charlotte burst out laughing, happy to have Karen back in her life. "You can have whatever you want. Just as long as you're there. Oh, and mum's the word on the engagement. We're trying to keep the press from finding out as long as possible."

"I'll take it to the grave. Besides—can't have my best friend getting married without me. What would people say?"

Charlotte fell silent. "That you're the best friend a girl could ever hope for. And I *mean* that."

"Even when she's being a jackass, huh?"

"Even then."

"Tell me all about how Mr. Wonderful proposed."

The two friends spent the next two hours howling on the phone as Charlotte shared how David had put the ring in a Cracker Jack box, and Karen caught Charlotte up on her latest dating escapades. By the end of the conversation, all was right in the world again, as Charlotte got her best friend back and Karen promised to come down one day soon for a celebratory dinner.

Charlotte was humming "Moon River" and folding laundry when David returned from William's.

"Well you're in a good mood. Can't all be because of me."

"Nope. I finally talked to Karen today. We're good."

"Ah, I'm so glad to hear that. I know how tough it's been not having her in your life."

"Yeah," she mused. "Sometimes you don't realize how much a person means to you until it's too late." She turned to David. "I promise to never take you for granted."

"I know you won't. Nor I you."

The first time Charlotte got married had been at city hall. She wore a simple white suit, and her wedding reception consisted of sharing a slice of cherry pie at a diner near Ben's house. They'd never taken a honeymoon. Ben had reasoned because they had small families, it made more sense not to make a fuss, and why waste money on a honeymoon when they could save their money and take a trip later? Charlotte had gone along with it, but deep down she'd always felt cheated that she had never gotten a proper wedding. And that delayed honeymoon consisted of a day at the Santa Monica Pier six months later.

While Charlotte knew she didn't want a big to-do, she definitely wanted to be an actual bride, which is what led her to the bookstore in search of bridal magazines and books. She got giddy as she collected a stack of magazines and pored over them in the café, her mind reeling with the possibilities of dresses and bouquets, and DJs versus bands. She bought five magazines before she headed to the grocery store to do the shopping for the week. As she drove, she kept stealing glances at her ring and smiling, a habit she'd slipped into quite easily since becoming engaged.

"Charlotte King," she said out loud, relishing the way the name sounded. "Mrs. David King. Charlotte Taylor King." Charlotte smiled at the different incarnations, excited to spend time thinking about which one sounded best. It was midmorning, so the market was quiet, and Charlotte took her time filling her cart, visions of her and David saying, "I do," dancing in her head.

Once Charlotte had checked everything off her shopping list, she headed to the checkout. Without even thinking, she glanced at the magazine stand and gasped. Her and David's pictures were splashed across every rag in the rack. Some were the entire cover and promised "the real scoop on David

King and his new lady love." Others were smaller pictures of them from places she'd never even realized there'd been photographers—trips to the bookstore, even them entering the movie theater a few days earlier. Charlotte shook her head and grabbed copies of every magazine with their picture and tossed the stack on top of her groceries.

Back at home, she spread the magazines across her dining room. The pictures were pretty good; she was pleased to see she'd been caught at good angles most of the time. It was the headlines, though, that pissed her off: David King Dates Erotica Writer! King Captures a Cougar! David and Charotica Out and About!

She choked on the last one. "Charotica?" she mouthed to herself. She leaned back. "That has to be the dumbest thing I've ever heard."

She couldn't help herself—she was dying to know what the articles said, so she read and reread each one at least three times. She wondered what had incited this sudden flurry of publicity over her and David. For the most part, they were benign, how they'd walked the red carpet in New York and had been spotted all over L.A. together. There was precious little information about her other than she was a writer. Charlotte cringed at the sight of the covers of some of her books blown up to almost gigantic proportions. The article that really bothered her the most was the one that implied David was in need of a mother figure. Charlotte was startled by her cell phone's chirp.

"Hello?" she answered in a huff.

"Is Charotica home?" Karen teased. "I have to say, you look pretty smokin' in those photos. Love looks good on you."

"How much do you think the genius who came up with 'Charotica' got paid?" Charlotte asked, too irritated to have heard anything Karen said.

"Too much. Besides your new name, how are you?"

"Would you believe I bought a stack of bridal magazines today?"

"So you're really getting into this bride thing, huh?"

"Yeah." Charlotte chuckled. "Who would have thought?"

"Just remember not to get carried away and pick out some fugly *maid of honor* dress."

"You can wear whatever you want. Even a poncho."

"Well, I won't go that far. I'll do you proud. Promise."

Charlotte heard the front door open and saw David come in. She smiled, and he came over and gave her a peck on the neck before he signaled that he was going to take a shower.

Charlotte sighed. "Listen, Karen, I gotta go. I'll call you later."

"So long, soon-to-be Mrs. Wonderful," Karen sang before she hung up.

Charlotte laughed and went to put her groceries away. Fortunately, there wasn't a whole lot of damage done by her leaving everything out on the counter while she'd taken her trip into the land of tabloid trash.

David came out wrapped in only a towel, his chest glistening with drops of water, and Charlotte almost dropped the bottle of wine she was holding. He came over to give Charlotte a proper kiss when he walked by the pile of tabloids splayed across the dining room table.

"What's all this then?" he asked as he riffled through them and picked one up. He chuckled as he read the cover of one.

"Let me guess...Charotica?"

"Come on, you have to admit it's rather clever."

"No, it's stupid."

"Okay, we do look happy in this picture, though." He held it up for her inspection. It was a shot of them stealing a quick kiss at a farmer's market. "I just might want it framed."

Charlotte snorted. "So, do I leave 'Charotica' in the picture, or should I crop around it?"

"Oh, leave it in, please."

Charlotte rolled her eyes and joined him at the table.

"Did you read the articles?"

Charlotte wrapped a chunk of hair around her finger. "I skimmed a few."

David tossed the magazine back on the stack. "You know, Charlotte, someone gave me good advice once, which I'm now going to pass on to you. Don't read the articles. Look at the pictures all you want, but don't read the articles."

"Sage advice."

✦

Charlotte adjusted her laptop again and tried to will the words to fill the page. She'd hit a bit of writer's block, and all she wanted was to flop back into bed and wait for inspiration to strike.

"Too bad David's busy," she mumbled to herself. William was starting him on a press junket for his new movie, which was coming out in a few weeks, and he was having lunch with a reporter in Beverly Hills. Then he was off to make the rounds of a few entertainment shows. Her e-mail dinged, and she saw a note from her publisher.

Hey Charlotte,

Awesome news! Just wanted to let you know we've seen a huge spike in sales for current titles, and there's been crazy demand for some of your backlist. Stores are having trouble keeping you in stock—woo hoo! I'll keep you posted, and look for a big fat check soon!

Dale

Charlotte shook her head, disgusted. "Whatever happened to the days of selling your books on merit and not tabloid glory?" And what was that crack about expecting a "big fat check?" Like that was the only reason she was with David. The e-mail was enough to spur some words for the page, and Charlotte went on a writing tear for the better part of the day. David showed up around three, exhausted.

"Hey, babe, how'd it go?"

David plopped down on the couch and closed his eyes. "The next time I say the words 'To Have and To Hold,' I better be standing across from you at an altar with an *officiante* of some kind."

Charlotte snuggled next to David on the couch. "Considering that its weeks before the movie comes out, my guess would be no such luck."

"Killjoy."

Charlotte laughed. "So I've already set the DVR for *Access Hollywood, Entertainment Tonight, Extra,* and *E! News Live.* Am I forgetting anyone?"

"Who knows? Who cares?"

"I care. I love watching you be interviewed. You're quite charming."

David grinned. "That so?"

"Uh-huh. And sexy. Very sexy."

"I need to ring up William and tell him to book me on about a million more shows then, huh?"

"At least."

"I noticed your bridal magazines last night. You look like you're really getting into it."

Charlotte twisted her ring around. "I told you, I never had a real wedding. I want this to be extra special."

"How about I come out wearing a powder blue tux? That would be special."

The doorbell rang. Charlotte frowned, wondering who it could be. "No, that would be disgusting," she said as she stood up to answer the door.

"What? I've always been told blue is my color!"

Charlotte rolled her eyes and opened the door and saw an impossibly tall woman with a swell of blonde waves cascading down her shoulders, puppy dog brown eyes, a black tunic, and a pair of skintight jeans that ran into over-the-knee black boots. Charlotte's face fell as she realized who it was.

Olivia.

The woman smiled, her teeth sparkling in the late afternoon sunlight. "Hi," she purred, her voice deceptively smoky. "Is David here?"

Charlotte could only stand there, gaping at this beautiful freak of nature. Charlotte was mesmerized by how stunning she was.

"Who is it, love? You forget to pay the milkman?"

Charlotte's hand flew to her throat, and Olivia's smile grew even bigger upon hearing David's voice from the living room.

"Charlotte, who—?" David peeked around Charlotte and stopped in his tracks when he saw Olivia. She leaned against the doorjamb, smiled, and cocked her head to one side.

"Well hello, lover. Miss me?"

"What the hell are you doing here?" Charlotte heard David hiss over her shoulder. Charlotte was rooted to the spot, transfixed by the glossy Olivia, who merely kept her dazzling smile trained in David's direction.

Olivia ran her tongue across the front of her tile-white teeth, reminding Charlotte of a toothpaste commercial. "What do you think? Looking for you."

"For what?" The hot rage of David's voice made the hair on the back of Charlotte's neck stand at attention.

"Well, I finished my movie, just got back into town this morning, and"—Olivia smiled again—"I missed you."

"How'd you find me—us?"

"I have my ways."

"Fine. Now leave," David said in a low voice.

"For what?" Olivia said, mocking David's earlier words.

"Because my fiancée and I don't want you here—that's why."

For the first time, Olivia's gaze flicked over to Charlotte, who gulped. She felt like a ten-year-old with braces and greasy hair. Charlotte looked down at her feet.

"Well, well, well," Olivia said, her voice a seductive taunt. "Looks like I've missed quite a bit while I've been gone."

David placed a protective hand on Charlotte's waist. "Yes, you have."

Olivia narrowed her eyes. She glanced at Charlotte one more time before locking eyes with David. "Well, lover, I guess congratulations are in order."

"Stop calling me that. And your leaving will be congratulations enough."

"Aren't you curious why I'm here?" Olivia pressed, not willing to be dismissed so easily.

"Not at all."

"You know, I could really use the little girl's room. Why don't you be the gentleman I know you are and invite me in?"

"No."

Olivia turned her attention to Charlotte, forcing her to acknowledge her, as if Charlotte could possibly be unaware of her presence.

"I *really* need to pee. You understand, right? You know how it is with girls." Olivia winked at Charlotte, like they were two girlfriends sharing a delicious secret. Charlotte squirmed, her unfailing sense of decency gnawing at her. She heaved a big sigh, her shoulders slumping in defeat.

"You can use the guest bathroom. Second door on the left," Charlotte said as David poked her in the back. Olivia's face broke out into that large, high-wattage smile once again as she slithered past David and Charlotte, into the house, the scent of gardenias trailing after her. Charlotte closed the door, and David shook his head in disbelief. Olivia strolled toward the bathroom, her eye darting around the living room.

"Well, this is really…cute." Olivia cast a sideways glance at David. Charlotte winced at the open disdain Olivia had for her home. "Nothing at all like that mansion you were renting in Malibu. Remember that place? Practically needed a map to find your way around, huh? How long are you renting this place for?"

"We're not renting. We live here together."

"Oh. Oh, wow—okay. Makes sense then," Olivia said as she gave Charlotte the once-over again.

"Bathroom is second door on the left," David said, his jaw clenched in fury.

Olivia winked at him before giving Charlotte the sweet yet deceptive smile she'd perfected before pivoting on her heel and heading to the bathroom. David waited until she closed the door before looking at Charlotte.

"Why the hell did you let her in here?"

Charlotte pushed her hair behind her ears. "It's just the bathroom. What harm could that do?"

"Should have sent her to the gas station on the corner." David shook his head and looked in the direction of the bathroom. "She's up to no good," he murmured. "As usual."

They heard the toilet flush and the faucet shut off. Within a few moments, Olivia emerged from the bathroom and once again gave Charlotte's living room a snide appraisal with a slight sneer on her face.

"All right." David marched over to Olivia and began to hustle her to the door. "You've used the bathroom. Now go."

"But I haven't told you why I'm here," Olivia protested as she wrenched out of David's grasp.

"I already told you, I don't care why you're here."

Olivia looked at Charlotte. "Do you mind? David and I have some business to discuss."

Charlotte felt like she'd been punched in the face. Had this woman just come into her house and ordered her out?

David scoffed. "Oh no. You've got something to say to me, you say it in front of Charlotte."

Olivia narrowed her eyes at David and then at Charlotte. "Charlotte. Charlotte. Oh, right. *Charotica*, because you write dirty books..." Olivia chuckled. "Clever."

Charlotte inhaled sharply and felt the color drain from her face. David spoke again.

"*Charlotte* and I have no secrets, so whatever you have to say, you can say in front of her."

Olivia sighed and looked down at the floor, nodding. She snapped her head up. "Well, lover, I need a place to stay."

"I'm not going to tell you again—stop calling me that. And so what, you need a place to stay?"

"So I need to bunk with you for a bit."

Charlotte gasped, and David looked like he was about to choke. "Stay here? With us? Good God. I didn't think even *you* had that much gall."

"My place is being renovated," Olivia continued as though David hadn't said a word. "I got back before they finished."

"Come off it, Olivia. You haven't had a 'place' the entire time I've known you."

Olivia chuckled. "All right, so the Beverly Wilshire was all booked up."

"Call your agent."

"We've had a mutual parting of the ways."

"You mean he finally dumped you."

Olivia shook her head and laughed. "Oh, lover. You really do like to cut to the bone, don't you?"

Charlotte looked at a confident Olivia using every trick in her book and then at a pissed David holding himself back from throwing her out. Charlotte stood in the middle of it all like a spectator at a tennis match gone berserk.

"I can't help you. You'll have to figure out something else."

Olivia's bottom lip began to tremble, and her brown eyes dissolved into pools of melted chocolate as they filled with tears. Within seconds she was heaving uncontrollably, a weeping, watery mess. Charlotte looked at her, disturbed, while David just dropped his head in frustrated defeat.

"David, you just don't understand how terrible things are right now," Olivia sobbed. "Ira's being just *awful*. He called me this morning to tell me he was 'terminating' me as a client. And that was after he promised I could stay in his guesthouse when I got back to town. And all the money I've made him!" Olivia wiped her nose with the back of her hand, and Charlotte fought the urge to hand her a tissue.

David just leaned against the couch, his arms folded in disgust. "You knew that day of reckoning was coming."

"But not now! I just...I just need some time to figure things out, get my head together, you know?" Olivia gazed at David, her eyes glassy with tears. "Let me stay here. Just for a little while."

"Forget it."

"You're just going to turn me out onto the street like some awful homeless person with nowhere to go?"

"Olivia, I know I can't possibly be your only option, not with the literally *hundreds* of hotels in the Greater Los Angeles Area that are more than up to your exacting standards. Besides, what happened to that big fat paycheck you just got?"

Olivia scoffed. "Oh God, David. I was behind on *sooooo* many bills. I had to pay Ira his share, my business manager, my PR person, my lawyer..." Olivia snapped her fingers. "I got left with nothing!"

David rubbed his eyes, and Charlotte peered down at the floor, wondering when her life had become an episode of *Days of our Lives*.

"Unbelievable," David muttered.

"So," Olivia sniffed, sensing a softening in David's stance, "can I stay? Just for a few days?"

"How much of that money got snorted up your nose?"

Olivia's mouth gaped, and she swallowed. "None. I told you after the last time that that was the last time."

"And so what? After a few days, what's your plan?"

"I've got a few prospects. Just waiting for a few things to come in—that's all."

David smiled and clapped his hands. "Forget it, Olivia. I'm done."

Olivia shook her head, a torrent of tears spilling down her face. "Please, David! I honest to God have *nowhere* else to go! Just for a few days." Olivia whipped her head around to Charlotte, her eyes pleading. "Can David and I get just a few moments alone? Please."

Charlotte sighed, actually thankful for the chance to escape. "As a matter of fact, I do need to run to the drugstore—"

"Charlotte—"

Charlotte held up her hand to stop David's protests. "No, really, we need toothpaste...and aspirin." Charlotte picked up her keys and purse from the side table in the foyer before she gave David a quick peck on the lips. She glanced at Olivia.

"Nice meeting you," she whispered before she headed out the door.

Charlotte had filled up her little red plastic basket with more toiletries than she would use in six months. She was still shaking over the encounter with Olivia and trying to keep her frayed emotions in check. Olivia was so beautiful it was almost sick. She was a strange case of being even more dazzling in real life than on-screen. Charlotte could understand why David's head had been turned by her. But in those few moments, as David had said, Charlotte could tell all that beauty and charm was but a thin veneer stretched across a manipulative and shallow charmer. With all she'd come to know about David, looks aside, those two were a terrible match.

Charlotte peeked at her phone to see if David had called or texted with an update. Nothing yet. It couldn't be avoided—she had to go back home. Charlotte checked out, cringing at the nearly $300 tab. The sun was setting in L.A., and a cool breeze had slipped in. Charlotte embraced the chill as she pointed her Jeep toward home, her anxiety mounting with each rev of the engine. She rounded the corner onto her street, her eye searching her driveway. Olivia's rental car gone. Charlotte breathed a sigh of relief. All was well again.

Clutching her plastic bags, Charlotte unlocked the front door and listened for any sound of David.

"David? Honey, are you home?" Charlotte's heart lurched at the silence. She set her bags on the couch and went through the house in search of David. Empty. Charlotte took a steady breath and forced herself to stay calm. She went about the methodical task of putting her things away while maniacally checking her phone every two seconds. Just when she was about to call David, the phone rang.

"Where are you?"

"On my way home. I checked her into the Marriott on Sunset."

"Oh." Charlotte sat down to the couch. "For how long?"

"A few days. That's all."

"What happens in a few days?"

"I'm trying to sweet-talk her agent into letting her move into his guesthouse."

"What if that doesn't work?"

"It will. Trust me."

Charlotte rubbed her forehead. "David, I—" She stopped herself. "Nothing."

"Come on, don't do that. David *what?*"

Charlotte pursed her lips and closed her eyes. "What is this hold she has over you? I mean, I get that she's gorgeous and everything, but…do you still have a thing for her?"

"I can't believe you'd ask me that."

"Well? Do you?"

"My answer is an unequivocal no. I told you she hasn't got anybody else. I'm just trying to help her along is all."

"It seems to me she's pretty resourceful and always somehow manages to live another day."

"Charlotte, that's not fair. What about you and Ben—"

"*Ach*! Stop right there. Ben and I were married, so even though our marriage was a complete shambles, he was still my husband. So yes, because of that, I felt a certain obligation to him. You and Olivia were never married—no kids. It has to stop somewhere."

"Would you rather she stayed with us?"

"No, of course not. Look—all I'm saying is that if you keep rescuing her every time she crashes, she'll never stop hounding you. I mean, hell—she's gotten this far in life without you."

David was silent on the other end as Charlotte's words sank in. Charlotte was quiet, not sure if she had any words left on the subject.

"I'll be home in a few minutes," David said before the line went dead.

Charlotte was sitting on the couch and sipping a glass of Chardonnay in silence when she heard the front door creak. A lone table lamp illuminated the room. She waited for David to come in. His face was as wan and as tense as that night he'd shown up at her doorstep in the middle of the night to plead his case. So much had happened since then that it was easy to forget this weird air between them by the name of Olivia.

"Hey," David said.

"How'd you get home?"

"Taxi."

"You get Olivia all settled in?"

"Charlotte, it's not like that."

Charlotte dipped her head back and sighed. "David, I just can't help but wonder why, when Humpty Dumpty falls apart, you feel obligated to put her back together again."

"I told you—"

"I know, I know; she doesn't have anybody."

"Charlotte, please...I know it's a lot for me ask you to put up with this on top of everything else, but I'm just trying to do the right thing."

"David, believe me when I tell you that, in many ways, this does go against my nature, but if you and I are gonna have any kind of life together, you've got to cut her off."

"I know, I know. Believe me, I know. And I've tried!" David flopped down on the couch next to Charlotte. "She's just insidious."

"Stop making excuses for her! She's figured out how to play you like ten fiddles. Once you take the hard line and stick to it, she'll stop."

David dropped his head on Charlotte's shoulder. "I'm so sorry, Charlotte."

Charlotte shook her head and took a sip of wine.

"Me too."

The green face of Charlotte's alarm clock bore a hole in her face. When David had gone for a run, Charlotte had crawled into bed, exhausted by the way the day had unfolded. She heard David come in and take a shower, and she held her breath, uneasy. Charlotte watched the minutes on the clock tick past, listening to David shut the water off, brush his teeth, and swish mouthwash around his mouth. The bathroom door opened, and a flash of light hit Charlotte's back. She was lying perfectly still and had squeezed her eyes shut. David's feet sank into the carpet, and he cleared his throat. He slipped into bed, pressing his naked body against Charlotte. The hot scent of Irish Spring and Jergens lotion enveloped Charlotte as David planted cool kisses on her neck. His hardness poked against her. She bit her lip. All she wanted was to turn around and beg David to screw her brains out until she forgot all about Olivia and his strange allegiance to her.

But she didn't. Instead, Charlotte feigned deep breaths, the glowing green light of her clock trying to pry her eyelids open. David sighed and slumped against her before he rolled over to his side of the bed. Charlotte expelled her breath in a slow, silent stream. It was the first time she'd ever turned David down. It was the first time she hadn't felt like getting lost in his scent, his taste, his touch, his sound.

It was the first time Charlotte wanted to be alone.

"Morning."

"Morning," Charlotte said as she poured a cup of coffee from the pot David had made. He watched her as she mixed in cream and sugar.

"I can make you some eggs."

Charlotte shook her head. "No thanks."

"I think there's a box of muffins in the pantry."

"I'm not really hungry."

"I don't like things being so stiff between us."

Charlotte drew circles on the counter with her fingers. "Me neither. But it is what it is."

"How do we fix this?"

"I already told you."

"You know William has me booked for a few meetings today, but I can cancel. We can hop on the bike, head to the beach…"

"I've actually got a lot of work to do today, so you should keep your meetings."

David's face fell, and he nodded, quiet for a moment. "Yeah, okay. I'll let you get to it then."

"Thanks."

David's gaze lingered on Charlotte before he quietly went outside to wait for the car that ferried him around town. Charlotte sipped her coffee in silence, the tension in her shoulders sliding away with each swallow. She took her time showering and dressing, afraid almost to get on with the business of the day. She opened her laptop and stared, lost in the black-and-white photo of the Eiffel Tower that was her desktop picture. Charlotte chewed on her thumbnail for a bit before she slammed the lid shut and grabbed her purse.

What the hell good is it to work for yourself if you can't play hooky once in a while? She queried herself as she put her sunglasses on. She stepped outside into another postcard-beautiful Southern California day. Feeling better already, Charlotte walked to her Jeep, keys jangling between her fingers. She'd put the key in the lock when she heard a clicking sound. Charlotte stopped and listened. *Click, click, click.* There it was again. She whipped her head around and saw a photographer draped in camera equipment standing at the edge of her driveway, snapping away. Charlotte gasped and ducked into the Jeep, her heart pounding. She started the Jeep and screeched backward, trying to shield her face with one hand and maneuver the steering wheel with the other.

"Hey, come on, Charotica! Why don't you smile for the camera?" the intruder yelled into the open window.

The invocation of the hated "Charotica" blew Charlotte's top sky-high. "Hey asshole! This is private property!" she screamed as the guy jammed his camera in her face, her sunglasses no match for the glare of camera flashes.

"I'm standing in the street, so that's public property. What time is David getting home, huh? How long you guys been shackin' up?"

Charlotte growled and peeled off down the street. She put her hand over her heart to try to slow its zealous rhythm. She took a deep breath, her mind racing with all sorts of sinister possibilities. How long had paparazzi been staking out her house? How on earth did they know where she lived? Charlotte turned on the radio, jacking it up to near-earsplitting levels.

If only drowning her feelings were as easy as listening to music.

CHAPTER 12

"Where've you been? I thought you had a lot of work to get through today."

"I spent the afternoon at Santa Monica Pier. Went to the aquarium, checked out a photography exhibit. Had lunch."

"Oh. Was it fun?"

Charlotte nodded and put her purse and keys on the coffee table and sat on the chair opposite the couch where David had been sitting, watching TV.

David turned the TV off and looked at her. "Charlotte, sweetheart, talk to me. I hate it when you're mad at me."

"I'm not mad. I'm just...disappointed."

"God. That's worse."

"David, one of the things I love most about you is how big your heart is. I mean, when I was walking around the pier today, I was thinking about when we were at the lake and how...*accommodating* you were. Wanting to know more about everyone, cooking and cleaning and just being so...*decent*."

"You make it sound like I've got a disease or something."

"No, David, nothing like that. It's just that I hate to see you being taken advantage of, and that's exactly what Olivia is doing—taking advantage of your big, wonderful, open heart, and I'm just disappointed that you're letting her."

David reached for Charlotte's hand and pulled her over to join him on the couch. He kissed her on the nose. "I don't want this to come between us."

"David, I think you need to work out whatever it is with her. Figure it out."

David pulled back. "What do you mean 'figure it out'? What are you saying?"

Before Charlotte could answer, her BlackBerry started to ding from deep inside her purse. She rolled her eyes. "Hold on. My editor's been texting me all day. Let me see what she wants."

David sighed and waited while Charlotte pulled out her phone. It was a message from Karen: *Having a bad day Charotica? K xoxo*

Charlotte clicked on the link Karen had sent and groaned. It was the picture of her from this morning when she yelled at the paparazzo—mouth agape, nostrils flaring, fury seared into her forehead.

CHAROTICA—HOPPIN' MAD! the headline screamed. The ensuing story speculated that David must have done something to unleash Charlotte's wrath, but didn't say what, of course. Charlotte threw the BlackBerry aside, disgusted.

"What's the matter?"

"There was a photographer outside the house this morning, and he took a really bad picture of me screaming at him to get lost. And now, of course, it's all over the Internet."

"Damn. Sorry."

Charlotte rubbed her eyes and took a deep breath, suddenly too tired to move. "David, I need a little time to myself."

"What?" David said, shocked and angry.

"There's just so much to deal with between Olivia and the tabloids every time I turn around…"

David shook his head. "No. Charlotte, please. I already told you, I can walk away from all of this, but I can't walk away from you."

"I just need to get my head together. That's all."

"Don't do this. Please."

Charlotte blinked, and a tear ran down her face. She ran her palm against her cheek to stop the flow. "I'm going to take a shower and go to bed." Charlotte rose from the couch, and David tugged on her hand, his fear radiating with each touch.

"So that's it? We can't talk about this some more?"

"I'm just so tired, David."

Without another word, Charlotte began to walk back toward the bathroom, when David ran up behind her and grabbed her by the waist. He nuzzled her neck, and Charlotte intuitively leaned back against him. David began to rub her breast, and she moaned. His hand flicked over the top button of her jeans for a moment before he undid them and slid his hand into her underwear. Charlotte whimpered as he fingered her, pulling her against him. He turned her around and pressed her against the wall. He grabbed her lips with his, his hands stroking her nipples until they became stiff as diamonds beneath his frenetic touch. Charlotte flung his shirt over his head and did the same with her shirt before unhooking her bra, leaving the cups to flap around the sides. She guided David's mouth to her breast, and David whimpered as his tongue made contact with her nipple. He stopped for a moment to push her jeans and underwear to the floor, commanding her to step out of them. His lips finding hers again, he unzipped his jeans and pushed them and his underwear down in one swift motion. David flicked one of Charlotte's legs up and lifted her to meet him. As he plummeted into her, she screamed. He grunted as he continued his upward thrusts into Charlotte.

"I need you, Charlotte," David panted into her ear.

Charlotte gulped and closed her eyes, letting the moment carry her away. She held David to her, too overcome to say anything. She felt the swell rush forth and clenched as it broke free. Within seconds, David, too, tensed up and burst inside of her. They stood there for a few seconds, holding each other before David eased out of Charlotte. He pulled up his pants and handed Charlotte her shirt.

"I'm sorry," he said sheepishly. "I shouldn't have done that. Especially when you said you needed space. I just needed you."

Charlotte pulled David to her and drew him into a kiss. "I wasn't complaining."

David touched his forehead to Charlotte's. "I'll call William. Stay with him. You take all the time you need," he whispered.

They kissed again. "You're amazing," she said.

David shook his head. "No, I'm not. Everything in me is screaming to stay, but I'll respect your wishes."

"Thank you."

"And no matter what, just don't forget that I love you."

"I know. I love you too."

❦

Charlotte tossed the towels from the bathroom into the laundry basket. She purposely didn't look at David's side of the counter, which he had depleted of his most basic toiletries the night before when he left for William's: toothbrush, shaving gel, comb. A half-full bottle of Hugo Boss still stood guard over his mouthwash, razor cartridges, and the industrial-size bottle of body lotion Charlotte had picked up for him at the drugstore. She went around the bedroom, plucking forlorn socks, shorts, and T-shirts from all sorts of nooks and crannies. One thing she would say about David: housekeeping wasn't his strong suit.

She was about to head to the washer when she snapped her fingers and went behind the bathroom door in search of her terrycloth bathrobe. Her heart stopped when she spied one of David's plaid shirts keeping the bathrobe company on the next hook. Charlotte dropped the laundry basket and reached out to the shirt, tears stabbing her eyes. She laughed. Why was this stupid shirt, of all things, making her cry? She reached out to touch it. The soft, worn fabric felt lush between her fingers, and Charlotte edged her nose beneath the folds to inhale David's lingering scent. She unhooked the shirt and slid one arm and then the other into the limp sleeves, David suddenly all around her. Even though she'd asked him to leave, she missed him, missed him so much that it squeezed her insides and caused her to gasp from the pain. Charlotte grabbed a tissue from the box on the counter, dabbed at her eyes, and blew her nose. She picked up her basket and headed to the laundry room.

Charlotte swirled her spoon into the pint of soupy strawberry ice cream before she extracted a frozen chunk of fruit and popped it in her mouth. It had been almost two days since David's departure, and for almost two days, Charlotte had puttered around the house and slept in his plaid shirt. It was no longer awash in David's musk, but rather in Charlotte's funk. The TV was on a low hum, and Charlotte had been mindlessly flipping through the channels for the better part of the evening. She slurped up the rest of the ice cream and put the empty carton on the coffee table. She picked up the remote again and stopped when Olivia's face filled the screen. She was being interviewed by someone on the red carpet. Charlotte turned the sound up.

"Well, Olivia, we know you just completed *Black Knight, Dark Knight*, which comes out next year, but we just got word today that you're going to star in the new romantic comedy being directed by Lowell Henderson, which is quite a departure from the horror and action flicks you're known for. Why the change?"

"Because I'm funny!"

Both women chuckled as if Olivia had just told the most hilarious joke in the world.

"No, seriously, I've always wanted to do comedy and work with Lowell, so this is the best of both worlds. And you know, I want to do all types of roles, not just be known for one thing."

"Now, we know you and David King had tried to work things out, didn't last, and that he's moved on. What about you? Who are you getting romantic with these days, Olivia?"

Olivia smiled and winked. "Oh, Sherry, I don't kiss and tell, but hey, if I ever do decide to tell, I've got you on speed dial!"

Both women laughed again as if Olivia were the wittiest female to ever walk the earth.

The scene cut back to an anchor in the studio.

"And in addition to all her work on the silver screen, that Olivia Hudson has just signed a multimillion-dollar multiyear deal to be the face of Chelsea Cosmetics. Congratulations to her. Up next, we'll give you an inside view of George Clooney's fabulous Italian villa."

Charlotte clicked off the TV. She wondered if Olivia was Irish, because she sure had their luck. Charlotte got off the couch, restless. She paced each room of her house, twisting her engagement ring around her finger. It seemed like she and David had overcome so much in such a short amount of time. She knew David loved and adored her; she felt the same way about him. But love wasn't always enough. Charlotte meandered into her bedroom, and her eye fell upon the small black gift box David had given her for her birthday. Charlotte swallowed and picked it up with trembling fingers. The tiny piece of paper was still wedged inside, the folds fuzzy with wear. She opened it and smiled.

"I love you," she whispered. Charlotte refolded it and used the hem of David's shirt to swab a tear. She ambled to the bathroom and turned on the shower.

Maybe love was enough.

※

"Who is it?"

"It's Charlotte."

Silence.

"Just a second."

Charlotte looked around and fingered the frayed strap of her black straw purse. The door swung open, and there stood Olivia, blonde hair streaming down her shoulders in careless waves, brown eyes wide with curiosity, the aroma of gardenias wafting around her.

"What are you doing here?" she asked in that smoky voice that didn't quite jibe with her Barbie Doll looks.

"Can I come in?"

Olivia gestured for Charlotte to enter, and she shut the door. Charlotte saw several suitcases scattered around the room in various states of packing or unpacking—she wasn't sure which.

"I'd ask you if you want something to drink, but David said no booze."

Charlotte flinched, and Olivia shrugged.

"Bad joke. Have a seat."

Charlotte perched on the one corner of the room that was clear, the plush champagne-colored chair near the window. Olivia picked up a bottle of water from the nightstand and shoved a suitcase aside before sitting down. Charlotte cleared her throat as Olivia stared at her, slurping her water.

"You're probably wondering why I'm here."

"I think that's fairly obvious. You want to talk about David."

Charlotte forced a smile, wondering if this had been a good idea after all. "Right. Um. Well. You know that we're engaged."

"Right."

"And, I, well, I'm just trying to understand what the deal is with you two," Charlotte blurted out.

Olivia looked at Charlotte for a few moments before she flipped a chunk of glorious blonde tresses over her shoulder. "Okay. David and I met. We hit it off, and we dug each other."

"And?"

Olivia swished some water around her mouth before she swallowed. "The truth is, I was head over heels in love with David. Stupid in love. And he didn't feel the same way. But I didn't want to accept that. And yeah, I did some crazy stuff. You gonna tell me you've never tried to get a guy back even after he said he didn't want you?"

Charlotte looked up at the ceiling and chuckled, a long-forgotten memory struggling to the surface.

"There was this one guy, in college. He was in my Philosophy 101 class. He smelled like suntan lotion and cherry lip balm. Anyway, we were paired up as part of the same study group, and we spent hours discussing philosophy. I was enthralled by his arguments for free will versus determination. One thing led to another, and we slept together. Only, he wasn't all that interested, and I did some pretty stupid things to try to get his attention back on me." Charlotte raised an eyebrow. "So, yeah, I guess I can understand that you did some wild things to get David back."

"Maybe you and I are more alike than we realize."

"Except you like to manipulate people."

Olivia cocked her head to the side and narrowed her eyes at Charlotte. "Well, you just cut right to the chase, don't you? I admit, at first I wanted to get him back. Then I wanted to torture him for not wanting me. Then I needed his help. And he's just so fucking upstanding that, of course, he wanted to do what he could to help me. He's a giver, if you haven't noticed."

"You needed his help with the drugs."

"Yeah. The drugs. Look—it's the same sad story we've all heard about a million times. My mom was loony tunes, and my dad split when I was eight, except that he wasn't my biological dad, and my mom has no idea who the winner is on that one, though she had no less than six boys running the race. I never had anyone to take care of me. I left home when I was fifteen to live with my alkie aunt. It was only when some photographer caught me trying to steal some cheese and bread at a 7-Eleven when I was sixteen did I get a break. He turned out to be some big-time guy. He took a few pictures, sent them to a few agencies. Boom. I'm a model. And it went on from there. He's also the same asshole who introduced me to coke."

"And you got hooked."

"Yep, I got hooked. And I meet David, and he's kind and caring and amazing. Absolutely amazing. And damn, it hurt like hell that he didn't love me. That he didn't want to take care of me. When was it gonna be my turn?"

Charlotte nodded, suddenly beginning to understand the motivation behind Olivia's antics. She was still a scared and lonely little girl who just wanted to be loved.

"I tried and tried to get him back, to make him understand how much I needed him. And then I found out from a paparazzo that he was living with you, and, yeah, I wanted to push his buttons by saying I wanted to stay with you. And...I did try and get him into bed the night he checked me in here."

Charlotte's heart stopped. "You did?"

"If he could have punched me, I think he would have. He told me he was crazy in love with you. God. He wouldn't shut up talking about you." Olivia's voice quivered. "He talked about you the way I always wanted him to talk about me."

Charlotte unconsciously fingered her engagement ring. "You still love him."

"You know, I'll probably always love David, but I guess I have to move on. He didn't give me much of a choice. He doesn't want me." Olivia looked down and shook her head. "He never did. Not really."

"What made you finally realize that?"

"Honestly? Seeing the two of you at your house. He looked at you like you had hung the moon. Like I said, he talks about you in a way that…" Olivia's voice trailed off as she waved her fingers in the air like she was sprinkling fairy dust.

"Are you done with the drugs?"

Olivia chuckled. "Yep. Have to be. Too much at stake."

Charlotte nodded. "You'll find someone who'll love you the way you deserve to be loved. We all deserve that," she said finally.

Olivia sniffed and laughed as she tried to catch a tear before it dropped from her eyelid. "Well, maybe I'll find him in New York. That's where I'm headed. Ira's decided all is forgiven and is gonna let me stay in his Park Avenue apartment. He's also threatening to find me a good shrink, but we'll see. Anyway, my new movie's filming there. And I'll be starting my new ad campaign. I'm the new face of Chelsea Cosmetics, in case you hadn't heard."

"I heard."

"They've got all kinds of kick-ass things they're gonna do for my campaign. You know I'll get to do shoots in Paris, Rome, and London?" She laughed. "Not bad for trailer park trash from Miami."

"Not bad at all."

Olivia stood. "I hate to kick you out, but I've got a lot to do. I'm catching the red eye to New York tomorrow night, and I have loose ends to tie up before then."

Charlotte followed suit and slung her purse over her shoulder. "I'll let you get to it. I can show myself out."

Charlotte made her way toward the door, when Olivia called out to her. "Yeah?"

"David's a good guy, and he really loves you. Like I said, I can tell that you make him happy."

Charlotte mulled this over and smiled. "He makes me happy."

Olivia nodded, and the two women looked at each other for a moment.

"Good luck, Olivia. With everything. I really mean that."

"You know, somehow I think you do."

"Take care, Olivia." Charlotte stepped into the hallway and heard the door shut. She pulled out her BlackBerry as she waited for the elevator. She dashed off a quick text to David, and it didn't ding in response until she reached the lobby. She smiled at his reply, and as she joined the hustle and bustle of Sunset Boulevard, Charlotte felt like Charlotte again.

CHAPTER 13

Charlotte speared a juicy crumble of sausage with her fork and blew on it to cool it down. She waited a few more seconds before biting off a corner. She groaned with pleasure before she put the rest of it into her mouth. She looked at the clock. Just a few more minutes. She rummaged around in the junk drawer of the kitchen until she came up with a book of matches, which she used to light the two white tapered candles on her dining room table. She did a quick check around the kitchen. The stuffed manicotti that was cooling on the stove had come out beautifully, as spicy and pungent as the one that David had made for her at the lake. The red wine was breathing, and the chocolate-covered strawberries were perfectly chilled and arranged on a plain white plate in the refrigerator.

Charlotte wrung her hands and went into the bedroom, nervous now about whether this would work. She quickly splashed some cold water on her face and ran a bit of pressed powder across her nose and a touch of mascara across her lashes. She finished with a smear of lip gloss and a swift rake of the brush through her curls. Charlotte changed into a little black dress that had been one of her Vancouver purchases and spritzed herself with Chanel No. 5. The scent always made her smile; it had been her mother's signature scent and on special occasions was Charlotte's as well.

Charlotte heard the doorbell ring and placed her hand to her chest. She took a few deep breaths before she shoved her feet into the sandals she'd worn on the red carpet in New York. She smoothed down the front of her dress, made her way to the front door, and opened it.

David smiled, and Charlotte had to grip the doorknob to keep herself upright. He wore a simple blue linen button-down shirt and black pants. He held a bouquet of yellow calla lilies—Charlotte's favorite—bursting with color and fragrance.

"Why did you ring the doorbell?"

"I thought I'd treat this like a real date and act like a gentleman for a change."

"Cute."

David stepped inside and circled Charlotte. "My, my, my. Don't you look scrumptious."

Charlotte blushed. "Thanks. You don't look so bad yourself."

"I'm humbled to be in the presence of such sexiness."

Charlotte took the flowers and went in search of a vase. "I could say the same thing, you know."

"I won't stop you."

Charlotte giggled and filled a tall, clear vase with water before she unwrapped the flowers and placed them inside. "Can I get you some wine?"

"I'll get it." David sniffed. "If I didn't know better, I'd say that smelled suspiciously like stuffed manicotti."

"Guilty. I hope I did it justice."

"Well, we'll see if you picked up any tips."

David handed Charlotte a glass of wine and invited her to toast. "Here's to a lovely dinner."

Charlotte clinked glasses with his. "Cheers." They both sipped, and Charlotte set her glass down on the table while she grabbed the plate of bruschetta from the counter.

"Right down to the last detail, huh?" David said as he took one.

"Oh, I may throw a surprise or two in there just to keep you on your toes."

"Ah, so the shoe's on the other foot now, huh?"

Charlotte bit on a piece of bread. "It's good to change things up once in a while."

"Indeed."

As Charlotte dished up the salad and then the manicotti, they made easy, breezy small talk. William was in love with this month's conquest, and Karen's latest book had just hit the *New York Times* bestseller list. Charlotte even wiped away a smudge of tomato sauce from the corner of David's mouth, trying not to laugh at the image of the international movie star with sauce all over his face.

"I was thrilled to get your text last night. I will never delete it."

Charlotte cut a bite of pasta with her fork. "Oh, come on. All I said was 'the pleasure of your company is requested for dinner tomorrow night at Chez Taylor.' You had the better line."

"What, 'I'll be there or be square'? I thought it was a bit corny."

"It made me smile."

"My target hit the mark."

Charlotte chewed a bit and swallowed. "I went to see Olivia last night."

David choked on his wine, and Charlotte waited for him to regain his composure. "Come again?"

"I felt like she and I needed to talk, woman to woman."

"Was it a girl fight? You get down in the mud?"

"Sorry to burst your bubble, but no, there was no hair pulling, no mud-slinging. Just two adult women talking about you."

David took another sip of wine. "So? How'd it go?"

Charlotte folded her hands underneath her chin. "I get that she's spent most of her life feeling lost and alone. She somehow saw you as her savior, the man who would put all the pieces together and make her feel whole. She admitted she wanted to manipulate and torture you."

"I could have told you that much."

"Yeah, but it was *her* admitting to it. I don't know. Maybe this is the first step to her really turning her life around."

"You were right, you know."

"About what?"

"She does somehow always manage to land on her feet. She doesn't need me to hand her the parachute. I guess she told you about her cosmetics gig and the like?"

"Yeah. Sounds fun."

"And she's somewhat right about me as well. On some level, part of me did feel as though I had to 'rescue' her. I'm a giver, and Olivia's a taker, and the two should not meet." David reached across the table for Charlotte's hand. "I think that's why you and I worked so well together. You didn't need me to give you anything. You didn't need me to save you from anything. You saved me."

Charlotte shook her head, lost in thought. "No. You saved me from myself. The truth is, as much as I went around in the world like I didn't need anything but my books and occasional glasses of wine to keep me company, I was lonely. And people aren't meant to be alone. We're meant to laugh and live and, most of all, love. We're meant to love, and I'd managed to convince myself I didn't need that." Charlotte squeezed David's hand. "*You* taught me to love."

David looked down at his plate, and Charlotte realized it was because he was trying to keep himself from crying.

"Charlotte, I promise never again to let anyone or anything come between us. No more rescue missions or mystery trips or anything like that. Ever."

"I can live with that."

"I should hope so."

"Okay, and I promise to lay off the age thing, lay off the weight thing, and not be such a jerk."

"I can live with that." David kissed her hand. "Do you mind if we skip dessert?"

"But I had strawberries!"

David stood up and motioned for Charlotte to do the same. He blew out the candles before he bent down and lifted her off her feet, which made Charlotte yelp with laughter.

"We'll have them for breakfast," he said as he kissed her nose and whisked her toward the bedroom.

"What's that scar?"

"I tripped on the sidewalk and ripped a tiny little patch of skin off my foot."

"Sounds ugly."

"It was. I mean, look at the scar."

"Okay, what about this one, over here on your thigh?"

Charlotte giggled. "Are we going to spend the morning playing 'Let's dissect Charlotte's various scraps and mishaps'?"

"Sure, why not? I don't have anything to do today."

Charlotte laughed again as David continued tracing her nude body with his fingertips like an artist pushing his paintbrush across a blank canvas with light, sure strokes. They'd spent the better part of the morning examining each other's assorted bruises and marks and telling the stories behind them. David's best story had been about the scar on his knee that he received when a toddler in one of his movies had bitten him a little too hard in a scene.

"Oh." Charlotte's stomach fluttered as he grazed a nipple. "You're not playing fair."

"Feels like I am."

"No, seriously—you're going to make it so I don't want to get out of bed."

"That is the general idea," David said as he bent down to chew on Charlotte's ear.

"Well, I want to get started on a new manuscript idea I have."

David pulled back. "What's this one about?"

"I'm trying something different."

"I'm intrigued. Go on."

Charlotte propped herself up on her shoulder. "I've loved my books, each and every one of them, but I've been writing the same type of stuff for over twenty years. I'm ready to try something different."

"What'd you have in mind?"

Charlotte licked her lips, her excitement mounting. "I'm going to try writing a suspense novel. It'll still have romance elements, but less sex, more secrets, more lies, more murder."

"Anyone in particular you're trying to get some aggression out on?"

Charlotte laughed. "No, no, no. Nothing like that. It's just time to try new things."

"I'm proud of you for having the courage to step outside of yourself."

"You want to know a terrible secret?"

"Oh dear. *You're* a murderer?"

"Yes, that's it exactly. No. I've been thinking about this for a long while. The last five years, if not longer. But I've never had the courage. My books have always done well, allowed me to make a nice living, so why rock the boat? Ironically, it was Olivia who gave me the push I needed."

"Now you're really confusing me."

"I was watching her be interviewed about her new movie and how it's totally different from anything she's ever done, and it stuck with me. I just need to stop being afraid of life and just go for it."

"Let me see if I've got this straight. My ex-girlfriend inspired you to take your career in a different direction."

"Nuts, I know. However, if there's one thing I've learned in all these years of writing, it's that you never know where inspiration will come from."

"Indeed."

"Anyway, I had a couple of ideas that I wanted to make sure to get down. I'll need to talk to my publisher, see if they're on board. And I'll need to finish the draft of my current manuscript. I need to get all my work done, and fast."

"What's the rush?"

"I'm going to be on my honeymoon."

David tilted his head to the side, a small crease between his eyes. "Finishing the draft of your current book and writing down some ideas will to take you a year?"

"No."

"What are you getting at?"

"I changed my mind about waiting. Hell. Waiting for what? We love each other; we want to spend the rest our lives together. Well, I guess *I'll* be spending the rest of *my* life with you—"

"Stop it," David warned.

"All right. I'll shut up."

"I thought you wanted a proper wedding this time around. You know, Karen standing next to you in a horrific aqua dress, a hundred doves being released into the air, a twelve-piece orchestra—"

"Cut that out! I never said I wanted any of that."

"Okay, okay," David laughed. "So what kind of wedding would you like?"

"As long as it doesn't involve city hall and a honeymoon at Santa Monica Pier, I don't care what kind of wedding it is. Just soon."

David jumped up. "Today?"

Charlotte yanked David's arm down. "No, silly. Of course not today."

"Tomorrow?"

"Oh, *jeez*. How about after the movie premiere?"

"You're serious?"

Charlotte slid out of bed and dropped to one knee, the rough fibers of the carpet digging into her skin, threatening to give her a scar of her own. "David King, will you do me the honor of marrying me sooner rather than later?"

David reached down and grabbed Charlotte's hand, pulling her back into bed as he did so. "Where's *my* ring?"

"*Mmm*...how about a strawberry?"

David's eyes widened. "Strawberries. I'd almost forgotten."

"Don't ever forget the strawberries," Charlotte said as she scrambled out of bed and darted toward the kitchen, David hot on her heels.

"Still can't believe you're going to be a missus again."

"You and me both."

"I don't like that one. Makes you look 'hippy.'"

Charlotte screwed up her face as she looked in the mirror to examine the strapless white number that did indeed make her look like a wide load. "Where's Evelyn when you need her?" Charlotte mumbled to herself as she stepped off the small wooden platform in the bridal shop she and Karen had wandered into. Karen had come down from San Francisco so they could go shopping and have a big lunch later. This was the first store they'd gone into, and Charlotte about had a heart attack as she drank in the monstrous white dresses looming in front of her. Charlotte was afraid she'd be swallowed up by the countless rows of voluminous confections of tulle, taffeta, silk, satin, and chiffon, only to be spit back out on her wedding day looking like she'd been smeared in lace and white frosting.

"Who says it has to be white? Who says it even has to be a wedding dress?"

"I told you, the one 'wedding' thing I want is to feel like a bride. And that means *dress*."

Karen snorted and went back to appraising some of the dresses the sales clerk had brought out for their approval. The woman was busy digging up dresses for Karen to try on, but based on the current wedding dress selection, no one was holding out hope. Karen pulled one down from the rack and held it up for Charlotte.

"What about this one? You may avoid looking like you belong on the top of a cake."

"Gee, thanks."

"Can't say I'm not doing my official diva of honor duties."

"All right, I'll give you that. You are being a trooper." Charlotte looked at the dress again and discarded it. "Looks boxy."

Karen shrugged, and Charlotte took her turn thumbing through the rack. She found one and disappeared into the dressing room. She emerged a few moments later for Karen's inspection.

"*Eh*," Karen replied.

Charlotte looked in the mirror. "What's wrong with it? I think it looks nice."

"Too plain. You went too far in the other direction. Maybe you won't look like you belong on top of the cake, but people might think you're supposed to serve it."

"Ouch."

Karen shrugged. "I call it like I see it."

"Tell me about it."

Charlotte tried on no less than ten more dresses, but couldn't find one she liked. She almost wished she could fly Evelyn in from Vancouver to help her. Karen didn't fare much better, though it was mostly due to her own stubbornness. Even though Karen still had the same petite figure from her modeling days, give or take five pounds, she insisted on wearing her clothes three sizes too big. They gave up on finding anything in this store and went to three other bridal shops, each one more dismal than the last.

Almost out of desperation, they decided to try their luck in a department store. Amazingly, Nordstrom proved to be the pot of gold at the end of the rainbow, as they each found the perfect frocks. Karen settled on a sophisticated crinkled chiffon knee-length cocktail dress with an embellished neckline in black, the only color she deemed acceptable for a diva of honor. Charlotte squealed when she put on *the* dress: it was tea length with an overlay of tulle on satin. It had a beaded Empire waist and an A-line shape that made her look neither hippy nor too plain. The ladies couldn't help themselves—they high-fived each other in the store and decided to stop into one of Charlotte's favorite spots for margaritas, chips, and salsa.

They took a table outside, happy to lap up the waning sunlight of the early evening. Karen held up her margarita glass, the salt crystals around the rim glistening in the sun.

"To the future Mrs. Wonderful," Karen said.

Charlotte rolled her eyes but nonetheless clinked her glass with Karen and took a sip of her margarita, closing her eyes in ecstasy as the liquid slid down her throat.

"*Mmm*, that's a good margarita." Charlotte set her glass down and looked at Karen. "I wanted to thank you for today. I know tromping around bridal stores is your least favorite thing to do."

"About as much as pulling my fingernails off."

"I know, and I appreciate you taking the time to come down here and be a real diva of honor. Means a lot."

Karen took a healthy gulp of her margarita. "Listen—I know I can be opinionated and loud and raunchy, but I hope you know, at the end of the day, I just want what's best for you. Sometimes that comes out...opinionated, loud, and raunchy, but I always have your best interests at heart."

Charlotte smiled and grabbed Karen's hand. "I wouldn't have it any other way."

The waiter arrived with a sizzling skillet of beef fajitas for Karen and a massive chicken taco salad for Charlotte.

"Thank God," Karen said. "For a minute I thought we were gonna have to sing 'Kumbaya.'"

CHAPTER 14

"**D**avid! Over here!"

David turned on the red carpet and flashed a brilliant smile toward the innumerable cameras that were in action.

"Show us the ring!"

Charlotte held up her hand for inspection as an explosion of camera flashes went off in her face.

"When's the big day?"

David wagged his finger. "Like we'd tell you. We'll send you an invitation when it's all over!"

The assembled mob laughed, and David and Charlotte posed for a few more pictures. Charlotte even allowed herself to bask a bit in the attention, smiling and cracking a few jokes. This premiere had necessitated another shopping trip, but this time around, Charlotte couldn't wait to treat herself to a glamorous dress and a trip to the day spa. She had to chuckle over how much she'd changed in just a few short months. David guided her inside, where William was waiting with the flavor of the month, a redhead with alabaster skin, cherry red lips, and orbs of green glass for eyes. William swallowed his martini, kissed Charlotte, and slapped David on the back.

"Hey, kids, this is Ivanka. Ivanka, David King and his fiancée, Charlotte Taylor."

Ivanka gave them a bored, sullen nod as she picked up her just-arrived martini. "Yes, congratulations," she drawled in a thick Russian accent before rolling her eyes and finishing the martini in two gulps and signaling the bartender for another. Charlotte and David stole a glance at each other, trying to bottle their laughter.

"My friends, the jungle drums are telling me the critics are in love and the test screenings are through the roof. We should open the weekend number one when this comes out next week and will probably stay there."

"Well then, I should thank you for moving the script to the top of the pile."

William winked. "I've been tellin' you for years to stick with me. I'll never steer you wrong." He turned his attention to Charlotte. "What about you? You ready for the big day?"

"*Shhh*! Someone might hear you," Charlotte joked.

William scoffed. "Dear Charlotte, by the time I'm through, I'll have them thinking you're getting married in J-Lo's backyard next month."

Charlotte laughed and kissed William on the cheek. "Excellent!"

The houselights dimmed, and ushers moved through the throng, herding everyone inside to the theater. David looked over and saw that Ivanka had ordered another martini. He clamped a hand on William's shoulder.

"We'll save you a seat."

William nodded his understanding, and Charlotte shot William a sympathetic look before David guided her toward the theater.

"When is William going to stop wasting his time with these coat hangers with hair?"

"Probably not till they roll him into the grave and maybe not even then."

Charlotte and David sat in reserved seats near the front, and the theater began to fill rapidly. Darkness descended, and a hush fell over the crowd. The lights dimmed, and the screen went ablaze with David's name. Charlotte let out a little squeal and squeezed David's knee, who kissed her forehead in return.

Charlotte loved the movie, though it was hard to watch him make out with his beautiful costar. She held her breath during those scenes, watching them through semi-closed eyes. David grasped her hand and snuggled closer to reassure her. The audience seemed to adore the movie as well, screaming with laughter during much of it. When it was over, David and his costar, and eventually the rest of the cast and the director, stood to thunderous cheers and applause, and Charlotte's heart swelled with love and pride. David really was a phenomenal talent.

They mingled at the after-party for about an hour, one well-wisher after another coming over to gush all over David's performance. There were still more pictures to take, and Charlotte even chatted with his costar, Jillian, and her hunk of a husband, both of whom turned out to be lovely people. Charlotte saw Ivanka sulking in a corner, still pounding martinis and having a one-sided conversation with one of the busboys, whose head kept darting around in search of an exit. William was a few feet away, glad-handing a studio head. The party was in full force, but Charlotte was tired. She tickled the inside of David's hand, her signal to him she was ready to go home. He squeezed back, and they said their good-byes, making William their last stop.

Charlotte kissed William on the cheek. "We'll see you soon."

William winked. "You got it, sweetheart." He shook David's hand and clutched his shoulder. "Good job...I'll be backing the money truck up to your front door tomorrow."

"See ya...and tell Ivanka it was nice to meet her."

The two men nodded and laughed at each other, and Charlotte and David ducked out a side door where they'd instructed their limo to pick them up.

Charlotte leaned against David's shoulder. "What a night. I'm so proud of you."

"Oh yeah?"

"Oh yeah."

"Proud enough to become Mrs. David King day after tomorrow?"

"And then some. I know we wanted to head up to Lake Arrowhead first thing in the morning, but it's not going anywhere. How about we sleep in and hit the road around noon?"

"Whatever you say, Mrs. King-to-Be."

CHAPTER 15

Charlotte stood in front of the window and gulped coffee. She smiled at the lush needles dripping from the redwood trees around the lake. Had it been only mere months when she'd seen the first bursts of green spring forth from those trees as a single woman? And now she was moments away from becoming Mrs. David King. Funny how the world worked.

Charlotte slurped down the last bit of java and started humming to herself, bracing herself for the onslaught of "help" that would be arriving soon. Hendra, Emma, and Karen had appointed themselves as her court, insisting they would help the bride get ready to walk down the aisle. Charlotte really couldn't think of anything she needed. Her manicure and pedicure from the spa a few days earlier had held up, and she planned to pile her curls atop her head—befitting, she thought, for an afternoon wedding at the lake. Her dress was pressed and ready to go, and she'd go for just a touch more than her usual minimal makeup. Certainly not enough to warrant a gaggle of hens clucking over her.

Charlotte's phone rang, and she smiled when she saw it was David. The ladies had insisted on housing him in another cabin overnight.

"Don't tell me. You decided you'd rather run to the justice of the peace instead."

"Bite your tongue, Mrs. King."

"Not yet! T-minus two hours to go."

"Can't get here fast enough."

"I know. I tossed and turned all night. I couldn't wait for the sun to come up."

"Do me a favor and look outside the door."

Charlotte frowned and shuffled over to the cabin door; she opened it, and looked down. Sitting on top of the welcome mat was a blue box from Tiffany's swathed in their signature white ribbon.

"Come on, David. What is this?"

"You mean to tell me you have no idea what to do with a gift-wrapped box with your name on it?"

Charlotte snatched the box, undid the ribbon, and yanked off the top. She opened the snap of the small blue pouch inside and pulled out a sterling silver necklace with a charm dangling from the end.

"What? Oh," Charlotte gasped, her eyes brimming with tears.

"I take it you're not going to take me to task for this."

Charlotte bit her lip, the tears running into her mouth. "It's beautiful, David."

"I've told you. You saved me."

Charlotte fingered the lifesaver charm and shook her head. "You really do think of everything."

"I'll see you soon, Mrs. King."

"Not yet!" Charlotte said with an exasperated giggle. David merely laughed and hung up. Charlotte darted into the bathroom and smiled at the lifesaver charm again before undoing the clasp and securing the necklace around her throat. She swirled the charm around until it was nestled against her chest. She grabbed for a Kleenex and dabbed at her eyes, unable to take them off the charm.

Someone started banging on the front door moments before Charlotte heard it fly open.

"Hello? Is someone getting married today?" Karen bellowed.

Charlotte laughed and ran into the living room, where Karen, Hendra, and Emma had gathered.

"*Jeez.* What does a girl have to do around here for a little privacy?"

Karen flopped down on the couch. "Not get married."

"Stay on my good side, Charlotte. I'm trying to be a good Southern belle and forgive you for bewitching my man away from me," Emma drawled, and Charlotte giggled.

"I'll try to remember."

When Hendra clapped to get the ladies' attention, it elicited a roll of the eyes from Karen and a smirk from Emma. "Come now. We didn't come here to lollygag. We've got to get Charlotte ready to walk down the aisle."

"You know, Hendra, I actually don't—"

Hendra held up a hand in her infamous traffic-cop motion. "It's settled. We're staying, and we're helping."

Charlotte slammed her mouth shut as Karen snorted.

"Guess we should get started then," Charlotte mumbled.

The next hour was a flurry of preparation bordering on the preposterous. Emma, ever the women's magazine editor, appointed herself stylist for the proceedings, which meant reclining on a kitchen chair and telling Hendra and Karen what to do. Former model Karen took it upon herself to apply makeup to the face of a nervous Charlotte, who was surprised at how stunning the end result was. Hendra fussed over the bouquets and the marriage license and made sure that there were plenty of handkerchiefs on board.

Finally it was time for Charlotte to slip into her wedding dress. Her breath stopped cold in her throat as she examined herself in the bedroom's full-length mirror. The voices and images of the other women bustling around her fell away as Charlotte saw only marrying David. Her tears snapped her back to reality, and she signaled to Hendra for a handkerchief.

"I didn't realize how emotional I'd be," Charlotte said as she wiped away her tears.

"Weddings will do that," Karen said as she adjusted her own dress, a small smile tugging at the corner of her lips as she admired her form.

Hendra's frantic clapping broke the mood. "We're not done yet. Charlotte—living room."

"Oh dear," Charlotte mumbled, but followed orders.

Hendra pointed to the kitchen chair Emma had been sitting on earlier, indicating that Charlotte should now take up residence there. She cleared her throat and looked at Charlotte with laser intensity. "It's been quite a journey, hasn't it?"

Charlotte nodded. "You could say that again."

"Well, we just wanted you to know how much we love you and how happy we are for you," Emma chimed in. "Not every day one of us marries a movie star." She winked, and Charlotte blushed.

"Now you know I'm not one for tradition, but the Southern belle here tells me we've got to do the whole old, new, borrowed, and blue thing." Karen handed Charlotte a glittery gift bag. "So here goes."

Charlotte reached beneath the folds of silver tissue paper until her hand closed around an oblong box. The telltale pink stripes caused Charlotte to burst into laughter. "This better not be a thong," she said as she opened the box and pulled out a blue garter.

Emma and Hendra howled while Karen smirked. "Wouldn't you know they were fresh out of blue thongs?"

"I'll have to settle for this then!"

Emma extended her hand toward Charlotte. "Your something old."

Charlotte peered into Emma's hand to see a chunky silver bracelet.

"I was never much into diamonds—except my wedding ring, which I don't wear anymore. Anyway, my dear departed Edmund always gave me a piece of silver jewelry for our anniversary. He gave me this bracelet on our twenty-fifth. My wish for you is to have that many years and more with your movie star."

Charlotte's eyes shone with tears as she clamped the bracelet around her wrist. She reached out and pulled Emma into a fierce embrace. "Thank you."

Hendra tapped Charlotte on the shoulder. Charlotte tried stop tears from cascading down her face.

"Oh God, Hendra. I don't think I can take much more."

"Nonsense. Something borrowed." She thrust a red velvet pouch toward Charlotte, who undid the drawstrings to find a flower-shaped brooch studded in crystals. "This brooch was given to me by my mother-in-law on my wedding day. It was passed down through her family, dating back to the seventeen hundreds to hear her tell it. Every bride in our family has worn it as she went down the aisle, and we like to think it's a good omen for a happy marriage. And so now you'll be a part of our family tradition."

Charlotte shook her head. "I don't know what to say."

Hendra pinned the brooch on Charlotte and stepped back. "I've heard *thank you* is a good way to go."

"Ah. My manners. Thank you!" Charlotte held out her arms to her friends, her surrogate family, and they all embraced. "I'm so lucky to have you all. And thank you for being here today and for your lovely gifts. Most of all, thank you for letting David stay here last spring!"

"We do deserve some of the credit, don't we?" Emma mused.

"All right, all right," Karen clucked. "Enough with this lovefest. Let's get this show on the road."

The sun shone high and bright in the sky, and birds chattered incessantly, to Charlotte a sure indication they were as happy as she was. She peeked around the corner to the small cluster of chairs planted on the lush grass in front of the lake, the guests filling them looking at David, who stood ramrod straight at the makeshift altar. Charlotte tilted her head to the side, drinking him in. He wore a dark blue morning suit with a shiny gray shirt and matching tie. He kept fidgeting, rare for the normally confident David. It made Charlotte smile. William stood next to him in an equally dashing suit, though he seemed his usual relaxed self.

"Marry Me" by Train began to play softly in the background, courtesy of a local DJ, and Karen adjusted her dress one last time.

"You ready, Charotica?"

"Stop that. Now come on. It's almost time for you to go."

"See you on the other side," Karen said as she squared her shoulders and began her march down the aisle. Charlotte closed her eyes and took a deep breath.

It was time.

Charlotte stood at the top of the aisle as everyone rose and turned to look at her. As soon as David saw Charlotte, he couldn't stop smiling. She winked at him and gave him her own small smile before she made her way toward him. She ignored all the eyes on her; David was her sole focus. As she got closer, he held his hand out to her. She placed her fingers in his palm and joined his side. The music stopped, and Minister Lloyd, a friend of Karen's, cleared her throat and began. Charlotte didn't remember hearing her welcome everyone. She tuned back in long enough to hear Emma's reading of "I Promise." She zoned back out again as Minister Lloyd talked about the power of love. Charlotte just couldn't stop staring at David and thinking how soon they'd be husband and wife.

"Charlotte?"

She blinked and realized the minister was calling on her to say her vows. Everyone tittered, and David squeezed the hand he hadn't let go of the entire time.

"Sorry." Charlotte blushed and cleared her throat. She plucked the tiny square of paper she'd pinned to the underside of her bouquet and unfolded it, the creases sticking together. She opened her mouth to read, when she realized the flowers were in the way, so she turned and handed them to Karen. She looked back down at the paper, her voice quivering.

"David...I thought I had it all figured out. I was an independent woman who didn't need love. In fact, I had decided my chance for love had passed me by, and I was okay with that. At least I thought I was. And then you jumped into the back of my Jeep, of all things, and suddenly all my preconceived notions about, well, everything, changed. When you came into my life, you showed me how to love. How to be loved. You brought life into my life. And I thank—and will continue to thank—God, every day for the gift of being loved by you and the honor of loving you." Charlotte folded up the paper and looked at David. "I look forward to loving you, David, for the rest of my life," she whispered.

The minister nodded at David, who took Charlotte's hands in his. He looked at the ground, silent for a few moments, as he gathered his words.

"My dear Charlotte. From the first time we met, I knew you were special. You were unlike anyone I'd ever met before, and from that moment, I knew I'd never meet anyone like you ever again. And so I decided then and there I was never letting you go; I didn't care how much you protested. And my God, did you protest. Charlotte, you amaze me every day with your incredible reservoir of strength, your humor, your kindness, and your patience. Your love has been an astonishing gift that I will treasure until my last breath. Today and every day, I promise to love and care for you. I promise to honor and respect you and do everything I can to inspire and encourage you the way you've done for me. Forever doesn't seem long enough, but that's how long I will love you, with all my heart and all my soul." David kissed one of her hands. "I love you, Charlotte."

Minister Lloyd smiled. "David, Charlotte, the vows you have exchanged are but fleeting words, the sound of which is soon gone. It is your wedding ring that symbolizes the enduring promises you have made to each other." She looked to Karen and William. "The rings, please?" They obliged, and the minister turned to David. "Bless this ring that David bestows upon Charlotte; may it ever abide in unity, love, and happiness for the rest of your lives." She placed the ring in David's palm. "David, please place the ring on Charlotte's finger and repeat after me."

David chuckled. "Funny enough, I just did a movie in which I got married. It's going to come in handy now."

Everyone laughed as the minister turned the floor over to David. He held up Charlotte's ring: another eternity band of diamonds that connected to her engagement ring.

"I, David, take you, Charlotte, to be my wife. To have and to hold, in sickness and in health, for richer, for poorer, in joy and sorrow, I promise my love to you, with this ring, as long as we both shall live." He slipped it on Charlotte's finger.

Charlotte whispered, "That was pretty good. Hard act to follow."

David winked. "You'll do all right."

Charlotte took David's ring from the minister, a wide platinum band inscribed: *Love, Charlotte*. She asked the minister to repeat the words and slipped the ring on David's finger. She then looked to the minister.

"By the power vested in me, I now pronounce you husband and wife. David, *you* may now kiss your bride."

"Finally," David groaned as he drew Charlotte's face into his and kissed her long and hard before he dipped her to the delight of the crowd. He brought her back up and kissed her again, and when he started to pull back, Charlotte draped her arms around him and held on tight. They were both laughing as they broke apart, and the DJ played "She Will Be Loved" by Maroon 5 as they made their way down the aisle.

※

"I thought I'd never get you alone!"

"You want to have a go-round right here in front of everyone then?"

Charlotte rolled her eyes. "Oh yeah, the dream of my life is to get it on in front of everyone at my wedding."

"We almost sort of did when we were pronounced husband and wife."

"Good point. In all seriousness, I have something for you. Two things, actually."

"Pray tell?"

"I wanted to give this to you afterward, away from everyone." Charlotte handed him a small box. David hefted it and shook it. Charlotte giggled and slapped his shoulder before he opened it.

"Wow. Charlotte, this is…this is stunning."

"Turn it over."

David freed the heavy platinum watch from its case and flipped it over. "No more time to waste."

Charlotte snaked her arms around David's waist. "I promise you, today and forever, not to waste time on anything other than loving you and being the best wife I can be."

"I never had a doubt," David whispered as he put the watch on and kissed Charlotte.

"Part of that brings me to gift number two." Charlotte handed David a small envelope.

"I'm starting to feel like a lad at Christmas. Can I get a hint?"

"You know the drill. No questions. Open."

David ripped it open and pulled out two plane tickets. "What's all this, then?

Charlotte tried to keep from smiling, waiting for David to look at the destination. He gasped.

"My God. You booked us a trip to London?"

Charlotte nodded, giddy. "Surprise!"

"But you said you didn't want a big fancy honeymoon!"

"I lied. You said you haven't been back to London in years, and I've never been there, *sooo*…"

"You're already turning out to be the best wife a man could ever hope for."

"I'm glad you're pleased with the goods."

"Indeed."

Small tents had been set up on the lawn with tables for dinner and a wooden dance floor. Charlotte and David hired a caterer to recreate the first meal they'd had together at the cabin: old-fashioned spaghetti and meatballs, antipasti salad, and buttery garlic bread. Charlotte stood up to eat hers, wondering why on earth she'd thought a dinner full of tomato sauce and meatballs that might get a notion to sit in her lap was a good idea. She expelled a sigh of relief when she made it through without incident. The wine flowed freely, and just after dinner, William stood, clinking his fork to the side of his glass.

"Everyone, everyone…may I have your attention, *please*." A hush fell over the guests as William cleared his throat and held the stem of his champagne glass between both hands.

"What a day this has been. I've known David for more years than I will admit here tonight in front of all these lovely ladies. When David first told me about Charlotte, my God, I couldn't shut him up. How beautiful she was, how much she made him laugh, how much they had in common. No woman ever inspired such poetry out of this guy, so even before I met Charlotte, I knew she was the one. Charlotte, you've made David happy, which makes me happy, so I get the feeling we're all gonna be a bunch of smiling idiots for years to come." William raised his glass. "To David and Charlotte."

Everyone cheered and took a hearty guzzle of champagne before Karen stood and cleared her throat several times in an exaggerated effort to get everyone to quiet down.

"If I didn't know better, I'd think you all were trying to ignore me," she groused.

"We are!" Angela piped up, which drew laughter from everyone.

"Yeah, yeah, yeah. All right. Sometimes, when our friends and loved ones fall in love, you see changes in them, and not always for the better. But David, since Charlotte deigned to let you knock down that fifty-foot wall she had up around her heart, I've seen some pretty outstanding changes in her. She's confident and happy and content. The peace and serenity I see in Charlotte I know is all due to you. I'm not gonna tell you to live happily ever after because I don't believe in that. What I do believe in is letting each other know every day how much the other person is appreciated. Let the other person know how much his or her opinion matters to you, even when it is wrong. Most important, never forget the reasons you fell in love with each other in the first place. Charlotte, David, I love you both and wish you nothing but the best. Cheers."

The room exploded in applause, and Charlotte and David both swallowed Karen up in hugs.

"And all this time I thought you didn't get sentimental." Charlotte grinned.

"Only on special occasions," she muttered as she downed the rest of her champagne.

⚜

After David and Charlotte had their first dance to "You Really Got a Hold on Me," the reception turned raucous. David took a turn dancing with each lady to one rollicking rock-and-roll classic after another. A dateless William, "out of respect for the occasion," followed suit and burned up the dance floor as well, even leading a conga line at one point.

Charlotte was sipping white wine and chatting with Angela when David came up from behind and clamped his hands around Charlotte's waist.

"Do you mind if I steal my bride for a few moments?"

Angela took a swig of her wine. "All yours, babe."

Charlotte leaned against David, and they swayed together to "God Only Knows" by the Beach Boys.

"Hmm. That's interesting."

"What's that?"

David nodded his head toward Karen and William, who were playfully slow dancing and singing the lyrics to each other. "Sparks are flying."

"You think?"

"Oh yeah."

Charlotte tilted her head and considered this. "God—they'd be perfect for each other."

"Indeed. The perennial playboy and the sassy siren. Perfectly matched. Their chemistry is obvious."

"Think so?"

"*Hmm-mmm*. I do know a thing or two about chemistry. It *is* my business, after all. You and I had chemistry off the charts."

"That a fact?"

"Yup. I knew I was going to get you. You can't walk away from that kind of heat."

"Oh, so you were trying just to get into my pants?"

David nibbled on Charlotte's ear. "And then some."

Charlotte laughed. "Well, I and my pants are glad you succeeded."

"I can't wait to show you London."

"I can't wait to see it. Day after tomorrow—I'm so excited."

"Would it be rude if we left our own party early?"

"I think everyone will understand." Charlotte looked to see William and Karen duetting on "I Got You Babe." "Besides, what do they need us for when they have Sonny and Cher?"

⚜

"Close your eyes!"

"For what?"

"Because I want to do this right?"

"Listen, if you were doing this right, you'd have let me carry you over the threshold!"

"We can do that when we get home. Now come on, close them!"

David heaved a big sigh and cooperated. "Okay, they're closed."

Charlotte gave herself one last glance in the mirror before she turned out the light and stepped into the cabin's bedroom. A single candle flickered next to the bed, throwing Charlotte's shadow against the wall and illuminating David's perfectly still silhouette. Charlotte stood at the foot of the bed, placed one hand on her hip, and let the other fall to her side.

"Okay. Open."

David looked at Charlotte, his eyes bugging out of his head. "Oh. Wow."

"You like it?"

"That's not the word."

Charlotte looked down at the simple black Empire-waist nightie, its triangle cups trimmed in tiny ruffles, a little black bow nestled between her breasts. "Sounds like you approve."

"Is it new?"

"Yes. No. Sort of. I bought it a few years ago, for no other reason than I thought it was pretty. This is actually the first time I've ever worn it. Never had a reason to."

"Well, Mrs. King, I'm honored to be the first and last man to see it."

"For sure."

David held out his hand to Charlotte, who walked around to the side of the bed. His eyes shimmered with equal parts love and lust. "Turn around for me so I can get the full effect." Charlotte giggled as she did a slow twirl, which elicited a low whistle from David.

"As unbelievably sexy as this is, I hope you won't be disappointed, because you're not going to be wearing it for long," David said as he brushed his fingers against Charlotte's thigh.

"Oh, thank God. It was starting to get a little itchy."

David laughed and pulled her down on the bed. They began to kiss, and Charlotte moaned as David pressed his palm against one nipple.

"I want to make love to every inch of you," David whispered.

Charlotte held his face in her hands. "What are you waiting for?"

David needed no further invitation. As promised, he slid Charlotte's nightgown over her head and dropped it to the floor. He bent his head down to her unadorned breasts. He laid gentle kisses across the plump mounds, nuzzling his face against her nipples. Charlotte gulped and glued her legs around his waist, hoping she wouldn't explode too early. David continued to kiss the length of her body before masking his face with her now-throbbing center. He continued to nestle against her, his nose brushing against her. With a soft, juicy tongue, David slid inside her, and Charlotte gripped the side of the bed, the bomb seemingly ready to detonate whether or not she wanted it to. David wound his head around like a spinning top, and Charlotte rotated her hips to meet his movements. She was barely able to scream into a pillow before she came. David increased his sucking, and Charlotte lost control, the orgasm reverberating inside her like taut guitar strings being plucked. Charlotte began to convulse, and David released her, easing her down to the mattress.

"Good?" David whispered

Charlotte gave him a feeble thumbs-up, and David merely chuckled before he kissed her. She shifted a bit underneath him and wrapped her hand around him. She whimpered at how hard he was and raised toward him, guiding him inside her. It was David's turn to moan as he inched into her, relishing each descent. He hooked one arm under her leg and, mimicking his earlier movements, rotated, pressing against Charlotte with slow intensity. Revived, Charlotte pushed up, supporting herself on one leg, the other splayed toward the floor. David pushed harder, his sweat dripping onto her chest. Charlotte rushed to meet him, another orgasm on the horizon. They both grunted, and just as Charlotte tightened around him, David screamed and then let out a cry. They crumpled into the mattress, their frantic pants the only sound in the room.

"That was the best sex I've ever had," David gasped.

"Must be because we're married."

"My God. If I'd known that, I would have married you months ago."

"Gives us something to look forward to."

David snuggled against a limp Charlotte. "Rest up, Mrs. King. We've got a long night ahead of us."

CHAPTER 16

Charlotte frowned as she flipped through the electronic gallery on her computer. She could have sworn there was a picture of her and David in front of Big Ben. Several, in fact. She continued to click through the photos until she found them.

"Hiding at the end, I see," Charlotte muttered as she selected them to be a part of her album. She had decided to surprise David with a book of pictures from their wedding day and London honeymoon. Charlotte smiled as she thought about the seven days they'd spent there. They did all the touristy stuff, of course: Madame Tussauds, the changing of the guard at Buckingham Palace, Kew Gardens, Kensington Palace, now the site of Princess Diana's memorial, and lunch at Trafalgar Square, though Charlotte was disappointed they wouldn't be able to feed the famed pigeons, as the mayor had recently banned the practice.

Her favorite had been Piccadilly Circus. It was a lot different from when David had been there last, and certainly since his childhood, but he still loved showing her the various shops and stores. They'd taken two dozen pictures there alone. They visited his old neighborhood, and the administrators at the Royal Academy were all too happy to let one of their most famous alums poke around for a bit.

Charlotte liked the food better than she'd anticipated, having been warned by Karen about the bland, heavy cuisine the British adored. Karen had been to London on two book tours and had predicted that Charlotte would be "ready to buy, borrow, or steal a Big Mac, fries, and Coke before it was all over."

Charlotte adored afternoon tea, craved fish and chips—even a week after being home—and thought bangers and mash was about the tastiest thing she'd ever had in her life. Her only misstep had been the steak and kidney pie, which David scarfed down like a man who'd just been given his last meal. The weather had been a brisk seventy degrees with only one day of light rain. David had been overjoyed to be back home, and much as he had been in New York, he felt at ease walking the streets without fear of being mobbed by overzealous women.

Charlotte finished selecting her pictures and processed her order, choosing expedited delivery. In less than a week, her album would arrive shiny and new, chock-full of pictures documenting their relatively short time as husband and wife.

Charlotte switched her computer over to the outline she was working on for her new project. Her editor was flying from New York later that week to talk about the new direction Charlotte wanted to take with her books, and she wanted to have everything buttoned up before that meeting.

She spent the rest of the day in the zone, typing away on her outline and starting to develop character profiles. Charlotte was concentrating so hard that she never heard David creep up behind her and plant a kiss on her neck.

"Oh God, you scared me!" Charlotte whipped around to see David kneeling in front of her, a devilish grin on his face.

"Gotcha."

"Not funny." Charlotte looked at her computer clock. "Shoot. I planned to have this gorgeous meal waiting for you when you walked in the door. Looks like frozen pizza."

"Actually, I'm not all that hungry, but I am in desperate need of a shower in case you couldn't tell."

"Well, I didn't want to embarrass you…"

"I did say your kindness was one of the things I loved most about you." David stood and grimaced.

"What's wrong?"

David straightened up and groaned. "My back's been sore all day. Guess I slept funny. See what you're doing to me, woman?"

"I can call a chiropractor. I know a great one."

David waved Charlotte off. "I'm fine. The steam from the shower should fix me up. Why don't you fire up that pizza and break into a bottle of wine? By the time I get out, I should be ravenous."

"You sure? I mean, because it's no trouble."

"It's nothing…honestly." David tweaked her nose. "Can't wait to dig into that pizza." He winked as he headed to the bathroom.

Charlotte watched David's retreating back before she whirled around to her Rolodex and flipped to her chiropractor's number. She picked up the phone to dial, but then dropped the phone back in its cradle. David was right. It was a crick in his back—nothing to sound the alarm about. Charlotte launched herself out of her chair and headed to the kitchen to make dinner.

Charlotte leaned back in her chair and smiled. She hadn't felt this invigorated by writing in she didn't know how long. The meeting with her editor was tomorrow, and Charlotte couldn't wait to share what she had so far.

Satisfied with how her workday was shaping up, and thrilled at the new possibilities, she started to hum as she headed to the kitchen in search of some chocolate chip cookies. She went out to the living room and was surprised to see David drag himself in.

"Hey! What—What are you doing here? I didn't think you'd be home until after dinnertime."

David flopped on the couch and closed his eyes. "My back's still bothering me, and I'm feeling a bit run down."

"Again? You said the other day it was feeling better."

"Sadly, it's back to feeling not better today." David's face twisted into a slight scowl as he eased himself down on the couch.

"Enough said. I'm making an appointment with my chiropractor tomorrow. No excuses."

"Charlotte—"

"Silence. Mrs. King has spoken."

"You sure are turning into a bossy wife."

"Part of my charm. I bet I know what this is. We'd been back only about a day when you had to report to set, and you've been working nonstop since. You just need a few days to get your momentum back, that's all. You said you'd have this weekend off, right?"

"So they're telling me."

"All right then, we'll get you in to the see the doctor tomorrow or the next day, and then I'll spend the whole weekend fluffing your pillows and making you tea."

"Well the prospect of my pillows being fluffed…"

Charlotte giggled and joined David on the couch. "Now I know something's wrong. You didn't kiss me when you came in."

"Damn. I'm falling down on the job, and it's only been a few weeks."

"I'll let it slide since you're not feeling well. I'm just glad the job's here in L.A. We can stay put for the next six months. Play all night. Once you're better, of course."

David chuckled. "And then off to Chicago and Boston after that. Hope you'll come with me."

"I'm sure I can squeeze in a few weeks here and there."

"One can only hope."

Charlotte looked at David and noticed for the first time how pale he was. She cupped the palm of her hand against his forehead, which felt like an oil slick.

"David, you feel clammy. Maybe it's not fatigue. Maybe you're coming down with the flu."

"You're probably right. I'm gonna take a nap."

Charlotte frowned, still concerned over how he looked. "Okay. Listen, I'll take a crack at making you my mom's chicken soup. Always made me feel better when I was sick."

David smiled. "Sounds perfect." He kissed her. "See you later."

Charlotte checked her phone to see if the chiropractor had called back with an appointment time for David. He never woke up to have any of the chicken soup she'd made, and he barely trudged out of bed in the morning to make his call time on the set. She tried to convince him to stay home, but he insisted on going to work.

Charlotte smiled when she saw her editor, Tonya, making her way back to the table. She squeezed into the booth.

"Sorry about that. Our dog is sick, and my partner is no good in a crisis."

"I hope everything's okay."

"Oh yeah. She's just old. The dog, not my partner."

The women laughed, and Charlotte watched her as she took a sip of coffee. Tonya was far from the epitome of a glamorous New York City editor.

She was easily 250 pounds, still plagued with acne, and forever trying to contain her blonde Brillo-pad frizzies inside of a tight bun, but always to no avail. Unruly coils always sprang from her head like Medusa's snakes.

Tonya set her cup down. "I'm so excited about your project, and I can't wait to read your draft."

Charlotte nodded and sipped her coffee. "It's been a bit of a challenge, but in a good way. I haven't felt this invigorated in a long time." Charlotte chuckled and shook her head. "I don't think I've ever felt this wonderful. My life has finally fallen into place."

"Ah, yes. Wedded bliss to the gorgeous movie star. How *is* that going?"

"Heavenly. Well, except he's a little under the weather, but other than that, wonderful."

"Having known you all these years, I've never seen you look so happy. My grandmother, God rest her soul, always said a happy marriage was the fountain of youth."

"Well then, I guess I'll outlive David after all." Charlotte winked.

"Oh, honey, my sister married a younger man, and she says it's the best thing that ever happened to her."

Charlotte smiled. "Ditto."

❦

Charlotte turned over in bed and flinched as her knee hit a patch of cold, wet sheet. Her eyes flicked open. She sat up. David was drenched in sweat, and some of the moisture had seeped to Charlotte's side. He'd come home early again and had been asleep when Charlotte got back from her lunch with Tonya. She didn't have the heart to wake him and had fallen asleep next to him a few hours later.

Charlotte swung her legs around to the side of the bed and ran over to David's side. He was curled up in a ball, fast asleep.

"David. David, honey, wake up."

David didn't respond, so Charlotte grabbed a cold compress from the bathroom and riffled through the medicine cabinet for some flu tablets. She filled a glass with some water and went back to David. She placed the compress against his head, which caused him to stir a bit.

"Charlotte, I've never felt so sick. My legs and back are both sore, and I'm exhausted," he murmured. "Do you think I caught something in London?"

"*Shh, shh, shh.* It's probably something going around. Here, take this."

David popped the tablets and took a healthy gulp of water. He dropped his head back against the pillow, the sheer effort of that task draining him.

"I'll call William, have him call in sick for you—"

"No, no. I'll be fine. The show must go on."

"Not if you feel like crap."

"A lot of people are depending on me to be there. I have to push through, no matter how awful I feel."

Charlotte sighed, seeing there was no reasoning with him. "Okay. Make me a deal. If you're not better by the end of the day tomorrow, we're going to a doctor."

David closed his eyes and nodded. "Yes, Mrs. King."

Charlotte had been staring at her computer screen for the better part of an hour, unable to erase the image of a pale and shaky David peeling himself from his sickbed to report to the set. She chewed her fingernails and wondered if she should try calling him. Just as she picked up the phone, it rang, William's number flashing in front of her. Her heart lurched.

"William?" she asked, already knowing something was terribly wrong.

"Hey, kid…you need to get down here. David just collapsed."

CHAPTER 17

"He's going to be okay. He's probably just dehydrated or something like that," Charlotte said out loud to herself as she waited for the light to change. She pounded the steering wheel in frustration over David's stubbornness and her having accommodated it. She should have put her foot down that first day and made him go to the doctor. The light turned green, and Charlotte peeled out. The movie was doing some location shooting in Beverly Hills, so she didn't have to go far. Charlotte found the restaurant William had directed her to. Not that she could have missed it with all the camera crews, lighting, trailers, and trucks surrounding it. She screeched into an empty spot near a truck and bolted out of the car. William spotted her and motioned her over to him.

"How is he? Is he okay?"

"He's in his trailer; we've got the medics looking at him. He's on oxygen, but refusing to go the hospital."

Charlotte gulped as William led her to David's trailer, which was surrounded by paramedics. They parted when they saw William.

Charlotte had to keep herself from gasping at David's appearance. He was gray, and it looked like he'd lost twenty pounds just since that morning. An oxygen mask covered his face, and his black hair was plastered against his forehead like masking tape. He was propped up in bed, and two medics were taking his vitals. Charlotte took a deep breath and went around to grab his hand.

"Will, I told you, I'm fine. You didn't need to bring Charlotte down here."

"Listen, pal, you look like hell, and when you look like hell, I call the wife. End of discussion."

Charlotte looked at everyone. "Could we have a few moments, please?"

The paramedics started to protest, but William cut them down with a stare, and they all got up to leave.

"Charlotte, we'll be right outside."

David sighed and rubbed his neck.

"Is your neck bothering you?"

"A bit. Seriously, Charlotte, I'm fine. Will just overreacted."

"David, you need to go to the hospital. Let a doctor look at you and help you get well."

David looked at Charlotte. "Let's just go home, huh? You promised me some pillow fluffing and pampering."

Charlotte looked into his eyes. "David, this isn't a joke."

"Do you see me laughing?"

"Do you see *me* laughing? I want you well and whole again, and the only way that's going to happen is if you go to the hospital." A tear slipped down Charlotte's cheek. "Please. For me. Please."

David reached out to wipe away Charlotte's tears before he hung his head in defeat. "No tears, love. I can't stand to see you cry. I'll go to the hospital."

Charlotte closed her eyes, relief washing over her. "Thank you."

"On one condition, though?"

"I don't think you're in much of a position to negotiate."

"I don't want to be wheeled out of here like some invalid. I will walk out of this trailer, and either you or William will drive me. I can't stand to see my pale visage splashed across any tabloids."

"Okay. I think we can manage that."

David nodded and made an effort to stand before he grunted and toppled right back onto the bed.

"David!"

"No, no, I'm just a bit dizzy. Let me just get my bearings," he said as he struggled once more to get to his feet. Charlotte watched in horror as he collapsed to the floor like a rumpled sweater. She rushed over to help him, tears pricking her eyes once again. She helped him back up to the bed. David was panting like he'd just run around the block.

"Hold on, baby; we're gonna get you to the hospital," Charlotte said as she planted a kiss on his damp forehead. Charlotte flung open the door of the trailer and clambered down its steps. William and the two paramedics turned, startled. William grabbed her by her forearms, his face crinkled with worry.

"What? What is it, Charlotte?"

Charlotte tried to keep her composure, but it was too much. She broke down, sobbing. "We have to take David to the hospital. Something's really wrong."

CHAPTER 18

Charlotte had never been in an ambulance before. She'd been annoyed by them on occasion as they blared their sirens and flashed their lights to get people out of the way. They were too loud, or they made her late.

Never in her wildest dreams did Charlotte think her very life could hinge on an ambulance being able to get to the hospital in a timely manner. The paramedics had put David back on oxygen and kept monitoring his vitals. With his face obscured behind the mask and his dark swirls of hair now limp ringlets against his forehead, Charlotte barely recognized David. All she could do was hold his hand with as much assurance as she could muster, a faint smile painted on her lips. She didn't dare show him how terrified she was.

William had followed in his car and had called ahead to the hospital with explicit instructions about what should happen when they arrive. The ambulance pulled into the emergency room bay, and a cadre of nurses and doctors flooded out to meet them. The doors of the ambulance swung open, and Charlotte barely had time to scramble out of the rig before the wheels of David's gurney slammed against the asphalt. Charlotte's fingertips grazed the metal railing at his feet as she ran to keep up with him while he was rushed into the ER. The sterile, antiseptic smell mixed with the stench of vomit and urine ripped through Charlotte's nostrils, and she almost gagged, reminded of those days in the hospital with Ben's girlfriend. She blinked to clear her mind.

It wasn't going to turn out like that. It just wasn't.

"Ma'am, please step aside. We need to run some tests," one of the nurses shouted at her as the team began to hook David up to a mass of beeping, blinking machines.

"Please, I'm his wife...Let me stay with him."

One of the doctors nodded at the nurse, and Charlotte thought that meant she'd be allowed to stay. She didn't understand it was code for "Get this woman out of here now so we can work—I don't care *who* she is." The nurse took Charlotte by the elbow and gently guided her out.

"Ma'am, we need to stabilize your husband's condition first, and then we'll run some tests so we can determine what's wrong. The doctor will be out later to give you additional information."

Before Charlotte could open her mouth to ask what kinds of tests they wanted to run or what could be causing the problem, the nurse raked the thin yellow curtain shut with an authoritative snap.

Charlotte's shoulders sank, and her knees buckled. A hand reached out to steady her, and she gasped, but was relieved to see it was William. She shriveled into his arms, crying, as he led her to the waiting room. He sat her down in a chair, taking the one next to her.

"He's gonna be okay, Char. I've got the chief of staff in there working on him. The man's an institution. David's in good hands."

"I told him if he didn't feel better by today I was taking him to the doctor. William, what if I waited too long? What if—"

William held up his hand and shook his head. "You and I know better than anyone he's a stubborn son of a bitch. Believe me, when I showed up on set today and saw how bad he looked, I spent half the morning trying to convince him to go the hospital. I was arguing with him about it when he passed out. Don't you dare blame yourself. This isn't anybody's fault."

Charlotte shook her head. "But I knew something was wrong. I should have insisted."

William handed Charlotte a handkerchief. "Listen, the guy thinks he's invincible. He's probably in there right now arguing with the doctors to let him check out."

Charlotte laughed in spite of herself. "You're probably right."

The wait was interminable. The meager selection of magazines from at least two years ago held little interest for Charlotte. As did talking. As did nibbling on the pretzels, or M&M's, or the vanilla sandwich crèmes William offered her. She watched, unseeing, a relentless spool of afternoon court shows that sprawled across the screen of the waiting room's TV. If she'd cared enough, she would have asked them to turn the channel. Or better yet, to turn it off. The only thing Charlotte wanted was to have the doctor come out and tell her all David needed was some ginger ale, a few crackers, and a good night's sleep.

It was nearly eight in the evening when the tall, angular doctor who had subtly ordered Charlotte out of David's room earlier ambled out. His grim expression told her that this was more than ginger ale could cure. Charlotte gripped the armrest of the chair, suddenly afraid of the words this man would speak. William rose and greeted the doctor with a handshake. The two men murmured a few unintelligible words to each other before the doctor came over to Charlotte, taking the chair across from her. William remained standing.

"Mrs. King, I'm Dr. New, chief of staff, and I want to give you an update on David's condition."

Charlotte gulped and nodded. "Okay."

"Once we got David stabilized, we ran a series of tests, including X-rays and a CT scan. What we found is that David has an aortic aneurysm."

"A what?" Charlotte blurted out, her confusion and terror reaching a fever pitch. *Aorta.* That meant *heart.*

"What that means is his aorta, which extends from the heart and is the body's largest artery, is swelling. That's usually an indication of some kind of weakness in the wall of the aorta. If it ruptures, death is instant if it goes untreated. It looks like David experienced a tear, which caused him to hemorrhage and explains the pain he's been experiencing the past few days."

Charlotte's head was swimming in words as she tried to untangle what he was saying. *Aorta, rupture, aneurysm.* She was having a hard time trying to keep up.

"Dr. New, what are our options?" William chimed in.

"Surgery is the only alternative. David's pretty young to have this condition, since aortic dissections typically occur in people in their fifties and sixties, so my guess is that it's genetic."

"David's father was in his forties when he died of a heart attack," Charlotte said.

"Then that would explain it. It's a good thing you brought him in when you did. Unfortunately, most people die before they know what's happening. Because we're catching this fairly early, David's chances look good."

"What happens now?" Charlotte asked.

"He's in being prepped for surgery. Our chief cardiac surgeon, Dr. Curtis, will perform the surgery. She's the best."

Charlotte couldn't help it—she snorted. "People always say that."

"Come again?"

"How many times do you hear 'He's a gifted surgeon' or 'She's the best,' and then people die?"

Dr. New clasped Charlotte's hand, staring into her eyes. "Ten years ago my wife had cardiac arrhythmia, which meant her heart couldn't pump any blood. She had to have a transplant, which Adrienne performed. My wife just turned fifty-two last week, and she's never been healthier. I literally trust Dr. Curtis with my life. David's getting top-notch treatment. I promise."

Charlotte dropped her face into her hands, tears quivering throughout her. She blew her nose in the handkerchief William had given her earlier and shook her head. "I'm sorry. This is just all so much to take in."

Dr. New squeezed Charlotte's hand. "I know it is. But believe me, he's going to pull through."

Charlotte closed her eyes and nodded. "Thank you."

"Of course. I'm going to have the nurse take you up to surgery so you can see David before he goes in."

Charlotte offered a thin smile as Dr. New gave her a reassuring pat on the shoulder, and William shook his hand. Charlotte slumped against the hard chair, fear and exhaustion tugging at every fiber.

"It's all gonna be okay," William said as he sat down next to Charlotte. "David's a fighter. He's gonna pull through."

"I hope you're right," Charlotte whispered.

"Mrs. King?" a short bleached-blonde nurse with black roots and ruby red lips was standing in front of Charlotte.

"Yes?"

"Dr. New asked me to take you to surgery so you can see your husband." She gestured toward the elevator. William and Charlotte followed her, the click-clack of his loafers and the flip-flop of her sandals against the shiny tile floor a sharp contrast to the soft clomp of the nurse's bright orange Crocs. They all rode in silence up to the eighth floor. Charlotte kept her eyes trained on the elevator panel, while William checked his watch and cleared his throat at least ten times. The nurse merely stared straight ahead, cracking her gum.

When they reached the surgical floor, the ER nurse took them through a maze of hallways until they finally got to the pre-op room. David was propped up in bed, an oxygen mask a shroud across his face, his skin the shade of the stark white bedsheet. His eyes were sunken pits, and his entire body sagged like a rag doll against the bed. He held up a hand in a meek attempt at a wave. Charlotte rolled a stool to his bedside and took his hand. Charlotte was surprised at the strength of his grasp. She caressed his forehead, and David blinked his eyes in appreciation.

"You know, if you didn't want to do this movie, you could have just said so," William said.

David held up his other hand and gave William the finger. Charlotte giggled and William let out a hearty laugh.

"I knew you had to be hiding in there."

Charlotte looked into David's eyes. "Sweetheart, you know they said your chances with this surgery are really good since they caught it so early. You're gonna be just fine. You'll be back home before you know it."

David gave Charlotte a thumbs-up, and before she could speak, a stunning Asian woman with long, glossy black hair dressed in blue scrubs poked her head around the curtain.

"Mrs. King? I'm Dr. Curtis, and I'll be performing your husband's surgery," she said in the smoothest of English with a hint of Midwestern twang.

Charlotte and Dr. Curtis shook hands, and the woman looked at David.

"We're going to be wheeling you into the operating room shortly, Mr. King. You ready?"

David nodded, and Charlotte couldn't believe how brave he was being. Dr. Curtis turned back to Charlotte.

"If all goes well, the procedure should take about four hours. You'll notice a plasma screen in the surgery suite that will give you updates on the surgery."

"Wow...that's so high-tech," Charlotte said.

"We understand that friends and family want to be kept apprised of the situation. Just another evolution in the world we live in." She turned to David. "I'm going to scrub up, and I'll see you afterward." She looked at Charlotte. "I'll be out to talk to you when it's over...let you know how everything went."

Two nurses came in and announced they'd be by in a few minutes to take David to the OR. After the staff left, it was just the three of them. William looked at Charlotte and then at David before leaning over his friend's bedside.

"I'm gonna go hit up the vending machine. I'll see you when you're out."

David made the sign for okay, and Charlotte mouthed a silent *thank you* to William as he left. She resumed stroking David's forehead.

"Still beautiful."

Time crept. Charlotte could hear the hands of the clock in the surgery waiting room click by with each passing minute, each tick booming like a death knell. Charlotte watched the plasma screen, waiting each time for it to scroll through all the other surgeries until it got to David's. It would say things like "anesthetic administered," "procedure starting." About three hours in, Charlotte's eyelids drooped with sleep, and she sacked out on the buttery soft leather couch in the waiting room.

"Charlotte? Charlotte, honey, wake up."

Charlotte bolted up when she realized William was tapping her foot. She looked around, disoriented for a minute as she tried to figure out where she was before it all came flooding back to her. David. Hospital. Surgery. She looked down and realized William had wedged his suit jacket under her head and was dismayed to see a puddle of drool soaking into the expensive silk.

"Damn." She wiped her mouth with the back of her hand. "I'm sorry, William."

"No worries, sweetheart. I got thirty more just like it hanging in my closet. Just flashed on the screen that David's out of surgery, so Dr. Curtis should be out in a few minutes."

Charlotte stood to try to work the knots out of her muscles as well as to burn off her nervous energy. About twenty minutes later, Dr. Curtis emerged, her eyes red with exhaustion. Charlotte tried to read her face.

"Mrs. King, your husband did great." Dr. Curtis smiled. Charlotte's shoulders slouched in relief as William put his arm around her and squeezed. "It did take a bit longer than we had anticipated, but overall I'm very pleased with how he did."

"Can we see him?"

"In a little while. He's in post-op now, and later we'll move him to a private room. After that you can absolutely see him." Dr. Curtis gestured to the couch. "May we sit for a moment?"

Charlotte bit her lip and nodded, scared at what the woman was about to tell her. The three sat on the couch, and Dr. Curtis was quiet a moment before she spoke.

"Relatively speaking, the surgery was the easy part. Now comes the hard part, which is his recovery. I'm not going to parse my words—David has a lot of work ahead of him both physically and emotionally. Because of his age and because he's a man, he's going to think he'll just bounce back from this like nothing ever happened. He's going to find the simplest tasks will take Herculean effort. Walking across the room will wipe him out. Eating will be exhausting. He'll probably cry. Loud noises will frighten him. Taking a shower will be traumatic. You're both going to experience a wide range of emotions, and I want you to be prepared for them."

"Whatever it takes, Doctor. I'll do it, no matter what. As long as he's okay."

"You might consider hiring a nurse to help you. I just want you to be aware of the work that's on the horizon. It won't be easy."

"Like I said, whatever it takes."

Dr. Curtis patted Charlotte on the hand. "Good. I'll have a nurse take you to his room once he's settled in. I'll be going off duty soon, but my colleague, Dr. Anderson, will be monitoring David throughout the day, and I'll check on him when I'm back this afternoon."

"When can he go home?" Charlotte asked.

"Let's see how he does this week. We need to take it day by day."

Charlotte touched Dr. Curtis's arm. "Dr. Curtis, I can't tell you how grateful I am..." She couldn't finish the sentence, tears gobbling up her words.

The doctor smiled. "It was my pleasure. After you've seen your husband, why don't you go home and get some sleep, pick up a few things he might need. You're going to need every ounce of strength you have. Even some you didn't know you had."

Charlotte shook her head, adamant. "Oh no. I'm not leaving."

"Well, maybe your friend can grab a few things for you." She smiled again. "See you later."

The doctor went back toward the OR, and Charlotte leaned against the couch cushions. "She just said something completely logical, and I'm acting totally illogical. Of course David will need some things from home!" Charlotte shook her head.

"Don't worry about it. You got only two hours of sleep. I'll call my assistant and have her run up here, grab your keys, and get whatever you guys need from the house. Oh, and I can call Karen."

"Oh God. Karen. I hadn't even thought about that. If you could, that would be great." Charlotte went to grab her phone out of her purse. "Here… let me get her number."

"Oh, I've got it. We'd exchanged numbers for some wedding stuff."

Charlotte tried to keep from smiling. "Ah. Okay." Charlotte handed over her keys.

"Let me make some calls, get some things in motion. I'll run home and grab a shower; we'll get you taken care of." William winked. "Don't worry about a thing. And if one word about movies slips out of his mouth, you tell him I said to shut up. He's not to worry about anything but getting better."

"Deal."

"He's gonna be okay, Char. He's a strong one."

"I know."

William gave Charlotte a kiss on the cheek before he picked up his now-rumpled, spittled jacket and started to walk out.

"Wait! William!" Charlotte ran after him and threw her arms around him.

"I couldn't have made it through this awful thing if you hadn't been by my side. David and I are both so lucky to have you."

William returned her embrace. "Let's just say that luck is a two-way street."

Charlotte paced. David still hadn't been brought down from surgery. What was taking so long? Charlotte poked her head outside the door and looked down the hall. Nothing but nurses and doctors milling around, and none of them were bringing David to her. She let the door swish shut before she flopped down on the oversized chair next to the bed. The door swung open, and Charlotte jumped up. Two orderlies backed David's gurney into the room and eased him over to the bed. A tube jutted from his mouth, and he was sleeping. Charlotte placed a hand over her chest, forcing herself to stay calm.

"He dozed off again post-op, but he should be coming around soon," one of the orderlies informed Charlotte. "The doctor will be in shortly."

Charlotte nodded, her eyes glued to David's chalky face. "Thanks," she murmured. She sat back down in the chair and took David's hand, limp inside her own. She grasped it, brushing her lips against his ring finger, which was bare. She remembered the nurse had pulled his wedding band from his finger and had handed it to her right before he had gone into surgery. Charlotte reached into her pocket and slipped it back on him. She closed her eyes and leaned against the bed rail, never releasing David's hand. She flinched when the door opened again and burly black man in blue scrubs came in. A nurse trailed after him and busied herself checking vitals and changing banana bags. The doctor held out his hand to Charlotte.

"Mrs. King? I'm Dr. Anderson."

"Oh yes. Hi. Dr. Curtis said you'd be looking after David."

The doctor looked at the nurse, who rattled off a bunch of stats. The doctor noted them all, nodding his head as he wrote them in a chart, pleased with what he was hearing. It sounded like alphabet soup to Charlotte.

"Why's he still asleep?"

The doctor had moved over to examine the bandage plastered across David's incision. Charlotte stared at the thick wad of gauze, mesmerized.

"Perfectly normal. He's just gone through a fairly traumatic event and is tired. The good news is his vitals are strong, and we expect his incision to heal nicely."

Charlotte chewed her thumbnail and looked at David, not convinced he shouldn't be awake.

As though he could hear Charlotte, David's eyes flicked open. The doctor smiled, and the nurse took a whole new set of vitals.

"Mr. King? Hello!" Dr. Anderson boomed. "How are you feeling?"

David held up a shaky hand and formed an "okay" sign. He patted his throat, agitated to find that a tube prevented him from speaking.

"Hold on, Mr. King. You're intubated—don't try to speak." Dr. Anderson whipped his stethoscope from around his neck to listen to David's heartbeat. Charlotte was rooted to her position, and David's eyes darted around the room. Dr. Anderson nodded, obviously happy with the beats thumping through the stethoscope.

"Mr. King, we're going to go ahead and extubate you. I'll count to three and pull the tube out, and I want you to cough, all right? You ready?"

David nodded, and the doctor pulled the tube out. David's lungs expelled a waterlogged cough. Charlotte instinctively went for the pitcher of water on the nightstand, but the nurse stopped her.

"He needs to get this out first, and then we can get him some water."

Charlotte shoved her hands into her pockets and watched in agony as David continued to hack and grimace. Finally, the nurse poured a bit of water into a cup and threw a straw in before handing it to Charlotte. David sipped greedily for several seconds. Finally he cleared his throat and collapsed against the mountainous white pillows, drained.

"My God. I feel like I've just run around the block ten times." David's voice was thin and raspy. "When can I go home?"

"Mr. King, we need you to take it easy for the next few days. All goes well, you can go home at the end of the week. You try to push it, and you'll be calling this place home."

"Well, don't want that." David looked to Charlotte. "I have a feeling someone will be keeping me in line."

Charlotte glanced down, embarrassed as David gave her a languid smile. Dr. Anderson patted David on the shoulder. "All right. You get some rest, and I'll be back to check on you later."

Charlotte murmured her thanks as the nurse and doctor exited the room. She sat down in the chair next to the bed.

"How are you? Really?"

David gulped and closed his eyes. "Thankful," he whispered.

"Me too."

They sat in silence, both in contemplative thought.

"I'm sorry," David finally said.

"For what?"

"For being so stubborn. Probably could've avoided all this if I'd gone to the doctor when you wanted me to."

Charlotte pressed her fingers against David's cracked, peeling lips. "*Shhh.* Don't talk like that. The main thing is we made it over the first hurdle. We'll make it over all of them."

"You really do have nerves of steel, don't you?"

Charlotte stroked David's damp hair. "Only sometimes."

"There's something else I'm thankful for."

"What's that?"

"That we got the honeymoon over first."

"You really do have a one-track mind, don't you?"

"Says the woman who jumps my bones every chance she gets."

Charlotte chuckled. "Guilty."

"It's going to be a long road, isn't it?"

"Yes…yes, it is."

David sighed and reached for Charlotte's hand. Tears stained his eyes. "Well, we did say for better or for worse."

Fatigue knotted Charlotte's shoulders, and she felt a pinch in her neck as she picked up her tea. The hospital had arranged to move a cot into David's room, and for the past few nights, sleep had proven to be a futile quest. Worry kept Charlotte alert and staring at the ceiling. She'd grown accustomed to the hum of the machines and David's still-labored breathing. She still railed against fluorescent rays from the hallway that snuck underneath the door and flooded the room, as did the cascading rainbow of lights splashed across the various machines plugged into David. Nurses were in and out at all hours to check David's vitals and monitor his condition. Charlotte was exhausted.

She took another sip of tea and searched among the sea of white coats and green scrubs for Karen, who had gone through the cafeteria line for a full-fledged breakfast. Charlotte spotted her and waved her over to the table. Karen slid into the chair across from Charlotte and dug into a plate piled high with gooey pastries.

"You sure you don't want one? For a hospital, these are pretty damn tasty."

"Uh-huh. I haven't had much of an appetite lately."

"Is that why you're drinking tea all of a sudden?"

"Coffee smelled a little suspect."

"Well, other than not digging the coffee, how are you holding up?"

Charlotte raked her hands across her face. "Totally and completely wiped out."

"That's no surprise. You haven't been home in days."

"My place is here. Still, it is starting to take a toll."

"You know, no one would think you're a bad wife if you went home and took a nap in your own bed for a few hours. You don't have to be the martyr."

Charlotte shrank back, hurt. "Is that what you think?"

Karen shoved a finger into a pile of red raspberry filling and spooned it into her mouth. "Let me rephrase that. If you fall apart, you're not going to be any help to David. All I'm saying is it would do you some good to go home, get some sleep, recharge your battery. You've got a long haul ahead of you."

Charlotte ran the tip of her finger around the rim of her teacup. "David was napping yesterday afternoon, and as I was watching him, I was struck by how ironic this all is. I spent—no, *wasted*—so much time worrying about how I was going to be seventy-four when he was sixty, that he'd have to be the one to push me around in a wheelchair and watch me dribble oatmeal down my chin and..." Charlotte's tears surged forth, the dam demolished.

"And now you'll be taking care of him," Karen finished as she handed Charlotte a wad of stiff white napkins.

"It just never occurred to me it would be me in this position. It was natural to assume it would be the other way around."

"That's life. We can't predict the curveballs. We've either got to hit them or get the hell out of the way."

"It's really hard, Karen."

"Well, honey, that's marriage. The bitter and the sweet. The good, the bad, and the ugly. Can't all be rockin' sex."

Charlotte laughed in spite of herself and blew her nose again. "No, no—I guess not."

"Go home. You're fried. Take a shower, get some sleep, and watch a few hours of really bad TV."

"Don't ever change."

Karen shoved the last of a cheese Danish into her mouth. "Wouldn't dream of it."

※

Dr. Curtis nodded to herself as she listened to David's heartbeat. She smiled and eased David back against the pillows.

"You've made amazing progress this week, David. Barring any complications, I don't see any reason why you shouldn't go home tomorrow."

"Seriously?" Charlotte asked.

"Yes, but he's still very weak, and he must follow my instructions to the letter. Overdoing it, even in the slightest, can sabotage your progress and cause a relapse. That's not the result we're going for."

"Scout's honor, I'll stay in bed. However, would it be all right if Charlotte climbed in with me?" David winked.

Charlotte slapped his arm, embarrassed. "David..."

"Oh, come now. Good for the heart, right?"

Dr. Curtis chuckled and scribbled a few notes on David's chart. "All in good time, David. About six weeks, to be somewhat exact anyway. About the most cardiovascular activity I want you doing for the time being is walking around the block."

David saluted her. "Aye, aye."

"Thank you so much for everything. I can't tell you how much I appreciate everything you and your team have done. Truly."

"Are you kidding? It's not every day we get a big-time movie star in here."

"No offense, but let's hope it's the last time *this* big-time movie star comes through here."

"Actually, if I could impose on you for one thing."

"Anything—name it," David said.

Dr. Curtis hesitated a bit before going into the pocket of her white coat. "Sorry, this is all they had down in the gift shop. Anyway. Today's my daughter's birthday, and it would make her day—better yet, her year—if I got your autograph. You might even make her naggy mom a hero."

"Oh, well, only if it will make you a hero, of course." David winked. "I'll even go you one better. When I'm back on my feet, bring her over to dinner. I'll tell her you're *my* hero."

"Ha! If you do that, my husband and I just might make it out of the teenage years unscathed."

Dr. Curtis handed David the magazine she'd pulled out of her pocket. He looked at it and chuckled. Across the cover was his favorite photo of him and Charlotte kissing at the farmer's market, with a smaller one of him in the inset.

"What's your daughter's name?"

"Lindsay."

To Lindsay, Happy Birthday! David King, David scrawled with a pen across the cover and handed it to the doctor.

"Thanks so much!" She smiled at Charlotte. "See you later."

David held out his hand to Charlotte. She sat down next to him and laid her head in his lap. David caressed the back of her neck.

Loving David

"Hell of a way to start off a marriage, eh?"

"No kidding.

"How are you? I mean really?"

Charlotte lifted her head and looked at David. "I'm okay."

"Honestly?"

"Honestly. I'm just so happy you're coming home."

"That makes two of us. Say...I was thinking you could buy a naughty nurse uniform."

"Six weeks minimum!" Charlotte laughed. "Besides, I've gotten you a perfectly lovely nurse. Her name's Kate, and she, Karen, and William have been getting the house ready."

"Karen and Will seem to be getting on, huh?"

"I haven't asked either of them about it yet, but there does seem to be something brewing there."

"Well, it would appear, Mrs. King, that not only did we save each other, we might have saved our two best friends."

Charlotte nodded, considering this. "I guess everything really does happen for a reason."

CHAPTER 19

Dr. Curtis hadn't been joking—taking care of David required Charlotte to tap into strength she didn't know she possessed. She had a hospital bed set up in the living room so David would be more comfortable while he slept. The nurse came during the day to help David with his breathing exercises and monitor his vitals. William had surprised her by arranging for a cleaning lady to come a few days a week, a perk she hadn't realized she'd be grateful for until the day she was faced with mounds of laundry. Each day, Charlotte took David for a walk, though when they first got home, he couldn't go any farther than the end of the driveway. The paparazzi had been curiously respectful; Charlotte hadn't seen any lurking around since they'd been back.

Some days had been an emotional struggle. There were times when David was as chipper and as charming as ever, glimmers of his old self shining through. Other days he sat in bed for hours, not saying a word, just staring at the ceiling. The first time he took a shower, Charlotte heard him crying. He told her later he never expected a shower to be so traumatic—as the water felt like a hundred little knives ripping into his skin. He was terrified his incision would split open and he'd bleed all over the bathroom floor.

Charlotte never let David see her own tears. She'd make up silly little errands like needing to buy stamps or get her oil changed. In reality, she'd drive two blocks over, sit in the car, and cry for thirty minutes.

But once David no longer needed the hospital bed, his mood lightened. He'd taken to sitting by the window and leafing through potential scripts. He found a few comedies he liked—he was too afraid to venture into heavy dramas—and asked Charlotte to read to him. They sat in the matching shabby chic blue chairs of the bedroom, the afternoon sun blanketing them before it faded into nothingness. Charlotte read all the parts, making embarrassingly bad attempts at accents and comedic timing. She didn't care. It made David laugh, which was all that mattered to her.

Charlotte was curled up in one of the chairs, watching David as he napped in their bed. The doctors had discouraged sleeping during the day, but he hadn't done much sleeping the previous night. It had been a fitful night for them both; Charlotte had woken up every half hour to check on him as he tossed and turned, adjusting to being back on a regular mattress.

David stirred and opened his eyes. He looked around and spotted Charlotte.

"Aren't you a sight?"

"How'd you sleep?"

"Like a dream."

"What can I get you?"

"You."

Charlotte went to crawl into bed beside him. She took care not to bump against his chest, gently laying her head against his shoulder.

"When this is all over, we're going on a long holiday."

"Where?"

"You ever been to Greece?"

"Until we went to Canada, I'd never been out of the country. My passport was quite empty until you."

"Seriously? Charlotte, you need to get out more, my love."

"Isn't that why I have you?"

"Yes. Okay, back to Greece. The beaches are amazing. Pristine white sand, water so clear you almost want to drink it right out of the sea. And the food! My God, the food is just...I can't even describe it."

"Sounds amazing."

"It is. I can't wait to show it to you. In the meantime, how about a trip to the couch? I feel like watching the sappiest, syrupiest, most sickeningly sweet romantic movie we can find on the shelf."

Charlotte helped David out of bed. "I may have just the thing," she said as they ambled toward the living room.

"I'm listening."

Charlotte fluffed some couch pillows, and David slumped against them, the short trip seeming to wipe him out. Charlotte frowned.

"You look tired. Are you sure you're up to this?"

"Yes. I'm tired of lying in that bed. Now, what's the movie?"

"*Somewhere in Time.*"

David covered his eyes with one hand before peeking out at her between fingers. "No."

"I know, I know. It's terrible. I can't help it. I love it."

"I thought you were going to say something like *The Notebook* or *Sleepless in Seattle. Bridges of Madison County* even."

Charlotte shrugged and plucked the DVD from the bookshelf. "Laugh all you want. I absolutely, one hundred percent, love this movie."

"This better be worth it."

"You mean you sit here and make fun of my movie selection and you've never even seen it?"

"Guilty."

Charlotte pushed the play button in defiance. "That's all about to change, Mr. International Movie Star. You're going to watch this movie, and you're going to *love* it."

David rubbed Charlotte's knee. "We'll see."

The last thing Charlotte remembered before dozing off was the portrait scene. The music for the closing credits woke her up. She looked over at David and giggled. He was crying.

"I knew you'd love it! It is a pretty romantic—" Charlotte stopped as she realized something was wrong.

"I'm so sorry, Charlotte," he choked, barely able to get the words out.

Charlotte took David's face in her hands. "What's the matter? What do you need?"

"I love you," he said with a deep sigh as he closed his eyes, his shoulders sagging.

Charlotte shook his shoulder, her tears clouding her vision. "David!" No response. Sweating, Charlotte bolted for her phone, frantically dialing 911. She held David's hand.

"Please don't leave me," she whispered.

Charlotte refused to cry. She would not cry, because it would be an admission of sorts, a truth she just couldn't face.

David was going to die.

Dr. Curtis came out. Charlotte looked at her, struck by how she was moving toward her in slow motion. Panic washed over Charlotte

"How's David? Can I see him?"

The doctor sat down, her face drawn. She rubbed her eyes for a moment before she spoke. "The blood isn't flowing properly through the graft we put in, and that blockage has caused a rupture. It's a rare complication, but unfortunately it does happen. We could do more surgery, but it would only be putting off the inevitable."

Charlotte stared straight ahead, hearing the words, not quite believing them.

"How long?" she whispered.

Dr. Curtis hung her head. "No more than a day."

"I see." Charlotte stood. She felt as if she were drowning in a river of sweat, and her mouth exploded with cotton.

Charlotte fainted.

※

"Mrs. King?"

Charlotte opened her eyes, blinded by the overhead fluorescents. A nurse was standing next to the gurney she was amazed to find herself lying on.

"What happened?"

"You fainted. The doctor will be in in just a sec."

Charlotte groaned and leaned her head against the pillow. The curtain snapped back, and

Dr. Curtis strode in.

"You gave us a scare. We want to run a few tests, because your blood pressure was bit elevated."

Charlotte started to get off the gurney. "No, I don't have time for this; I have to—"

The nurse laid a hand on Charlotte's shoulder and gently pushed her back. "We're just going to run a few standard tests. I promise to be quick so we can get you back to David."

Charlotte started to protest, but then relented.

"Fine. But please hurry. I can't waste time."

CHAPTER 20

Charlotte slid her chin into the palm of her hand. The sun was just starting to come up; she wanted to push it back into the night. Smash the clock to remain forever frozen in another, happier time. Not this moment.

David's leg twitched under the sheet, and Charlotte's head jerked up. He was moving. He unglued his eyes and looked at Charlotte. In an all-too-familiar sight, an oxygen mask cloaked his face.

"I'm here, sweetheart. I'm right here."

David blinked to show Charlotte he understood. She leaned in, knowing she had to talk fast.

"David, I need to tell you something. I found out today I'm pregnant."

David's eyes grew wide, and Charlotte laughed and cried all at the same time. "I know, I know. I couldn't believe it either. I thought I was too old, but the doctor said it can happen. I'm about six weeks along."

David squeezed Charlotte's hand and closed his eyes again. A single tear streamed down his cheek.

Charlotte leaned in farther and whispered in David's ear. "I love you so much, David. I always will. And I'll tell our baby all about you. He or she will know who you are. How amazing you are."

David took a deep breath and shuddered. He closed his eyes, and Charlotte heard the monitor behind her expel one long beep. A nurse swept into the room and whisked a whimpering Charlotte aside. More doctors flooded the room, and all Charlotte could do was stand in the corner and watch, sobbing.

"Good-bye," she whispered.

CHAPTER 21

Charlotte had come to realize time was a funny thing. She'd met David almost two years ago. They'd fallen in love. Married. In the blink of an eye, he was gone.

And now she had a newborn.

Charlotte bounced Frances Marie on her hip as she paced the cabin. She'd named the baby for her and David's mothers, though she was nicknamed Frankie by William and Karen, who relished being her godparents.

She'd be scattering David's ashes across the lake soon, and she was steeling herself for the task.

It had been a year since David's death, a year Charlotte could both scarcely remember and would never forget. In the days following David's passing, she and William had planned a public memorial. It seemed grief had enveloped the world, as Charlotte heard from people as far away as Japan, Spain, and of course, London, expressing their sorrow and condolences. She was still amazed by how many people attended the memorial, so many people touched by the man with the beautiful smile and amazing talent. David had more money than Charlotte knew what to do with. She donated a large chunk to various heart-related charities, set up a college fund for the baby, and established a scholarship in David's name at the Royal Academy.

Intent on protecting her pregnancy, Charlotte had gone into near seclusion. Because of her age, it had been a high-risk pregnancy, and she couldn't have afforded the stress of dodging overzealous photographers salivating for a shot of the widow King and her burgeoning belly. She rented a house high in the Hollywood Hills, behind a massive iron gate, and hired a battalion of extra security to keep the paparazzi at bay.

William, of course, had been a godsend, doing everything from dealing with the mainstream media, getting David's estate settled, and finding her the best medical care. Karen had been in the delivery room with her while a nervous William marched around the waiting room. Charlotte cried from joy and sadness as her daughter was born. Frankie had the same shock of black hair and sparkling emeralds for eyes as her father. Sometimes her laugh even sounded like David's.

There was a knock on the door, and Karen poked her head in without waiting for an invitation. "Need any help?"

"I'm okay. Just trying to mentally prepare myself."

Karen made goo-goo eyes at the baby. "You'll be okay. Look at how you've handled this past year."

Charlotte kissed the top of Frankie's head. "If it weren't for her, I don't know if I would have made it."

"Babies will do that."

"It's funny. When David and I fell in love, I always wished I was younger so we'd have more time. And then, when I knew David was going to die, I wished I was older so I wouldn't have to be without him too long. Before I knew about Frankie, of course. Isn't that strange?"

"Actually, I think it's nice. He was your soul mate, and you wanted to be together." Karen looked at her watch and reached for Charlotte's hand. "It's time."

Charlotte drew up her shoulders and hugged Frankie to her a bit closer before placing one hand in Karen's. She took one last look around, David's spirit wrapping around them both.

Karen and Charlotte walked down to the shore of the lake, where William was waiting with the other ladies. He held a wooden box with David's ashes. The sky was clear and blue, and the birds chirped a little louder. It was the perfect day. Emma and Hendra embraced Charlotte and jiggled the baby's fingers while William and Karen shared a brief hug. Charlotte smiled. David would be so happy William and Karen had become close.

Hendra placed her hands on Charlotte's shoulders. "You ready?"

Charlotte took a deep breath and nodded. She handed Frankie to Karen and took the ashes from William. She clutched the box and looked down, thinking about her words.

"This lake meant a lot to David and me. It's where we met, fell in love, and got married. I couldn't think of a better place to lay him to rest. And I want you to know how much all of you meant to David. Mostly he was glad you didn't kick him out that first night."

A small twitter of laughter passed through everyone.

"Loving David was the easiest thing I've ever done. It was effortless. I fell more in love with him every day, to the point where I thought I would burst. I'm so fortunate to have known a love like that, even for a little while." Charlotte looked at her daughter. "And of course, the greatest gift—little Frankie. David will live on through her smile, her grace, and her spirit. I've been doubly blessed."

A small breeze whispered by. Charlotte said a silent prayer before she opened the lid. Swallowing the lump in her throat, she held the box up to meet the breeze. David's ashes left the box in a perfect swirl and flew over the lake until they vanished.

Karen sighed and shook her head, an ironic laugh bubbling beneath her words. "Still beautiful."

Charlotte chuckled. "Indeed."

The End

lovingdavidnovel.com
Cover photograph by:
Elizabeth
Hummer

CPSIA information can be obtained at www.ICGtesting.com
Printed in the USA
LVOW132254210612

287183LV00008B/100/P